THE
STOLEN
SKY

ALSO BY HEATHER HANSEN

THE SPLIT CITY SERIES

The Breaking Light

THE STOLEN SKY

HEATHER HANSEN

SKYSCAPE

SKYSCAPE

Text copyright © 2017 by Heather Hansen
All rights reserved.

Published by Skyscape, New York

www.apub.com

Amazon, the Amazon logo, and Skyscape are trademarks of Amazon.com, Inc., or its affiliates.

ISBN-13: 9781542046817
ISBN-10: 1542046815

Cover design by Mike Heath | Magnus Creative

Printed in the United States of America

For my husband, Steven. Thank you for filling my life with joy, laughter, and selfless love. There is no one else I'd want to walk this life with. You make everything better.

Chapter one

They were being hunted. The pressure of the chase and the exhaustion from battle felt thick inside Dade, slowing his movements. Numbness made it difficult to think. Still, he did not stop. They had to keep going. The govies could catch them and blast them full of phase-fire at any second. Fear, not for himself but for the girl in his arms, pushed him onward, straining his body past the limits of its endurance.

He held Arden against him, his arm wrapped around her back. The wet tackiness of her blood coated his fingers from where a phase-fire blast had ripped open her side. Around the wound, her suit had been cut away to expose the injury. Her skin was charred and puckered from the in-field attempt to cauterize the damage. She felt cold from the chilled air and loss of blood.

It was a real possibility she would die.

His worry increased. They'd managed to get halfway across the city through the Lower Levels without incident. He'd have considered their escape a success except they had nowhere to go—no friends, no one to rely on. Even their families wanted them dead.

Arden leaned heavily into his side, her eyes closed. Dusky lashes contrasted against the bruised purple translucence of her skin. She sighed shallowly, making her breath rattle in her chest, which was followed by a pain-laced whine.

Their running suits were charred. The material regulated their body temperature against the extreme chill of the Lower Levels and helped repel phase-fire. It wore like a second skin, moving with their anatomy as if it were part of them. The fabric was black, created with nanotech that swallowed light.

Like Arden's, his suit had been compromised as well. He'd taken repeated fire blasts that had broken down its synth-fibers. He felt the cold to his bones along with the chapping wind against the exposed parts of his face and hands.

Dade stopped to adjust the long blast-phaser that lay strapped across his back, while maneuvering Arden to the center of his chest so she wouldn't fall. He had a smaller phaser tucked into the palm of his opposite hand. Both hands were bandaged, broken fingers taped together.

His plan was simple: get themselves lost in the Lower Levels of Above. There were always so many people here, struggling to survive as a fluid jumble, bodies packed together. He had used this tactic to disappear many times. It was easy enough to become invisible even with the city's vid-cams perpetually monitoring the streets. The govies used these cams to keep the people in line. But Dade knew they weren't the only ones with access. Piggybacking on signals was a given by anyone with technical ability. This made discovery by the govies not the only thing he feared.

Today was different, though. Not only because they were bruised and broken and he was half carrying Arden, but also because the entire citizenry seemed to have flooded outside to watch the destruction they'd left behind. Those in the crowd craned their necks for a better view. Others, covered in debris, screamed for help, not knowing which way to head for safety. Govies and emergency vehicles swarmed, adding to the pandemonium.

Dade pushed against the crowd, descending farther down into the Levels. He tuned out the sounds of chaos, the smell of rotting garbage, and the lingering tang of sulfur from the static cloud that surrounded the planet, cutting it off from the sun. The cloud sat thick in the atmosphere, covering the planet in darkness and chilled fog. All except for the Sky Towers that rose above it.

He hoped that the lower he went, the easier it would be to cross to the other side of the city. But the throngs of people pushed back their progress. Tucking Arden closer, he shoved his way through. Using his free arm, he landed blows when he needed a hole to open in the crowd. Fighting aggressively until he was able to he maneuver himself and Arden into a commercial space and the corridor that led into the center of a building.

Businesses lined either side of the hall. Most were closed for the day, their lights off. From here, he could continue his route through the city as the buildings slipped one into another, their entrances and exits interconnected.

"I'm cold." Arden's voice was thready over the chattering of her teeth. She'd not spoken for miles, pained gasps being the only sound she'd made.

"We're almost there," he promised. Though he had no idea where "there" was or even if they'd find someone to help her in time.

Being indecisive wasn't his usual weakness. He'd been born to luxury, inside the Sky Towers. With unlimited access to the cloudless purple sky, blood-orange sun, and two moons. He hadn't understood the depth of his privilege until he'd walked away from that life. Perhaps he still didn't understand the extent of his loss.

It didn't change the fact that he'd make the same choice again, all circumstances being what they were. Because he could not embrace the life his father had set out for him. Eventually he'd figure out where he fit in.

Helplessness felt like a monster inside him. The feeling grew and pulsed, filling his mind with desperate thoughts. It reminded him that he was a tiny cog in a big organized machine. Power had been an illusion. One he'd believed in until reality had shown him otherwise. Dade had known that providing the poor with the VitD he stole was just a bandage on a significant problem. Yet now the wiped-out VitD refinery meant the end of anything good he'd set in motion. He'd have to figure out where that left him and what his new purpose would be.

He could live with his decisions that had forced him away from his family, into a life and circumstances that felt unstable. Dade had made the choices, knowing their consequences. Though he clung to the hope that he wouldn't lose the two things most important to him: his sanity and Arden.

Arden made a tiny motion with her arm, indicating the blackout band on her wrist. It was strapped there to keep the govies from accessing the implanted data sensor they used to monitor citizens. She swallowed several times before she managed, "I have credits."

The credits would be off grid if they were keyed to the band instead of the chip beneath her skin. And hopefully not attached to Lasair's black-market accounts. Dade nodded. That was good.

Dade kept credits under an assumed name to fund his activities as well. He'd put away a vast sum of money into the account for his planned escape from his family. But his codes didn't work after the fall. He wasn't really sure how it had happened. The blackout band wasn't damaged, but he'd been unable to access the funds when he'd tried to do so before rushing to the joint refinery to find Arden.

For now, they could use some of her credits to get her medical attention. Any credits remaining could be used on a place to hole up. And then when he gained access to his, they'd be okay.

He hoped.

"How much do you have?" he asked.

She shook her head, her eyes closed. "Not a lot. I didn't plan."

He knew she'd meant to die when Lasair had attacked the joint refinery. Dade was still angry at her for attempting to throw her life away. His blood still sang with anxiety at the thought of not getting to her in time. And when he had, she'd been hurt.

Swallowing back the fear that once again threatened to crowd his thoughts, he focused on this task. Recriminations needed to come later.

The hallways became gloomier the deeper they went into the expanse of interconnected buildings. The tracked domes in the ceiling were powered by poloosh, a glow stone from the Wilds. The domes didn't do much to pierce the darkness that the closed and shuttered storefronts created.

Just when Dade had reached the point of exhaustion where he didn't know whether he could continue to walk himself, let alone carry Arden's weight, hope appeared. Ahead, a medical sign caught his eye, a caduceus, two snakes winding around a winged staff, bolted to the wall. The paint had been rubbed half off, and a solid metal grate had been tacked up in front of the cracked moonglass window. But he could see light from inside still creeping through the edges.

Arden must have been at the end of her endurance too. Her body sagged heavy against him, her legs no longer working to support her. Suddenly, she slipped from his grip to land on her knees. Dade went down with her, gathering her into his arms to keep her from hitting the floor.

"Arden," he said sharply, lowering her the rest of the way. He slid his hands to her face. His thumbs brushed her cheeks. When she didn't open her eyes, he pulled up her lids, only to see sightless, dilated pupils.

He shook her. "Wake up."

Fear, which he'd managed to ignore for the most part, bloomed hot and snaked its way through his chest with a searing burn, making it difficult to breathe. Here they were exposed—he could practically feel eyes on them—through the city's vid-cams, or from curious strangers in the darkness who might sell them out for credits. He needed her to wake up, to help him take a few last steps.

Arden's eyes finally opened. Her gaze was hazed and unfocused. He gave her a moment to wake fully before he dipped his shoulders under her arm and then hefted her to her feet.

"Dade?"

"I'll get you help," he promised, leaning in to kiss her forehead. Her skin was feverish against his lips. Already infection might be setting in, her body too damaged to fight it.

At the door of the med center, he placed his hand against the scanner, but the door didn't open. He tried again. Nothing. Frustrated, he gently propped Arden against the wall and then banged against the metal door.

Someone had to be inside. He refused to believe otherwise. There was nowhere else for him and Arden to go. He knocked on the door again, even louder than before. Using his full forearm, he put his weight into it. Dade's already-strained muscles ached.

A speaker clicked, static crackling.

"We're closed," said a muffled voice. "There's an emergency med center on Aurora Passage, about three blocks west."

He glanced at Arden, noticing that her breath had thinned. Staccato gasps punching through her body interrupted the stillness of her chest. She was now slumped over, her head hung low and her body curved in. They'd never make it to another med center.

Dade searched the doorway for a vid-cam centralized to the facility, not one of the cams connected to the city grid. Even so, he didn't like showing his face, because this feed could be hacked if his enemies were persistent enough in wanting to find him. Locating the tiny black lens with its telltale pinhole red dot, he looked directly into it while twisting his shoulder so that the blast-phaser strapped to his back wasn't visible.

He attempted to even his breathing. The vid-cam system would monitor his voice inflection, his breath pattern, the flush of his skin, all to determine if he meant harm. Given this was a high-crime area, it was a good precaution, just not one that worked in Dade's favor.

"I need a doctor." He let just enough desperation bleed through so that hopefully the person on the other side of the door would feel compassion for their situation. But he also knew he was covered in grime from the battle, making him appear objectionable. And if the person had seen their weapons—

No, he'd focus on talking their way in. He had to because Dade wouldn't accept defeat. Not now that they were so near help.

The speaker crackled. "The doctor isn't here."

"Then let me buy supplies," Dade begged. He leaned forward into the cam while making his voice soft with promise. "I can pay you. I have off-grid credits. They can be yours. No one has to know."

Appealing to greed was a tactic that had often worked for Dade. If he could somehow convince this person that it was in his best interest to open the door, they'd have a chance. Dade didn't need a doctor. Gaining access to a med pod would be enough.

There was a long pause. Dade could almost feel the hesitation on the other side of the door. Then he heard the words, "You'd better have the credits."

The door slid open to reveal a boy. He was about Dade's age, but shorter, with blue scrubs that hung on his lanky body. His hand twitched before reaching up to run his fingers through his overgrown hair. It took him only seconds to assess the situation, to see the shape Arden was in and the phasers Dade carried. His eyes opened wide.

Dade was ready, though. He pushed his foot into the doorway so that it couldn't slide closed, then bent to pick up Arden. "Thank you for helping us."

The boy startled, and his eyes got wider as his gaze bounced between them. "You're one of them." He gulped and then let out a pant. "You tore up the city." He took a second step back, his voice turning into a whine. "Don't kill me."

Dade didn't have time for this. Holding Arden's limp body in his arms, he didn't offer explanations or reassurances as he stepped fully inside. He pushed past the boy who tried to block his entry.

The door autoshut behind them.

"I can't help you," the boy babbled.

Dade walked through the front office and into one of the exam rooms. It appeared sterile, the surfaces empty. He laid Arden down on a shiny metal table. "Where do you keep your bandages? Do you have a suture gun? Hook her up to the med pod and start the scan."

The boy stood just inside the door. His eyes were wide, and his face had lost its color. Instinct, rather than any intent to help, had probably made him follow Dade into the room. He shook his head once, briefly, then shook it again harder as Dade stared at him. He turned to leave.

Dade aimed his phaser at the boy's chest.

The boy squeaked. Tears gathered in his eyes as he swallowed. "Please, I don't want to die."

"I won't shoot if you do as I tell you." Realizing that the boy was growing more agitated, Dade made his words soft and reassuring even though he kept an edge of commanding sharpness. "Relax, take a deep breath. We'll be gone soon. Do as I say, and you'll live. Plus, I'll leave you the credits I promised."

Arden coughed, snagging his attention. Blood stained the table beneath her. It reminded him that they only had a precious few minutes to stop her blood loss. He prayed it wasn't already too late.

Flicking his phaser toward Arden, he indicated that the boy should go to her. Repeating his previous directive, he said, "Get the med pod hooked up."

The boy's lip quivered, but he did as Dade told him. He placed his hand against a scanner located on the wall next to Arden's head. A strip of light ran under the boy's palm. On either side of the table, a wall of plasma emerged. It stretched over Arden, connecting in the middle. Then the plasma solidified to create a dome.

It looked as if a clear coffin had formed over the top of her body. She lay pale and broken inside it, like a discarded doll. Her eyes were open, wild with pain, as she fixed her stare on him. She reached out to touch the solid plasma shield, sliding her finger against it.

His heart twisted. Clearing his throat, Dade told her, "Stay still."

She closed her eyes.

The boy started the scan. They didn't speak as the med pod processed her body, vibrating at a low hum. When the scanner beeped, the boy studied the light readout projected on the side of the plasma shield. "She doesn't have any broken bones."

That was a minor miracle.

Dade had taken a few classes in field patching and knew the basics. But he wouldn't be able to help Arden beyond getting her stabilized. He appreciated that the med pod was intuitive. The projection labeled the information it had gathered. He focused on the readout since the projection indicated her numbers in comparison to a normal baseline.

If Arden had broken a bone, he would have been in trouble. Dade had no knowledge of how to set the fracture before calibrating the med pod, connecting the med wire, and injecting the appropriate number of nanites to speed the process. A scan and pain management, he could do.

He checked Arden's vitals. Her blood count was low. The red numbers blinked in warning. He knew they didn't have the time, nor he the expertise, to perform a transfusion. Dade doubted the boy knew how to administer one either. The best he could do was patch her up and trust the scan when it said she had no internal injuries.

"Open the med pod, we need to stop the bleeding," Dade said. Quick-seal wasn't going to cut it. But first he was worried about her pain level. "I need a pain blocker and an antibiotic."

With the hand that wasn't holding the phaser, he opened drawer after drawer. He looked through their contents quickly, throwing anything interesting onto the counter.

"Hey," the boy protested.

There. Dade grabbed a little white packet. He was already ripping the seal with his teeth as he made his way over to Arden. A strong alcohol smell singed Dade's nostrils. He slapped the anesthesia patch onto her neck, making her moan, but her eyes didn't open.

Then Dade picked up the suture gun loaded with cryo-staples. He knew from personal experience that they would go in with an ice-cold bite, delivering nanotech to her bloodstream to speed healing, then would melt into her body after her skin had enough time to knit together. He handed the suture gun over to the boy, instructing, "Staple her up."

The suture gun shook in the boy's hands. "I've never used one of these."

"Have you watched the doctor use it?"

The boy licked his lips. "Yes."

"Then it'll be fine." Dade hadn't ever used one either. His experience had been on the receiving end while he'd been in pain. He figured the boy would know how to use it better than he did.

Dade turned back to the drawers, looking for antibiotics and more pain blockers. He gathered up his loot, also snagging blood meds to speed up her body's regeneration and hopefully help with his fingers. It had to be enough.

The boy had finished by the time Dade turned back. He'd squeezed Arden's wound so that the edges came together, and then pressed the end of the suture gun against her skin. It wouldn't heal straight, but Dade was pretty sure Arden wouldn't mind a mean-looking scar.

Dade pointed his phaser directly at the boy. He needed to tie him up before he and Arden made their escape, and leave the credits he'd promised. "We're going to need some scrubs. And the keys to your vehicle."

The boy gulped and nodded.

"Thank you for your help," Dade said sincerely.

There was still the better part of the night left ahead of him. Thankfully, Arden was now unconscious. He had to find somewhere safe for them to hide. It was going to be a long few hours.

Chapter two

Arden licked her lips, trying to ease the dryness. She reached for the glass of water Dade left on the dresser beside the bed each morning. Her side tweaked at the movement, sending fiery tendrils shooting through her body as her skin pulled taut against the slow-healing wound. She swallowed back the pain and the hiss that wanted to escape.

They'd holed up in a low-end boardinghouse. Like so many other rooms in the city, it had no window, leaving her blanketed by darkness and the ever-present dust that overran this hole. It wasn't located very far from where the joint refinery had stood before it had been blown to bits. Arden had no recollection of how Dade had gotten her here. He didn't want to tell her particulars and seemed nervous that he might have been seen.

She'd been feverish for days. Time had slipped by. She honestly couldn't pinpoint how long they'd been there. All she was certain of was that she'd been awake and aware for the last five days. She was slowly getting better too. When she'd first woken, it had been difficult to move. But by now, she'd managed to get herself to the bathroom on her own, and she could stand steadily for an hour at a time.

Creatures scurried on the other side of the room. Their yellow-tipped claws clacked against the floor and their red eyes reflected in the dull glow of the lamp. Every once in a while, she'd catch the flash of their iridescent scales and tusked teeth as they braved their way closer to her.

Stupid vermin. Hunting them from her spot on the bed helped to fill her day. Patiently waiting until she got a clear shot with her phaser. It even kept the dwindling credit supply from disappearing completely when she cooked the little animals for dinner. They weren't the tastiest things, a bit gristly to be honest. But she'd had worse.

While shooting things was awesome, Arden would have preferred instead to be wherever Dade was. Boredom gnawed at her most days. She hated that she was confined to the room. Even though she felt better, her stamina still wasn't at its optimum level. If she left the boardinghouse, she had to be sure she could escape from danger.

She spent most of her time stewing with anger. Being physically weak didn't help her overall mood. Inactivity was the antithesis of who she was. She hated it. Hated being here, hated everything that had forced them into this stupid, stupid place.

Before this nightmare had unfolded, she'd questioned her life's choices. Now she wasn't sure whether she'd gotten herself into even more trouble. Her brother, Niall, had come up with the bright idea of pissing off the Solizen by attacking their joint refinery. This left the city and her in a deep well of crap. They'd taken out the only VitD manufacturing plant. This meant that not only did they condemn the entire population of the city to Violet Death, unless another source of the drug could be found, but Arden had also been hurt and left without her gang.

Someone moved outside the door. She tensed like she always did, waiting for whoever it was to continue on. When they didn't this time, the shadow at the door shifting, Arden glanced at the clock. It was too early for Dade. She didn't expect him back for at least another two hours.

Beeping, the entry scanner pinged. The sound blasted the stillness, each discordant number ratcheting up her blood pressure.

Adrenaline rushed through her, heating her blood with taut anticipation. Her heartbeat sped while her body went loose as satisfaction thrummed. Maybe today she'd prove she wasn't totally useless.

She raised the phaser, pointing the muzzle at the thin particleboard that separated the room from the hallway. She thought she heard the sound of another person breathing, panting softly. But maybe it was her own breath stuttering out as her excitement grew. She leaned forward to aim, ignoring protestations from her battered body. Pain would not steal her focus.

Whoever it was on the other side of the door entered the key code, and the door slowly opened. She waited. The door's movement synced with the beat of her heart. One heartbeat . . . two . . . She could almost see the figure that stood in the shadowed doorway.

She tucked her phaser close, using her other hand to grip the barrel. Squinting, she sighted the target. *Wait, breathe*—she exhaled her coiling excitement, calming her thoughts. Her finger tightened on the trigger, not quite squeezing.

The figure cleared the doorway.

"Stop right there." Arden wasn't messing around.

The shadow jolted. Yet he ignored her warning and took another step into the light, holding up his hands.

"It's me." The sides of Dade's lips kicked up with obvious amusement.

"Moons," Arden swore. "Did you want me to shoot you?"

Exasperated, she set the phaser down on the nightstand. She wanted to yell at him to take it seriously when someone aimed a phaser at his chest. When *she* aimed a phaser at him. Because truth be told, she was irritated enough right then to shoot him anyway. Arden had a reputation she was proud of, and it had been well earned. She'd been in the top tier of command in her gang, a spot she had not earned through nepotism but by proving her ability to be ruthless. If she had to kill someone, she would. Though she tried to have good reason if killing became necessary.

Yet she'd never successfully intimidated Dade and doubted she ever would. He saw only the good side of her, the kindness that sometimes she thought she'd lost.

Arden sighed. She loved that, even if it was dangerous. Vulnerability could be useful, but it could also turn you into prey instead of predator. It was a fine line to straddle.

Dade put down his hands as he walked closer, but his grin didn't fall away. Instead, it became soft as his gaze assessed her. "I thought you'd be asleep. Are you feeling okay?"

"I'm fine," she said, though she wasn't. She fell back onto the mildewed bedcovers, worn out by expending energy she didn't have. Her body ached and groaned. She fought not to grimace, without any luck.

"You need to sleep more if you want to heal."

Arden grunted. She didn't want to talk any more about her pain levels or how she feared that the wound on her side wasn't healing correctly. Or how she knew that she needed another session or two in a med pod.

The last thing she wanted to do was add to his concern with her own. Knowing she was worried too would only burden him. And there was not a damned thing either one of them could do about it. Dade's taking her to the med clinic in the first place had been risky enough. By now the city would be alerted to search for anyone who might have escaped the pandemonium. Walking in with her injuries was a surefire way to call attention to themselves. Besides, they didn't have many credits left, so they'd have to get medical attention by force. For that she would need to help him.

Arden took comfort in the fact that she should be up to it soon. After all, she was already walking. Plus, her injury didn't lessen her ability to hit a target. As soon as she could run and knew she'd be able to hold up her end of the escape, she'd ask him to break into a clinic so she could shake the last of this injury.

"If you're in pain, I can find something to help," he offered.

It meant that he'd have to leave again, which was the opposite of what she wanted. She craved the feel of him next to her. His warm, solid body reminding her that she was still alive. Giving her some of the hope that had dwindled a little more as each day passed.

Still, she refused to voice that need. The vulnerability embarrassed her. Besides, if he left, it wasn't likely that he'd be successful in procuring pain meds anyway.

"Why are you back so early?" she asked instead.

Not that he had a specific schedule. It was just that she was aware of every moment he was gone, alert in case something happened. And there was the ever-present knowledge that she should be with him, watching his back.

Dade grunted but ignored the question. Instead, he took off his cloak and began to strip his weapons.

They'd been doing that a lot lately—avoiding real discussions. They danced around each other, never shared their true thoughts. Each worried that their fears would burden the other. It was silly, because they both understood what was happening. Arden hated it, but she didn't know how to fix the problem. Not without being honest about her own feelings, both to herself and to Dade.

And that wasn't going to happen any time soon.

Dade stepped near to where she lay on the bed, allowing her to see him closely. Bruises littered his face. His lip was split and bleeding. And a dark patch shadowed his left eye, looking as if it would continue to blacken.

Arden sucked in a breath and then let out a low growl. "What happened?"

He placed the back of his hand on her forehead. "You're still burning up."

Oh no. They wouldn't be focusing on her. Not tonight.

She pushed his hand away. They'd been working up to this confrontation. Every day he'd come in looking a little bit worse, but never this bad. Her capacity for sniffing out trouble hadn't been compromised.

"Tell me what happened," she said. This time it was a demand.

"It looks worse than it is." He stuck out his tongue to test his swollen, split lip.

She didn't care for his deflection. "Stop it. Tell me the truth."

Dade sighed. His eyes became soft and pleading. "Don't give me crap, okay? I feel awful enough as it is."

"Then tell me what you've gotten yourself into."

"I was fighting."

"Obviously." She tried to keep control of her temper. Though he'd damaged his gorgeous face, she knew the injuries weren't serious. He didn't appear to have broken bones. Well, beyond the fingers that had been broken weeks ago. They'd been on the mend, but now she wondered if he'd reinjured them. "You know, you're not all that pretty right now."

"Are you saying I look tough?" He gave her a goofy grin, and then winced when it made his lip bleed.

Arden snorted. "As tough as a street thug."

"You like street thugs."

She shook her head. "I like *you*." Which was why she didn't want him hurt.

The two of them were a pair of pummeled messes.

Arden sat up, groaning as she moved to get out of bed. She hadn't managed to get her legs untangled from the bedding before he gently pressed her back into the pillows.

"No, stay there. I'll tell you everything, just let me clean up a bit first, okay?"

"Like I can go anywhere." She didn't want to wait. Wanted to interrogate him for answers. But if he was finally agreeing to talk to her, she figured she could afford a little patience, as much as she could spare anyway.

Dade picked up their wash basket with their soap and a towel. They had to use a communal bathroom down the hall. It was as disgusting as the rest of the place, but at least it had running water.

"I'll be right back." He locked the door when he left.

Arden leaned back into the pillows, closing her eyes. The hovel they were staying in had once been a private residence that now took on boarders. The walls were so thin, she could hear conversations from the surrounding rooms.

They would have to move soon. They'd stayed here too long. Too many had already marked their presence. She worried about finding another place, though. As crappy as this room was, the next place would likely be worse. There weren't many places to stay in the Levels, which meant they'd have to travel into Undercity.

The city was tiered. At ground level was Undercity, where Arden had been born and where if the government had its way, she should have stayed for the entirety of her life, as Undercity was enclosed and people weren't allowed to leave. Through Arden's former association with her gang—whom she still considered family even if they had turned against her—she knew the passages into Above.

On top of Undercity were the Levels, where they were currently. It was a dark and windy place. The cold here could flash freeze, and the population struggled for survival. The Levels were below the static cloud that cut them off from the sky.

Originally, the miners who ran the machinery during the terra-forming had set up base in Undercity on the crust of the planet. The Levels had been built for those seeking to colonize. But there was too much fighting for too little space. And so, the dome had been bricked between them.

Soaring above them all were the Sky Towers. The Solizen who lived in the Towers were the original benefactors of the mining colony. They'd held the money and power when the city had been built. And they still maintained that stranglehold over the citizens.

Dade looked fresher when he stepped back into the room. His wounds still appeared red and angry, but the smudges of dirt and sweat had been cleaned away. He walked across the small space, shedding his tunic and slipping off his boots as he did so.

Then he slid into the bed next to her. His movements were careful, and that slow, deliberate calculation drove her crazy. He constantly checked himself so that he didn't hurt her. There wasn't any need for that. She wasn't breakable.

Arden leaned against him. Her eyelids slid closed as she felt grounded for the first time that night. She found comfort in his soapy smell, the strength of his body, and his solid heat. He promised a place to rest, and she was so, so tired. She wanted this moment to last as long as possible.

Dade tucked his arm behind her to pull her closer. His leaned his face into her hair, and he rested his lips there, breathing in and letting the silence of the moment stretch. His other hand came up to play with the golden-brown hair curling over the side of her face. Then he pushed the thick mass behind her shoulder and slid his palm to her cheek. His thumb caressed her skin.

They hadn't gone beyond this careful cuddling since the night of the battle between the govies, the Solizen, and the city gangs over the destruction of the joint refinery. They hadn't kissed—not in any deep meaningful way that made her toes curl. Arden thought that maybe he felt guilty she'd been hurt. Not that he said as much, but the hints that he'd dropped had all pointed to that being the case.

His guilt frustrated her. Dade hadn't even been there when the battle had started. He couldn't have stopped it from happening if he had been. If anything, she was the one who should have figured out a way to stop it. And yet, Arden hadn't even been able to dissuade her brother even though she'd tried.

"When I wanted to leave my family, this is not how I pictured we'd end up," Dade said, breaking the silence.

She hadn't either. Her life was dramatically different now. She'd walked away from her family too. Her parents were probably wondering where she and her brother were. At this point she didn't know what had become of her brother either, if he was still alive. She didn't even know if he was still in charge of the Lasair. It was hard for her to think about who'd survived and who hadn't.

There was no way for her to go back. Arden could still picture Uri's face when he realized that she had betrayed them for Dade, a Solizen. He'd looked so angry. Her stomach squeezed, replaying it over and over, and she kept hearing the venom in his voice when he'd banished her.

Arden kissed his shoulder. "We have to give it time."

"I know. It's just that I want to help people. That's what the Ghost was about, you know? And now? How can I do that when there isn't even VitD in the city?" He referred to his vigilante work with his guard, Saben, stealing VitD from his father and redistributing it to the poor and the neglected children. That had ended badly with the Ghost being killed and Dade blown off a skywalk.

Arden sighed. She didn't know how to make it okay. And she wasn't exactly good at saying stuff that would make people feel better. Especially when she didn't think it was the truth. She kissed his skin again, instead.

"You need to go to sleep." Dade pulled away for a moment to shift things around on the side table. He made sure the phaser was where he could easily grab it. "I'll stay awake to make sure no one breaks in."

She didn't care about any of that. Reaching out, she turned his face to hers, demanding his attention. "Kiss me."

"You're hurt."

Arden laughed. "You are too. Kiss me anyway."

She thought he'd put her off. But Dade wasted no time pushing his mouth to hers. Their touch was soft at first, yet quickly turned hot and desperate. Arden moaned and clutched at the back of his head, keeping him there. Wanted his lips on hers forever.

This was what it felt like to come home.

Several minutes later, they pulled apart. Their mouths held inches from each other, sharing breath while their gazes connected.

"You're not going to make me forget that your face looks like it was used to stop a hovercar," Arden said.

Dade grinned and kissed her again. "I don't want you to worry about me."

That was all she could do, sit in this bed and think about what trouble he was getting into without her. "Tell me what's going on."

"Okay," Dade said. There was a look of regret and pain in his eyes. "But you're not going to like it."

She'd already figured out that part herself.

Chapter three

To call the boxing club "sleazy" would be an understatement. It wasn't like Breck's Gym that Dade and Saben had often used for cover when they coordinated the Ghost missions. This place didn't have a name or a storefront. It was off grid and illegal, not sanctioned by the govies. Which meant that there were no rules. Most of the competitors who fought here were indentured. Paying off debts with flesh and bone. The fights often ended in death because a winner wasn't called soon enough or medical treatment wasn't administered in time.

The club was dirty. Dade could practically smell disease. The air was thick with sweat and a musty odor that soaked into the walls. It was in the Levels, far into the Zero district where only the most disreputable went. The buildings had been neglected, adding to the cavernlike feel. Water dripped constantly from overhead, keeping the walls moist with condensation.

He led Arden through the back rooms, hoping that the activity surrounding them would cut off her questions until they were done.

Arden was smart, though. She knew what kind of place this was. He could feel her glare boring into his back.

He ignored it the best he could. But he knew that it was only a matter of time before she told him just how shortsighted he'd been to get caught in his current predicament. Telling her back at the boardinghouse had been one thing, but Arden's seeing it was completely another. It was so much worse being here.

She'd insisted on coming, partly because she wanted to know the entire scope of the problem and partly because she was stubborn, even if she was not well enough to walk for long periods of time. That didn't seem to be a factor in her decision. Apparently, sheer determination was enough to keep her moving. And she was pissed.

Dade let out a resigned sigh.

Arden glared.

He smiled sweetly at her. If the situation were reversed, he'd be every bit as angry. Dade hadn't told her why he'd signed this contract. Perhaps she thought that he'd concluded it was the best way to make credits. That wasn't it. When she found out what was really at stake, he was sure she'd forgive him.

Perhaps.

No one stopped them as he took her down the back hall. The owners of the indentured boxers used these tunnels to move their fighters to the public areas where the bets and matches took place. The fighters were easy to distinguish. They looked somber and mean, most with smashed noses that had awkwardly healed into flat shapes, their skin littered with scars.

Arden tensed when they entered the caging areas. These enclosures were used to keep the indentured fighters from fleeing. Most of them came from other cities, working here to pay off the debt of their tickets, though he was sure there were local fighters who'd incurred debts as well. It was illegal, this form of slavery, even if the govies did nothing to stop the exploitation. As long as it wasn't visible to the public, they could pretend it didn't exist.

"Why are we here?" she asked, her voice low and angry.

Dade gave a slight shake of his head. Answers meant seeing—understanding. No matter if it felt like his soul had cracked open.

He reached out to lightly touch her back and then steered her farther down the long row of cells. Most cages housed several occupants for cost-effectiveness. Each cage had a couple of sleeping pallets and a toilet.

The atmosphere was thick with despair. It pressed on Dade's nerves like a toothache. He hadn't gotten used to visiting here. It made him unsettled, and when a shiver wracked Arden, he imagined she felt the same.

As soon as they stepped alongside the first cage, the yelling began. The fighters catcalled and made profane suggestions. The sound reverberated, aching in Dade's skull.

Arden's posture didn't waver in spite of how tired she looked. She stiffened, and her chin tipped up while her gaze took in their surroundings. Anger burned in her eyes when she looked at him. "Why?"

He didn't know what she was asking specifically. Why they were here? Or how humans could treat other humans this way? The first she'd know almost immediately, so he didn't respond. The second he couldn't answer.

A quarter of the way down the row, he stopped and turned to look into a cage with a sole occupant. He sat on the cot, his large body hunched forward. Only his brown arms resting on his knees were visible. Dirty, unbound hair covered his face. His posture signaled defeat.

It took a moment, but when she was calm enough, she asked, "Is that Saben?"

"Yes." Dade stood as close as he could to the barrier that separated them without crossing it and getting shocked. It was made from an electrified plasma shield much like the one that was used on the med bed. A line ran on the floor, indicating where the barrier stretched. They could speak through it well enough, and the swirling blue sheen looked innocuous except for a faint buzzing that warned of danger. He called out to Saben, saying his name loud enough to be heard over the fractious noise of the cell room.

They'd taken away Saben's weapons and his X-brace, the strap that crossed his chest and back in an X. It didn't make Saben appear any less lethal. Dade knew that his friend had been better cared for than the others, having been allowed a shower once a week and given a tunic and cloak for the chill. Still, he looked haunted when he turned his glare on Dade. "I told you not to come back."

Of course that wasn't an option. Dade would never allow his friend to suffer when he had even the smidgen of a chance to make it better. There was heavy guilt that factored into it too. It was because of Dade that Saben had ended up here. Dade had asked Saben to dress up as the Ghost and attempt to fake Dade's death, leading to circumstances that had forced Saben to seek the help of his contacts in the pits. All the while, Saben and Dade had thought the other dead until Dade had found him here.

Saben had worked for his family. Had been his personal guard for years. Yet he meant more to Dade than simply an employee. He was a friend, a brother. Dade would do anything to right this situation that he'd inadvertently caused.

"What have you done, Dade?" Arden asked from behind him. "What have you both done?"

They'd made a deal with the devil. He knew it had been a fool's bargain when he struck it. But he hadn't seen any other way to get Saben out.

"I told you not to get involved," Saben accused, his gaze intense. "This is not your fight. Turn around and walk away from here. Tell Crispin that you changed your mind. Get out of your contract."

Dade blew out a breath and shook his head. "The day you came into my life and offered me friendship with no strings attached was the day I knew I'd fight to keep you in my life. You saved me . . ." He paused to think through what he wanted to say out loud, knowing that anyone could overhear. Then he spoke softly. "I wouldn't be here without you. So don't tell me what I can and can't do."

Saben shook his head. "You can't help me. You can only make it worse."

"I want you to trust me."

"This is more than stealing VitD, Dade, or even fighting in the pits for me. You have to be careful."

Arden stepped forward. Dade felt the heat from the plasma shield flare as she neared it. Addressing Saben directly, she asked, "What did he do?"

"Made a deal with Crispin to buy my way out," Saben told her. Then he looked at Dade. "You know he's not going to let either of us go."

"I didn't promise him servitude," Dade said.

Saben chuckled. It was a hollow sound. "It doesn't matter. That man can twist a bargain."

"Who's Crispin?" Arden asked.

"That would be me," said a jovial voice from down the aisle. "I've looked forward to meeting the infamous Arden Murray. The vid-feeds make you out to be a warrior goddess. I have to say, you're looking quite the worse for wear, darling."

Dade closed his eyes, his head slumped forward. Fantastic. They'd have this confrontation today too. He'd hoped that he could avoid this problem for now.

When he opened his eyes and lifted his head, it was to see Saben looking at him, amused. He stood up and approached the barrier directly in front of Dade. There was a sparkle to his eyes that hadn't been there moments before, a smirk that hovered on the corner of his lips.

Arden turned to the man behind them, the movement stiff. There was rage in her expression. She was lethal and cunning, which Dade had forgotten over the last few weeks.

Dade rolled his eyes at Saben's silent tease, then turned and stepped closer to Arden to make sure she wouldn't kill Crispin. They didn't need that quite yet. And honestly, he hoped to avoid that altogether, not that he hadn't considered it a time or two in the past week.

"Who are you?" Arden asked Crispin. Her hand had moved to rest on the phaser strapped to her side.

Crispin was unlike any crime lord Dade knew. He might be a devil, but he looked like an angel. Curly hair fell in ringlets around his face, framing eyes that sparked with mirth and a mouth that was always upturned. He was ever quick with a laugh, as if there were a joke others didn't understand. Showing off a pirate's smile that flashed three gold teeth, which oddly added to his persona rather than detracted from it.

There was something calculated about Crispin's appearance that bothered Dade. His features were so precisely cut that it was as if he'd been genetically altered. He was young to run such a vast criminal empire, but Dade didn't doubt that he'd controlled it using cunning and sheer determination.

This underground fight club belonged to Crispin. Though the fighters weren't his. Well, except for Saben and himself. Crispin was the man behind the curtain. He rented out the cages and pimped the fights. So far he'd treated Saben well, getting him medical attention and meals.

He also had legitimate businesses, ones that he publicly claimed. The most important of these were the casinos through which he funneled Solizen money. Dade was sure that Crispin had his hands in many other dark dealings.

In spite of all that, Crispin was insufferably likable.

Unlike the Twins who flanked Crispin on either side. The boy and girl were small and pretty. They looked maybe thirteen or fourteen. They had large round eyes and cropped short hair, and were dressed in identical dark tunics like little killer elves.

Dade didn't need to see them in action to know they were good at their job. The way they moved like liquid in glass—all flowing motion and grace—told the story better than words could. The arsenal of knives they'd strapped to their bodies underscored the point. Over the last week they'd appeared from seemingly nowhere, as if they were part shadow.

"I'm hurt that you've never heard of me." Crispin reached forward to take Arden's hand. He made an exaggerated show of leaning over and kissing it.

Dade felt his anger rise as he watched Crispin's lips meet Arden's skin and linger there.

"Now that we've finally met, I'm sure you'll find our acquaintance mutually beneficial."

Dade's mouth thinned. "Not likely."

Arden's only response was the tightening of her other hand into a fist. She didn't look away from Crispin. Then she did that thing where her stance subtly relaxed, and she suddenly appeared to be softer, nonthreatening. It was a lie, a cunning deception of femininity. Dade knew her to be viciousness ready to strike.

Crispin noticed the change as well, evidenced by his now-gleaming teeth. But he didn't seem worried in the slightest. He released Arden's hand and turned to Dade. "Your match is in half an hour. I thought you weren't going to make it. I was about to send the Twins to remind you that punctuality counts."

The Twins grinned.

Dade grit his teeth. "I wouldn't be late."

He couldn't read Arden's expression when she stared at him. It seemed to say all kinds of things. Mostly, *Are you dumb?* Which was something he'd found himself asking a lot.

"Ticktock," Crispin said in a singsong voice. "You should go prepare."

Crispin turned to Arden. He offered her an arm to escort her. "We can have a chat while Dade is working."

"Leave her out of this," Dade said. He fought to keep his panic from erupting. He didn't want her entangled in this web of lies and favors. "She's not part of our deal."

"I want to see Dade fight," Arden said, lifting her chin.

Crispin gave them both a fake pout. He said to Arden, "I'll let the Twins take you where you can watch. We'll have that chat later." His gaze slid to Dade. "Together."

That sounded marginally better. Dade needed to make sure he was still standing at the end of this fight. All bets were off if he got knocked out. He couldn't leave Arden to deal with Crispin alone. Not when it was his mess to clean up.

CHAPTER FOUR

Arden forced herself to look straight ahead and swallow back the sickness that climbed up her throat. The fight was horrible to watch. She wanted to cringe each time a fist struck flesh. The wet crunching sound followed by shouts of glee made her sick to her stomach.

She had never had a problem with fights before. Had been in many more than she could remember. In fact, if she'd been in the ring, she'd have no problem with it whatsoever. But this one was different. It was Dade in the ring because of some foolish manipulation. One she didn't know the context of, nor was there anything she could do to stop it.

Dade held his own even though he was unevenly matched. His opponent had at least fifty pounds of muscle on him. Dade was wiry and knew how to move, so that helped. He circled the ring on swift feet, returning more hits than he took. Still, the other guy's fist made forceful contact with Dade's face more often than Arden liked.

Her stomach twisted with each cracking thud. While her heart squeezed in her chest, making it difficult to breathe. But Dade didn't seem concerned, dancing forward to meet his opponent punch after punch.

Perhaps she would have understood if she knew why he fought. What deal he had made and how Saben was involved. If she had context for this craziness, maybe she could have helped Dade figure out another option. Not that she blamed Dade for trying to save his friend. She'd have done the same. Especially after seeing him in that cell.

Frustration filled her the longer she stood in this crowd. Did he not trust her? Perhaps he thought her weak. If she had pulled her weight since they'd decided to make a break from their previous lives, he wouldn't have had to make that choice.

And this was still the case. Being here drove home exactly how much her body had deteriorated. She hadn't anticipated just how much energy it took to navigate a crush of people. Arden had been on her feet too long today. Already a headache burned at the back of her skull.

As she watched the fight, she kept her eye on the crowds as well. Lasair, her former gang, might be here, and if any Lasair members saw her, she'd be dead. Crispin knew who she was, and that compromised her safety. He seemed slimy enough to sell her whereabouts.

She noted each exit. They were all too far away for her to make use of them, her escape routes cut off by the crowd and her inability to move quickly. Her best bet was to slip back the way she'd come, from behind the ring.

Yet the Twins flanked her. Clearly keeping Arden leashed.

That was how she thought of them: as capital "T"—Twins. As if they were one entity. A pair that had formed a unit in utero and could not exist as individuals each on their own. They communicated with each other silently, their macabre movements perfectly in sync.

They did offer her some respite from the crowd, though. Their presence created a barrier that she wouldn't have been able to pull off alone.

The match was coming to an end. She could feel it as she did with most fights. Though the outcome was yet to be decided.

She saw Dade's opponent move, his arm swinging in an upward arc.

Dade was too slow to avoid the fist to his face. It landed square on his jaw. His head snapped to the side, and blood and saliva spat from his mouth.

Arden cringed as the crowd went wild. Even the Twins grinned, their expressions vicious.

Dade shook off the punch and danced back. It was fancy footwork that wouldn't have worked in a street fight. Yet here it delivered just enough distraction that when he launched himself forward to deliver a blow, the other man didn't see it coming.

His hit had power behind it. It landed solid and clean. Even though the guy dwarfed Dade, the punch was substantial enough to take him down.

Arden was already moving before the opponent's body hit the mat, forcing herself to move faster than she should. Her body screamed in agony each time she was jostled by the crowd as she pushed her way through.

The Twins stepped up beside her. They blocked the unwanted elbows from contacting her seemingly without any effort. She wondered why they'd helped when they hadn't even spoken to her once.

They led her backstage, this time into an anteroom filled with people. It was as crowded as the club had been, but without the bloodlust that had stirred the audience. Some were fighters waiting for their turn in the ring. Others had been chained along a wall to await their return to their cells.

In front of them, their owners chatted with one another in a laughing camaraderie. They reminded Arden of the birds from the Wilds, the kind with teeth and talons and razor-sharp feathers, dressed in their slickly made tunics of brightly colored fabrics.

Disgust made her stomach sour.

Dade was already there. He sat on the floor with his back pressed against the wall. His head was tipped back, and his eyes were closed. The wraps, already taken off his hands, lay strewn on the ground beside him. He held a towel but hadn't used it to wipe the blood off his face yet.

Arden knelt next to him. She took the towel from his loose grip and began to clean his wounds, inspecting them as she went. The cuts were bloody but superficial. None of them would need quick-seal. Between the new cuts and the old bruises, his face was a mess.

Dade opened his eyes and watched her. He looked exhausted, his lids heavy and dark rimmed. She suspected that while some of his fatigue was from the fight, most of it came from keeping secrets. She should have pushed him for answers earlier. If this thing between them was going to work, they had to have trust.

"We work better together," she said.

He nodded.

She pulled the towel away to look at him directly. "You need to remember that."

He took her hand in his. "I will."

Arden squeezed his hand before letting go. She went right back to checking his bruises and split skin, making frustrated noises as she cleaned off the blood.

He asked in a dry, scratchy voice, "Are you okay?"

"Me? I'm not the one who just got pummeled."

Dade laughed. It was a brief sound, more of a croak than a chuckle. "I won."

This time she gave him a genuine smile. "Barely. We'll have to work on that."

"I thought you didn't want me fighting."

"I don't, but if you're determined to get yourself killed, you need to be better at it."

His eyes sparkled. He took her arm just above her elbow and steered her in closer. "I hurt, maybe you can kiss it and make it better."

"Yeah, where?"

He pointed to a spot just beside his lips. "Right here is the worst."

Arden managed to look serious as she leaned in. Her lips swept against his skin in a light caress. She didn't want to hurt him. There didn't seem to be any undamaged skin on his face. Not to mention, this wasn't the place for a make-out session.

Dade didn't seem to care, though. He turned into the kiss, his lips meeting hers, deepening it. His arms came around her, reeling her in.

She went along with it. Falling into his embrace was too easy.

He kissed her with intensity. It felt like a soul connection, full of need and want. His lips and his touch had become something she craved.

His hand reached up to gently stroke her cheek as he pulled away. Then he rubbed his nose against hers. "I love you, you know that?"

It was the first time he'd ever said the words out loud. Her body lit on fire near to bursting. The beat of her heart sped and almost swallowed her whole, but she managed, "Yeah, I figured."

"Oh, how's that?"

Her breath rushed out. "Because I love you too."

"It's me and you, right?"

"Forever."

Their lips met again, feverishly searching. This time the world fell away.

Turned out their moment didn't last long.

The prickling sensation of being watched tingled at her subconscious. It was like an itch that got stronger and stronger the longer their kiss went on, irritating her enough that she pulled away, though she was still caught in the traction of Dade's gaze. She blinked and scanned the area.

The Twins stood a foot away, shoulder to shoulder. Their heads tilted at the exact same angle, and their gazes watched them with an eerie intensity. They looked curious, as if they'd never seen anyone kiss before.

Arden shivered. The little freaks were totally skeevy. She leaned into Dade and asked them nastily, "What do you want?"

Dade's arms tightened.

The Twins grinned.

"Boss wants you both—"

"In the back."

"Come—"

"Quickly now."

The syncing, the way their speech went back and forth in the sing-song lilt, was not right.

"He said—"

"Not to let you dawdle."

"Time is money—"

"Money is time."

The Twins reached for both Dade and Arden, each offering a hand to help them gain their feet. They appeared slight, but there was strength in their grips.

Arden allowed herself to be pulled up, then followed them. She could fight, but it was best to save her strength for when she needed it. And she was interested in what Crispin had to say. She was mentally ready for battle by the time they'd left the crowded hallways and entered the inner sanctum.

Swaggering over, Crispin met them at the end of the hall and greeted them jovially. "There you are."

Arden didn't know what to think about Crispin. She didn't trust him, yet there was something likable about him. Under other circumstances, she'd find him entertaining. She wanted to know who he was beneath the crafted charm.

"As if we'd be anywhere else." Arden looked pointedly at the Twins before she looked back at Crispin with her eyebrow raised. "I agreed to talk. I don't appreciate the intimidation."

That earned a huge grin from Crispin. "You're feisty."

A slow blink later, she still stared at him. When he continued to look delighted, she realized that she amused him. Arden was positive that wasn't a good thing. Further, she didn't understand it. He'd anticipated her visit, and then he found her . . . engaging? She didn't think that had ever happened. It completely put her off her game.

Crispin turned to Dade. "That was an excellent match. I have two heavier-weight boxers in the lineup next week. Fighting them will make you a bigger profit. Or rather, will make *me* a bigger profit." He laughed at his own joke.

Dade grunted.

"Now that Arden has joined us, let's talk in my office." After a gesture down the hall, he led them to a door similar to all the others. Crispin slapped his hand on the scanner. The laser glided under his palm, and then the door slid open. "After you."

Arden felt thrown by Crispin. Unable to figure him out. So when Dade looked at her with an eyebrow raised, she just shrugged. She didn't understand what was going on either. Though whatever this was couldn't be good. One thing was for certain: Crispin had played this scenario nicely.

They all stepped into the office: Arden, Dade, Crispin, followed by the Twins. But Crispin stopped abruptly as soon as he entered, and his back went stiff. Arden looked across the room, wondering at his reaction.

Her eyes widened and then narrowed.

A girl stood at the desk, examining the knickknacks scattered there. She picked one up, testing its weight. Her back was to them, and she didn't bother to turn around.

Not that Arden had any problem identifying her. She knew that stance, knew that power packed in a little package. She knew the girl's seemingly benign behavior was false. She was a predator.

One that even Arden had a healthy fear of.

Arden's heart took a leap as adrenaline shot through her body. But she couldn't tell if it was from excitement or fear. Maybe both. Whichever, it felt good—like she was finally alive again. This was what she'd missed.

She'd last seen Mina on a buy for Lasair. Mina was a highly connected weapons dealer, one whom Arden met with often. At that meeting, the girl and her thugs had attacked her in order to make sure that Arden was who she said she was. Then, once reassured, Mina had given Arden a warning about the rumors of a mole in Lasair, as if they were friends. Maybe they were, sort of. They had a working relationship that Arden had trusted. At least until Arden had been attacked. Which was why Arden was confident the reason Mina now stood in Crispin's office had to do with her.

Mina turned and gave them a sharp smile. She carefully placed the tchotchke she was holding on the desk before she leaned her weight back against the metal surface and folded her arms, looking at Crispin first, then Dade, and then finally Arden. There her gaze stayed the longest, her head tilted with consideration. She appeared delighted.

Absurdly, Arden was too. There was a promise in that expression of fun or at least some sort of dangerous adventure. Arden craved that, though she knew to caution herself. Trust was tentative between them, situational at best.

Mina was pretty and petite with curly dark hair, dusky skin, and wide almond eyes. For a while, Arden had assumed this look was a synth-mask. But then she'd realized that no, Mina was crazy enough to walk around and do business without wearing a false appearance.

There were phasers strapped to her belt, and she wore a black running suit made to repel phase-fire. This wasn't a social call. Arden had seen Mina dressed in various outfits over the years, but never had she seen her dressed to do battle. And yet she appeared as wholly relaxed as when she wore her more usual bright sheets of color and glittering jewelry.

Crispin's skin had gone a blotchy red. His eyes burned and his jaw clenched. He didn't lose his cool—not yet. But he was close. The congenial veneer was gone, had slid away so completely as if to be forgotten.

Arden had to give it to Mina. She brought out the best in people.

"What are you doing here?" Crispin asked.

"Come now, Crispin," Mina tsk-tsked with a silky-smooth tone tinged with the accent of another of the planet's cities. "Is that any way to greet an old friend? I'm here for the same thing as you, a piece of the power couple."

Yep, things were about to get sticky. Arden grinned.

CHAPTER FIVE

Dade stood just inside the door, watching the exchange in Crispin's office from behind Crispin and Arden. He had been the last to enter and because of that, his view was obstructed. But he recognized the voice of the girl who'd crashed the party. It was one that he remembered all too clearly. A chill straightened his spine.

Not now. This was the worst timing.

The Twins moved around him with easy speed, flanking Crispin like avenging demons. Their demeanor had morphed from general oddness to a lethal promise in seconds. Their daggers were drawn, two each, the wicked-looking blades assuring a deadly end.

Dade inched around Arden's side and looked past her shoulder. When he saw Mina, he exhaled hard. Though he'd guessed, there had been a small hope that he was wrong. He hadn't expected to see her for weeks.

His stomach tightened with anxiety. He had yet to tell Arden about his business with Mina. Kept putting it off, convincing himself that there would be a better moment. Now the window of opportunity he had was gone, and the delay was going to cost him.

He cursed softly.

Mina didn't look bothered by any of them, not the Twins or Crispin, who glared, or Arden, who'd gone deadly still. She leaned on the desk, the side of her mouth curled slightly, and Dade realized she enjoyed creating chaos.

"Arden, you look like crap," Mina said.

"Why does everyone keep telling me that?" Arden folded her arms and glared.

The fact that Mina and Arden knew each other didn't surprise Dade. What caused the sinking in his gut was the confirmation that Mina most likely had manipulated his rescue—or maybe even his blast off the skyway—to trap Arden. He'd thought long and hard about Mina and her crew and why they'd picked him. Trying to reason out what they could want. Sure, he had knowledge of some privileged information because he was a Solizen, but not anything that they couldn't access another way. The only thing of value that Mina could want from him was his connection to Arden.

Seeing Arden and Mina adjust to each other in the room, Dade realized that they were more than just acquaintances. The way they moved, each seeming to anticipate the other, their unspoken communication, the narrowing of Arden's eyes, which made Mina laugh. Not friends exactly, but not enemies. Something in between.

"To what do I owe the pleasure of your company, Mina?" Crispin asked. The polished, sociable veneer was still in place, but Dade could tell that anger simmered under the surface. His voice had gone low and smooth, without its usual joviality. And his body tightened as he adjusted his posture.

It was a fighter's stance, Dade realized. He wondered then if Crispin had once fought in the rings himself, if maybe he hadn't always been the one in charge.

"Call off your children, Crispin," Mina said, the flick of her gaze indicating the Twins. "I've got no quarrel with you."

Dade heard the same unstated *yet* he was sure everyone else did. It was a threat that possibly only Mina could get away with.

Crispin and Mina were deadly players. They each had connections, and they both could make someone disappear with the snap of their fingers.

The tension escalated. For a moment, Dade thought Crispin would ignore her to prove that she wasn't in charge here. If something did go down, Dade didn't know whom he wanted to win or if he should simply hope for the best.

Arden didn't look concerned. She looked rather bored, actually. That more than anything settled him.

Finally Crispin waved his hand to dismiss the Twins. They obeyed, retreating into the hall. Crispin didn't look happy about it. His mouth puckered, and his eyes were slits. Though by the time he lowered his hand, he once again wore a smile. Only it had morphed, bordering on cruel with too many teeth showing and gold caps shining. "How'd you get past my guards?"

Mina's eyes twinkled as she straightened from the desk. "You know I don't like to gossip. But I'm sure we could trade secrets if you're so inclined."

Crispin grunted with what was supposed to be a laugh, but his tone expressed annoyance rather than mirth.

Arden watched in tense silence, so still that she seemed not to breathe.

Dade shifted, and that snagged Arden's attention. She looked at him, her gaze unreadable. Then she took two steps backward to stand at his side. Reaching out, she took his hand, sliding her palm against his. Her fingers gripped tight.

It felt like an assurance that they would get through whatever was happening here unscathed. That she would take care of everything.

Except she didn't know what he did.

Dade squeezed back, wishing she could hear the silent screaming in his head. The frustration churning in his gut was not something he enjoyed. There was no way to warn her of what was coming. He had to stand here and watch it happen with no way to stop it.

"Shall we?" Crispin held up his hand, indicating the sitting area.

Mina inclined her head. She slid away from the desk, and took a leisurely stroll through the room before she sat herself in the center of a couch. Dade and Arden positioned themselves on the couch across from her, while Crispin chose the chair closest to the door.

"Now that everyone is settled, care to tell us what you are doing here?" Crispin asked.

Mina shrugged with fluid grace. She tipped her chin at Dade. "I have a prior claim on Dade. I'm here to collect him."

Dade's stomach pitted.

Arden sucked in a harsh breath. He could feel when she turned to stare at him, but he refused to look at her. Didn't want to see the accusation or her disappointment. Moons, he'd screwed up so bad by not telling her. His mouth felt dry and his head a bit too light.

She turned back to Mina. Yet she leaned into him, her side glued to his. He couldn't read her intention. Didn't understand what it meant. Was she protecting him? Wanting to show a united front? Or maybe she was planning to kick his ass as soon as they left the room? Whatever the reason for her closeness, it made him feel sick to his stomach.

"What claim do you have on Dade?" Arden asked.

Mina blinked. The reaction seemed to show surprise, but Dade thought that it appeared way too calculated. "He hasn't told you that I saved his life?"

Dade's breath popped like a balloon. And now it began. He forced himself to sit up straighter. If Mina was making him do this with an audience, he wouldn't be a coward about it.

"When?" Arden's question was little more than a hiss of breath.

"When I fell over the skyway," he said, "Mina and her crew were the ones who put out the net. She saved me."

Arden shut her eyes, her face pinched in a moue of distaste. "Of course she did." When she opened her eyes, they focused on Mina, her stare unblinking.

Crispin leaned back in his chair, one leg folded over the other. For all intents looking like the king of the castle. "Dade is working for me. He's paying off a debt. As I have prior claim and am in need of his services, I'm sorry, but I can't let him go."

"It's his debt?" Mina asked. The toothy smile informed Dade that she already knew the answer. He wondered just how many spies she had.

Crispin looked reluctant when he answered, "No."

Mina clapped her hands like they'd reached an agreement. "Then he's free to go."

"We've struck a deal," Crispin insisted.

"A bargain that isn't his to pay," Mina pointed out. "A debt must be paid when the marker is called. You know this. My claim supersedes yours."

Dade didn't care for the way they spoke about him like he wasn't there. He wanted to say something, but he was indebted to both of them. His options were a bit limited. He wasn't sure whom he should pick.

Arden didn't speak up either. She watched them spar, her gaze intent. The warmth of her hand in his was something solid he could focus on.

"He's in my custody now," Crispin said.

"Is that really the case?" Mina asked. "He comes and goes. You allow him the freedom of an employee rather than treating him as if he's in service to you. I could have taken him anytime this week or last."

Crispin grunted.

"You had me followed?" The words were out of his mouth before he could stop them. It wasn't shocking that Mina's spies had kept tabs on him. What he couldn't get past was that he hadn't seen them or had any indication they were there. Dade knew the tricks to keep his dealings secret. It was how he'd managed to get away with his activities for so long. The fact that he'd had not one clue he'd been watched served to underline just how much he'd let slip in the last few weeks.

He should have at least expected it. Mina had implanted a tracker in him. He knew she could find him whenever she wanted. Yet at the time, it hadn't seemed all that important when he had things like his daily survival and keeping Arden alive to focus on.

"Of course she did," Arden said under her breath.

"But I didn't take him," Mina continued as if they hadn't interrupted, "because I knew you'd follow the code. Right, Crispin?" She raised an eyebrow.

Crispin's mouth pressed together. The silence was as good as assent.

"I'm not leaving without Saben." Dade couldn't leave Saben to rot. But he had no cards to play. Mina didn't have to help him, though he hoped there was some compassion inside her, even if her help would put him more in her debt.

"How much to buy out Saben's contract?" Mina asked Crispin.

Crispin was already shaking his head. "It's not for sale."

"Everything is for sale for the right price."

"There's nothing I want from you." Crispin's amused expression was back in place.

"We both know that's not true." Mina leaned forward and lowered her voice. "I know what you want—or should I say, I know *who* you want. I can get her."

Crispin blinked once, but that was all the reaction he showed. "I don't believe you."

Mina smirked.

There was an intensity to their stare. Dade couldn't help but feel he was the only one who didn't understand the deeper implication of what was being said. Even Arden had gone still, the hand not holding his clenched.

Finally, Crispin broke their stalemate by asking, "A favor for a favor?"

"Agreed," Mina said with a dip of her head. She glanced over at Arden and Dade. "It looks like you're coming with me, Dade, and we'll take Saben."

"First we need to make the terms of the repayment clear." Arden lifted her chin as she spoke to Mina. "What favor is required of Dade?"

"I'm not going to discuss my plans in present company, but I assure you, he'll only be needed for a single job."

"And the implanted tracker?" Arden pressed. "If he does this job for you, you take it out and the debt is paid."

"You tagged him?" Crispin interrupted, clearly impressed.

Arden sent him a scathing glare before turning back to Mina, pressing, "He does this for you, and then you have no further claim on him, agreed?"

"What about you?" Mina asked.

"What about me? I don't owe you anything."

"No . . ." She let her agreement hang between them for a moment. "You're going to let me take Dade? That doesn't sound like you. You gave up your family for him."

Arden flared her nostrils.

Dade's heart squeezed. Sun, he couldn't breathe. He'd known this would happen. But knowing and watching it unfold were two different things. Arden wouldn't leave him, just like he wouldn't leave her. He'd gotten her trapped. This was his fault.

"I will let Dade go after this job and remove his tag if you agree to join us," Mina promised.

Crispin whistled. "Nicely done."

Mina didn't acknowledge the compliment. She didn't gloat or crow. Yet she knew Arden didn't have any other choice, and it showed in how casually she offered the trade.

"I owe you nothing," Arden finally said. "I come and go as I want."

Mina nodded once. "Of course. However, you will wear a tag as long as you have access to our facility."

Arden's eyes narrowed. She let go of Dade's hand, sliding to the front of her seat, and leaned forward. "No."

Mina shrugged a shoulder. "It's nonnegotiable. You won't be able to set foot inside the facility without one."

Arden sat in silence for a long moment. "When we're finished, I want all of the tracers removed: Dade's, Saben's, and mine."

"If you want them out at that time, then yes, I'll remove them."

"Okay," Arden agreed.

Dade knew there was no going back. Whatever happened from this point forward, they only had each other.

CHAPTER SIX

Arden resisted the urge to look over her shoulder as they left the boxing club. Tension had been her constant friend for weeks, but now it seized her muscles. It was because of things like this—making a deal for their lives and not knowing if Mina or Crispin would keep their word—that kept her body from relaxing enough to heal.

"There's a hovervan waiting," Mina said. Telling them to hurry was implied. They were too far down inside the Levels for the hovervan to park directly outside the club. Hovertraffic was restricted to Level Three. As they were currently on Level One, this meant they would need to trek through the city and take a public quadralift to get there.

As they left the club, Mina positioned herself right in the middle of the group in a clear show of power. Her shoulders were straight, and she walked at a measured but brisk pace. Confident, as if this afternoon were merely another deal in a long line she had yet to accomplish before dinner.

Several times in the past, Mina had asked Arden to join her crew. Arden had repeatedly said no, of course. At the time, she'd thought Mina had no idea who she was, because Arden was always careful to wear a synth-mask and voice modulator. When she tried to avoid doing the exchanges with Mina altogether, somehow Niall always came up with a reason why Arden should be put on the task.

And now, here Arden was, trailing after Mina. This was what made her most suspicious. Mina's motives couldn't be trusted, at least not until Arden could see the full scope of her plan. Arden got a sense that Mina's calculation was too precise, too long-term, and Arden hated being included in other people's plans without her explicit agreement. It set her on edge.

When Arden and Dade had left their families, intending to create a new life, she'd known it wasn't going to be easy. And so far, between the two of them, they'd mucked up everything. If Arden had pieced together this con, or whatever it was, before Mina had set it into motion, maybe she could have altered its course. Now that she'd been outmaneuvered, she was in the worst possible position to defend herself.

Once they were clear of the club, Mina directed them through the streets of Level One in Zero District. It was the base Level directly over the dome on top of Undercity, so the street connected from one side to the other. Above them, the skyway was open to the static cloud. They crossed a walkway heading toward the center of the city and the quadralift.

They moved as quickly as possible through the crowd. Someone was keeping tabs on them. Arden could feel it in her gut, though she didn't see any evidence of it.

The air was still dusted with debris from the explosion weeks earlier. Damp from the static cloud, the wet ash stuck to the side of the buildings. The flecks that had made it to the ground had been trampled into a gray slush that swirled and kicked up under booted feet.

Arden maneuvered herself closer to Mina. "Where are the big dudes you're normally with?" Every time she'd seen her, Mina had been surrounded by goons. She'd expected them to converge on the group as soon as they stepped out of the club. That they hadn't was a decided change from the norm.

Mina shrugged. "They're back at the ship. It makes sense to use them when I deliver my goods. The muscles serve to deter most double crosses before they start." She wasn't from this city and kept a permanent dock at the skyport where she would park her jumper, the ship they used for planet-side travel. It made sense that she'd keep the muscle there to protect it.

"And now?"

"I'm running light with a smaller, less conspicuous crew in the city. It's easier to stay under the radar."

Excitement zinged through Arden when she realized she'd finally see Mina's real crew members, the ones she pulled jobs with. It was something she'd always been curious about. Yet sharing the knowledge of her inner circle also displayed a vulnerability to Mina's operation that made Arden ask, "You're going to let me meet them?"

"I am, and here's the first one now."

The girl stood at the edge of the crowd. Most people wouldn't have noticed her. She certainly had a way of blending in. But Arden recognized the small tells: a hand that kept straying to the girl's side where presumably she had a phaser tucked under her cloak, the way she watched the crowd without actually catching anyone's gaze.

Her hair was cropped, the ends spiked and dyed in a vivid shade of green. She was short and thick, with a strong face. Her combat boots were softly worn and dirty, and given the way she stood with her hip cocked, ready to strike, Arden knew she was a fighter.

When the girl saw them, her hand pushed away the cloak at her hip, resting her palm on the butt of a phaser. Yet her attention moved past them, tracking the street in the direction from which they'd come. The girl's eyes narrowed. "You have a tail of three, maybe four."

"Let's move swiftly, then," Mina said. "We can lose them in the riots to the south."

The girl pulled cloaks from a sack slung over her shoulder. She threw one at each of them. There was even one for Saben. Confirming Arden's suspicion that Mina meant to break him out the entire time.

Misgivings flared bright inside Arden. But she didn't say anything, just swept on the cloak and pulled the hood low over her head.

The girl seemed indifferent, not making a point to be friendly, but not acting overtly hostile either. She spoke into her comm before saying to the group, "The hovervan should be landing in ten." Then turned and melted into the crowd waiting for the quadralift.

When the disk docked in the station, Mina signaled with a slight tilt of her head that they should enter into the round tube first. She took up the rear position, stepping in last and making sure that no one got separated. The light door engaged, and the edges of the disk glowed blue before it began its ascent.

Arden found the jaunt through the city at this pace difficult. She leaned against the graffiti-scarred inside of the tubing and steadied her breathing. Normally she'd be able to traverse the city without any problem. She'd been too long on her feet, the excitement of the day too much past her new endurance. Her exhausted body did not follow directions, and her limbs felt shaky.

Dade looked over at her, his face pinched. But she shook her head, causing him to frown and look away.

The others began to look too, the new girl and Mina. She couldn't have that. Arden forced herself to straighten, having no choice but to press forward to reach wherever Mina deemed it safe. Yet as the minutes ticked by, she wasn't sure she'd make it. If Mina wanted to use Arden as a puppet, she might have to wait awhile until her strength returned. The thought of Mina getting damaged goods after all her machinations made a smile tug at Arden's lips. Served her right.

They exited the quadralift on Level Three and turned into an open storefront market. People were crowded into the space. They held signs raised high, while voices decried both the Solizen and the city government with chanting lyrics. They wanted fair wages and access to the sun, spurred on by the knowledge that the VitD refinery was no longer producing. Their deaths were inevitable, and they knew it.

There was a palpable feeling of anger in the air. It pulsed like a physical presence. Rioting hadn't begun yet, though Arden figured it might break out at any time. The crowd pushed forward toward cordoned-off areas. And several small fires had been set at their outer edges.

Govies lined themselves between the protesters and the shops, trying to curb the tension. There were too many people to clear the skywalk, their goal to redirect the crowd. Their presence only made the protesters angrier. The chanting swelled.

The people had always been oppressed by circumstances of their birth, but there had never been a reason for them to fight back. It was frightening and awe-inspiring. Maybe for the first time Arden realized that they were on the cusp of a revolution. It would take only one or two more incidents of corruption to push the citizens into an all-out war.

Niall had been right all those months ago that attacking the VitD supply had been the way to instigate change. The powerful drug was the only way people were able to stave off Violet Death, the horrifying illness that came from lack of sunlight. He'd managed this. In an indirect way, his actions had caused this chaos.

The truth was that VitD had always only been available in limited quantities, with profits and the majority of the manufactured drugs going to the Solizen. The govies distributed the rest with a strict priority system as a way to control the people. Everyone was ranked according to age and social standing, and how much they contributed to the city's economy. A manipulation that now couldn't stand up in the face of panicked citizens.

They were still in the early days of the crisis. The effects from the lack of VitD wouldn't be seen for at least a year, maybe two. Plenty of time for someone to seize control of the city. The question was, who would that person be?

She'd never felt unsafe in Undercity or the Levels. A lot of that sense of safety came from the knowledge that she could take care of herself.

This was different. Arden wasn't sure she could put up a good fight as exhausted as she was. And the animosity was higher than she'd ever seen. It set her heart to beating. She wanted out of this crowd right now. And she didn't much care at that point where they headed.

Tucking her face down, Arden tried to keep in the wake of Saben as he parted the protesters in front of her. Halfway through, the crowd began to roil. The anger ramped up, promising a bloody mess. Her body stiffened, reacting to the knowledge that she was stuck.

"Quicker," Mina said from behind her, and put a prodding hand at Arden's back. "They're going to block off the street."

Arden looked past the crowd to see that more govies had arrived. They flanked the skywalk in front of the far exit, spreading out to stop the crowd from moving forward. The crowd surged anyway, trying to make it through before being cut off.

She pushed herself faster. Each step was agony. Her body had taxed itself beyond her capability. Exhaustion threatened to black out her mind. And through that, the cold slice of panic carved at her chest, squeezing out the air she managed to pull through her lungs. She could not pass out here. The crowd would trample her without a second thought.

They finally made it to the line of govies. Mina pushed Arden through the ranks while using her shoulder to shove into the gut of a govie moving to stop her. They ran while the govies closed in behind them, facing the crowd.

Down the next section of skyway, the girl who led them there waited. Dade and Saben had just reached her when the girl pulled her phaser and looked back. She relaxed when she saw Mina.

"We pissed off those govies. Between them and the crowd, it should keep our tail busy for a few minutes. We need to get to the hovervan," Mina said. She'd kept her hand on Arden's back. Now it acted as both a brace to keep Arden from falling and a tether to keep her mind in the present.

Arden didn't tell her to drop it. She couldn't. Her entire focus had narrowed, concentrating only on putting one foot in front of the other. The panic attack had even helped to block out the fact that her body hurt.

Even then, she didn't want to ask for help. Mina seemed to know this. Her hand felt warm and reassuring against her back, and she shooed off Dade when he began to walk back to Arden, telling him that they didn't have time.

Three blocks later, they found the hovervan illegally parked against the skywalk, its side door open. A boy, dressed in a running suit so tight it showed every dip of muscle, stood beside it with his arms crossed over his chest. His dark hair had been slicked up into a pompadour, and his cloak blew in the wind. When he saw them, he grinned with blindingly white, perfectly even teeth.

Arden tried to decide if this was yet another meathead in Mina's seemingly unending supply. He seemed younger and quite a bit more lithe than the usual suspect, though perhaps not much smarter.

The boy saw her looking and flexed his bicep.

Arden instantly wrote him off. No, definitely not smarter.

"About time," the boy said. "What'd you do, go sightseeing?"

The girl who'd met them shoved him in the gut as she made her way into the hovervan. "Shut it."

CHAPTER SEVEN

Dade slid into the backseat of the hovervan next to Saben.

The girl in the driver's seat turned away from the wheel and gave them a little wave. "I'm Annem."

She was young, of average height, and extremely thin. Her dark skin looked like it barely covered her bones, as if she hadn't grown into her body yet. Her long, glossy black hair was braided in two rows secured with bright red ribbon. She bounced in her seat as if the excitement of the rescue were too much to contain.

Arden slid into the middle bench between Roan, the boy who'd met them at the hovervan, and Mina. Dade felt too far away, staring at the back of her head. He frowned. There was something going on with her. She looked odd, kind of pasty with her pupils blown too large, and she seemed to stare right through him. Dade wanted to get her alone and ask her what it was. They were a team, and he greatly disliked that they were already being split up even if it was by only a few feet.

The girl who'd met them in the city was named Coco. She finally introduced herself as she slid into the front passenger seat next to Annem. She gave the younger girl an indulgent smile before waving at her to roll out.

They slid into traffic with a zipping move followed by a thrust of power that pushed Dade back into the seat. The jarring motion made him realize he hurt in places he hadn't known were bruised. The smell of the ozone recycled through the filtration system. It blew cool air into the back of the hovervan, but it wasn't enough to stop his roiling stomach.

Annem dipped and swerved through the vehicles, as the hovervan barely missed hitting other drivers.

Roan swore and snarled at her from behind her head, "Stay in your lane."

"Stop yelling at her," Coco said with a glare. "She's ditching our tail."

Roan was having none of it. "There's no one behind us, and I don't want to die thousands of feet in the air because she can't control this vehicle. And why is she always at the wheel? Annem's the worst driver."

Coco showed him her teeth. "If you don't want Annem to kill you, I could volunteer for the job."

"Children," Mina chided with amusement. "You can drive next time, Roan."

He huffed and crossed his arms. "I will."

Annem darted straight up into the static cloud where hovervehicles were prohibited, then used the thick, gray, charged smoke for cover. It was cold and wet. Droplets of condensation covered the moonglass shields. Visibility was less than a foot, and yet Annem pushed the hovervan at top speed through it.

Roan swore.

Coco laughed.

Dade's heart felt like it sat in his throat for long minutes, only starting to settle when they began their descent into the Lower Levels. Visibility outside the vehicle improved. The static cloud began to wisp into lighter swaths of gray that caressed the vehicle.

The city came into view below them. He leaned into the moonglass that protected him from the outside rush of air to get a better look at the mass of moving bodies as they flew over yet another protest site. He now realized that the demonstrations hadn't been contained within the Level where they'd met the hovervan or even within that side of the city. Everywhere, it seemed, angry citizens held up signs.

Seeing the chaos made him think about all the things that he'd neglected. The weight of responsibility settled heavily on him. The people who counted on him to bring them stolen VitD—they'd probably die without him. The children and the sick wouldn't last as long as the healthy adults. They didn't have the two years to wait. Maybe a year tops. Not that he could do anything at the moment to help.

"The protesters are using the sun-star?" Arden asked, her tone thoughtful and her voice sounding like her own again. Her color seemed better too. She leaned over Roan to get a better look.

Dade looked to the window as well, searching the crowd to see that she was right.

The sun-star was the symbol used by the Solizen: a simple black sun, its center a perfect dark circle. Eight spokes surrounded the nucleus at equal intervals, the four points of the compass longer than the others. These spokes did not touch the center, leaving a rim of negative space to break up the design. The Solizen used it to signify that they were special, the only ones allowed access to the sun.

As the Ghost, Dade had used the sun-star as a declaration of war, spray-painting it in dripping red across the city. It seemed that the people had taken the appropriation of the symbol to heart. Several of the signs had been painted with the symbol, while larger versions decorated the sides of buildings.

It reminded him of things he didn't have anymore. Working as the Ghost for the last few years had given Dade purpose. It focused him and set the tone for his life decisions. He wondered what he'd do now and didn't like that he had no idea. It had been his plan that the Ghost would live while "Dade" would die. It hadn't worked out that way. As far as the city had been told, the Ghost was dead. He'd never meant to cut off that part of himself. It felt like a phantom limb, one he could feel but not use.

"The Ghost is their hero," Annem said, taking her gaze away from driving. Hovervehicles whipped around them as she strayed out of the line of traffic.

"Keep your eyes on the sky," Roan yelled at her.

The thought of the Ghost's memory becoming more than just a dead vigilante warmed Dade. He had done some good. Even as little as he'd managed to pull off had left a positive mark. The Ghost had become a symbol of a better life. Maybe he'd offered more hope to the people than he realized.

"I'm sure Dade has lots of thoughts about the Ghost and the sun-star." Mina glanced over her shoulder at Dade, the look she gave him inscrutable.

Saben stiffened beside him.

Dade's face went hot and then cold. He tried not to swallow or flinch or show any reaction to her comment whatsoever. Mina knew he was the Ghost. He'd questioned her awareness when she'd rescued him. Now it was quite obvious his intuition had been right. That was how she'd managed to be there at the right time. She must have figured out exactly what was going on between Dade and "the Ghost" when they fought, and she probably even had inside knowledge that the govies were going to take a shot at him.

If the Ghost were to rise from the dead, it wouldn't be in anonymity. The circle of those who knew his secret had spread wider. He didn't know how he felt about that. He'd always figured that eventually the identity of the Ghost would be discovered. But he hadn't expected it to be quite so soon. And he also hadn't expected that he'd consider going back to it, knowing full well there were people who knew exactly who was behind the mask.

Fear shouldn't play into his decision. Saving lives was worth fighting for when only he and Saben knew his identity, so it was worth fighting for now. The bigger problems he had, though, were his lack of money, his lack of gear, and the fact that VitD production was at a standstill. He needed to figure out these three things before he could move forward.

"They're tattooing their skin with the sun-star too," Coco said from the front seat.

"Who are?" Arden asked.

"The people, everyone."

Dade hesitated. "That's illegal."

"The sun-star isn't just for the Solizen anymore. Guess you're not so special after all," Roan said snidely.

Dade refused to give in to the impulse to touch his sun-star tattoo on the left side of his neck just behind his ear. It felt like a brand, telling him he was different, set apart, that he'd never outrun his birth.

"If everyone has them, then yours won't stand out anymore." Arden sounded satisfied.

Roan snickered. "You would think that, Sunshine, but anyone could tell Dade's a siskin from a mile off."

Dade glared at him. Then shook his head and looked back out the window. There was no point in fighting with the guy. Roan was the type who enjoyed saying all kinds of things just to get a reaction.

That didn't stop Arden. There was a growl in her voice when she said, "Don't call me that, and don't call Dade that."

Dade had to give her credit for not throwing a punch. He didn't so much mind being called a siskin, the derogatory term for Solizen. It was something that had happened more often than not throughout his life. To his way of thinking, he'd rather be a siskin than the douchebag that Roan clearly was.

He also understood why the Sunshine comment annoyed her. It was a slam, implying that since the sun was only for the Solizen, that she was a Solizen whore—*his* whore.

Mina made a humming noise. "The rebellion is getting worse. It hasn't spread into Undercity yet, but it will. We need to pull together:

Undercity, the Levels, even any Solizen who will join us." Her gaze met Roan's. "Let's not antagonize our allies."

Annem docked the hovervan on a stretch of landing pad designated for long-term public parking. The landing platform was located in the middle of several older buildings, carved away like an afterthought.

Coco was the first out. She grabbed a case from the hovervan and strapped it over her shoulder, and she and Annem proceeded to make their way into one of the buildings. They laughed and pushed at each other. Annem bounced, her red ribbons fluttering, while Coco shook her head. Then she reached out to twine their hands together.

Mina rounded the vehicle and Roan followed. They pulled a net out of the back, opening it between them, and then threw it over the top of the hovervan. It was thin, see-through, with a silvery sheen. The fabric moved like liquid, undulating through the air before snapping out and clamping into place around the sides. Then the silver simmered and disappeared.

There was still a hovervan parked in the space, but it didn't look like the vehicle they'd ridden in. It appeared as a duller, dimmer version, the blue paint having turned to dark silver. He stared at it and realized that his vision slid off, as if forced to the side. Dade kept looking back, squinting, always with the same result.

"What is that cover?" Arden asked. She too squinted, reaching forward to touch it.

"It's a form of net-tech," Mina said. "Venz's invention. You'll meet him soon. It hides things in plain sight. I haven't sold it yet because its value is in the fact that no one knows we have this ability."

The netting had disappeared, becoming part of the vehicle. The air around the hovervan felt colder than it should, frigid, with an electric charge that bit at his fingertips as he pressed against the metal. It tingled and zapped him, causing Dade to snatch his hand back.

Arden and Saben were doing the same thing. Touching and then pulling their hands back as if burned.

Mina proudly stood by, indulgent. "If you know the netting is being used, it's easier to train your gaze to land on it. Normally people walk by it and don't think twice."

Dade wondered what else this netting had been used to hide and how many things he'd walked by without noticing.

"What happens if someone sees through the camouflage and tries to dismantle it?" Saben asked.

"It hasn't happened yet, but if anyone tampers with the net-tech, it's rigged to explode," Roan said.

Dade thought about the innocent people who could get hurt. But he also realized they couldn't leave their vehicle vulnerable. Anyone discovering and logging their DNA was a threat. It relieved him to know that he, Arden, and Saben would be off grid and hidden from their enemies as long as they were with Mina.

"Come on. We need to get inside." Mina turned to walk toward the building that Coco and Annem had entered. "We can't stay out here in the open."

They weren't being treated like they were prisoners, which was good and odd and definitely suspicious. It warned Dade to be prepared for anything. He knew Arden and Saben felt the same way based on how they carried themselves—Arden with an attempted limberness to her body, prepared to strike, and Saben taking deliberate steps, his gaze alert and cautious.

The building they'd entered was standard for the area. Much of the siding had been replaced with large metal panels bolted to the walls. Inside looked tired and smelled moldy. The lighting was mostly busted, leaving the hallways in darkness.

"Cameras?" Saben asked.

"They're taken care of," Mina said. "We have control of this part of the grid."

They took the small inside stairwell. The metal stairs clanked as the heavy tread of their boots hit the metal skiffs. He tried to keep track of how far they descended. They'd started out on Level Three, but with forty stories to a Level, they traveled for some time. A thin sheen of perspiration coated his forehead, and his breathing was heavy by the time they stopped. He estimated they'd reached Level One.

Dade expected them to exit onto the street, but instead, the group turned toward the center of the building and entered a boiler room. It was filled with a maze of big machines that provided the building with ventilation and sometimes heat.

The room was hot and sticky. Dade's clothes sucked against his skin, and he wanted to remove his cloak. He wiped his brow as sweat began to bead down his face.

In the center of the room, Coco was already using a screw gun on the bolts of a machine while Annem stood beside her, humming, her tempo rising and falling with the action. Once the shielding was off, a panel was visible. Annem pressed her hand against a control pad, and then entered a series of numbers. The box pulsed once with light, and then the hatch opened.

It was dark inside the tube, but he could faintly make out a ladder. This looked to be much more technologically advanced than the bolt-holes he'd taken into Undercity with Arden. He realized that instead of using the old passageways, they'd reconfigured an air shaft.

Arden held herself stiffly. "Your base is in Undercity? How did I not know that?"

Mina gave her a smile. "There are a lot of things you don't know."

"For how long?" Arden demanded.

"Years." Mina shrugged. "Undercity gangs have always been at one another's throats, too preoccupied to notice I'd moved in, and the govies don't bother with what happens there."

Arden crossed her arms. She spread her legs slightly apart so that she appeared to be steadier on her feet than Dade knew she was. "I'll be shot on sight if I return."

"Then don't let anyone see you," Coco said, rolling her eyes. Then she opened the case she'd brought from the car.

"I can't walk the streets," Arden continued, not taking her eyes off Mina. "They have spies everywhere. If anyone recognizes me, I'm to be killed on sight. Or is that your plan? Do you want me dead?"

Mina sighed. "No, I want to heal you and then help you fight. I need you, Arden, or I wouldn't have wasted all this time and effort."

Shifting slightly, Arden relaxed so incrementally, it was almost unnoticeable. She nodded once. "If you screw me . . ."

"I won't."

"I'm ready," Coco said. Syringes lined the interior of the black bag she'd laid on the ground. The liquid inside the glass tubes was clear, with a metal ball the size of a pinhead floating within. Coco had extracted one of the cylinders and popped up the needle.

Dade's gut clenched. These vials weren't for him. He already had a tracker.

"You remember this, don't you?" Annem asked Dade, her eyes sparkling with merriment.

Arden, who'd stopped staring at Mina long enough to see what Coco held, said with a shaky breath, "No."

"We made an agreement," Mina reminded. "Tagging you is necessary. This tunnel and our compound are both wired to blow if you don't carry the transmitter. We all have one."

"You wired your facility?" Arden's eyebrow rose.

"I like to keep my things secure." Mina waved at Coco to come closer. "It won't even hurt."

Dade saw Arden's hand clench. The struggle it took for her to breathe. But she said, "Do it now before I change my mind."

CHAPTER EIGHT

Arden gasped in shock as the heavy metal door slid open with a silent whoosh, displacing the airflow between the tunnel and the cycled air beyond. The opening led straight into Mina's compound.

She'd expected that they'd come out somewhere in Undercity and then have to travel to the hideout, as the Lasair usually did. To have the bolt-hole lead directly to a safe house, if it were to be compromised—it was no wonder it was rigged to blow.

Mina's lair had been converted from an old mining facility. A smart choice, considering they'd been boarded up and abandoned. No one would look for her here.

These mines could go down several stories and were lower than the city. Undercity was built on the soil, while the mines dug into the earth. Though Arden didn't think they'd traveled too far into the underground. By her estimate, they should still be in the first shaft.

The blue rock and silt walls had been reinforced with sheeting metal that ran halfway up the enclosure. Over the top were metal staves that braced the sheets in place, keeping the soil from shifting and collapsing the mine. A salty, wet mineral tang hung in the air even though an air-vac system had been installed. The condensation stuck to her lungs like wet sludge.

Mines were notoriously unstable because they flooded with groundwater. Arden heard the low hum of a pump system used to divert that water. Even so, flash flooding was a real possibility. It could come with-out warning, and they'd drown in a matter of minutes. Even a pump system couldn't divert a river of water.

"Please tell me I'm not going to drown in my sleep," Arden said.

"We have a warning system and an exit into the city." Mina pointed to her left where a tunnel headed upward.

The room they were in was large, the ceiling high. There were other openings at various points within the room besides the one Mina had indicated. It confirmed Arden's assumption that they were in the first shaft before the tunnels angled deep into the surface of the planet.

To one side was a kitchen. The space had all the usual necessities: a stovetop, a refrigerator, a sink, a long bench that functioned as an island with flanking bar stools. The rest of the room had been left open. There were several chaise lounges and a coffee table. It looked comfortable enough, though not decorated for aesthetics. Still, it was a lot better than any of Lasair's hideouts.

There were modern touches throughout that spoke to Mina's tech-nical capabilities. Those were new, shiny, and sleek. Gadgets that beeped and whirled, and Arden had no idea what they did. A vid-projector played the news silently, words scrolled along the bottom. Next to that was a weapons wall on which tactical gear was hung. There were phasers of all sizes racked, but no locks to secure them.

Arden looked to Mina as she stepped into the room. "If I knew you had a sweet setup like this, I would have joined you a long time ago."

"No, you wouldn't have," Mina said. "I didn't think anything would get you out of Lasair. Turns out I was wrong."

Arden swallowed back the pain those words brought her. Mina was right. She'd never thought of leaving Lasair until Dade came into her life. She tried for a light reply to cut the tension. "I would have robbed you at least."

"That I could believe."

Coco folded her hands across her chest. "You could have tried."

Arden glared at her. She wanted to point out that she would have succeeded. This place might be secured to the devil and back, but Arden was nothing if not determined when she wanted to be. This girl did not intimidate her, and she needed to know it.

Annem laughed before Arden could say anything, and gave Coco a slight push. "Stop it. Be nice."

Nice? No one in Lasair would have said such a thing to Arden. It was kill or be killed. Cut the throat of the person who wanted you dead first. What was with Mina's group? They acted like they were friends. It was so strange. She didn't quite know how to assimilate this new information.

Moving up beside her, Dade bumped his arm against hers. When Arden looked at him, he raised his eyebrows in silent communication. *Don't start a war with them on the first day, please.*

Arden rolled her eyes and looked away. She wouldn't start a fight. Not until she felt better, at least. Then she'd worry about the battle over dominance that would inevitably happen between her and Mina. She didn't take orders well. It had only worked with Lasair because Niall was her brother. Here, she knew she'd chafe against it.

Another girl they hadn't met stood just inside the room, waiting for them, datapad in hand. She was as tall as Arden, which was unusual and which Arden appreciated. Her hair had been braided and wrapped, the severe style making her cheekbones appear sharp on her delicate face.

"This is Nastasia," Mina said, introducing her. "She runs things here and is my right hand."

Nastasia dipped her head briefly as if confirming the position. Then she pointed to a tunnel on the far side. "The residences and restrooms are that way."

"The facilities are a little crude here, but we make do." Roan stretched, then scratched at his stomach. He'd taken off his cloak and most of his gear.

Annem rolled her eyes. "Don't let him scare you. It's a composting toilet. And we do have running water."

Arden's attention had already moved on to Roan, who began checking the rounds in his phasers before putting them in the locked position. He then hooked them to the weapons wall. The only weapons he kept on his person were the knives strapped in a harness that crossed his back.

None of them seemed to be concerned that she had easy access to their weapons. Fools. It was as if they weren't afraid of her. Or, she supposed, more likely it was Mina making clear that she wanted to partner with Arden.

The only thing she'd agreed to do was to watch Dade's back. She needed to remember that. Because as much as this show of trust could lull her into complacency, if it came down to it, only Dade had her loyalty. The rest of them could rot.

Arden looked away from Roan and realized that Mina had been watching her eye the weapons wall.

Giving Arden a tiny smile, Mina said, "You're welcome to use anything there. Once you've recovered, of course."

Coco watched the entire interaction with crossed arms. Her gaze darted between Mina and Arden, and when it looked like nothing more was going to be said, she dropped her arms. "Okay, gotta run."

Annem gave a little wave as she followed Coco out of the room.

Arden watched them go. And then realized Dade was in the middle of a staring contest with Roan. This was all too much. A headache pounded the back of her skull. To Mina she said, "You all are nuts."

Laughing, Mina said, "You think this is crazy? Wait till you meet Venz."

"Enough for now. You can meet him later. Let's get everyone settled first," Nastasia said. She studied Arden. "You're a lot worse off than we thought you'd be."

Arden narrowed her eyes and grunted.

"Come," Nastasia said, "I'll take you to the med bay."

Arden's body screamed her discomfort. She was exhausted and barely functioning. Her shoulders were tight and aching from when she'd forced them to move in spite of the pain. Still, the thought of separating from Dade made her anxiety flare. "I don't want to leave Dade."

It cost her to admit that vulnerability. It wasn't that Dade couldn't take care of himself. It was more that she was afraid that if she backed down for even a second, she might not be able to muster the strength to start again.

Mina's expression softened. "We're not locking you in. He can visit you as often as you both like. You have to allow yourself time to recover."

Nastasia studied Dade's hands. "He'll be in the med bay too, at least for today. He needs a nanotech booster to repair those fingers."

Arden nodded, relieved. She ached to kiss him, to reassure herself that this had been the right thing to do. Not that there had been another choice.

To come out on top, they needed a better plan, needed friends who could help. She sighed. Maybe she could give it a chance. She'd wait and see before making any decisions.

Chapter nine

After her third session in the med pod, consciousness did not come back fast to Arden. She swam in the in-between for a length of time. It felt warm and weighted, but she forced herself to let go of the comfort it offered. At first she wondered where she was. Her eyes ached when they opened, though the light in the room wasn't bright.

Low-level ambient sounds were the first things she recognized. She fell into their steady beep and hum. Then noticed the temperature. It was a little cool, numbing her toes. There was also an antiseptic smell that singed her nostrils as she breathed. Between the sounds and the smell, and the fact that she needed a pair of socks, she finally remembered where she was.

She realized she lay on a bed with wires stretching from her. There wasn't exactly relief at knowing that she was safe. Her brain wasn't working on that high of a function level. Instead, she felt a muted calm, just enough to allow her brain to begin to assess other things.

Pain was next. She ached from lack of movement and exhaustion. Her limbs felt heavy, as if she'd been drugged. The prickles under her skin stung, as if her body wanted her to remember that it was there and she needed to pay attention to it.

Then she realized that someone else was in the room. Her eyesight hadn't fully focused yet. And there wasn't any noise that would indicate the visitor. So she couldn't say what had tipped her off. Perhaps it had been a shift in the room. Or maybe it was pure intuition. Either way, her body tensed, escalating her discomfort.

That at least helped her to finally manage to fully open her eyes and focus her attention. The light made her nauseated, and she squinted and swallowed against the curling in her stomach, breathing in deeply. Twisting her head toward where she sensed the person was in the room caused another roll to her stomach. When she saw who sat in a dark corner, she wondered why she bothered to put herself through the torture.

Roan aggressively leaned forward in his chair. He watched her intensely with a glassy gleam to his eyes. In his hand he held a large knife. When their gazes met, he leaned back and began to clean his nails with it.

Was that supposed to frighten her? Arden couldn't figure out why this farce was necessary. More dangerous people than Roan had tried to scare her, and they'd been unsuccessful.

He looked fresh, not like he'd sat there for hours or for however long she'd been out. Had he expected her to wake up, or did he just get lucky?

One thing was for certain: *she* wasn't lucky. Her first impression of him hadn't been good. And this move didn't improve on it.

They were the only two in the room. She confirmed the door was shut before she looked back at him.

Arden wanted to sleep. But she kept her eyes open and her stare level. Though it was hard to appear tough when she was draped across a bed and covered in med wire. Even as beat up as she was, she knew she could take Roan. The thought reassured her. So she didn't filter herself in any way. And if she provoked him, so what? She was pretty sure Mina had instructed her crew not to touch her.

Silence stretched to an uncomfortable level, but she remained steadfastly mute. She wouldn't be the first to break the stalemate. He came here for something—to grill her or to just be a pest—but whatever the reason he'd concocted, he wouldn't get the upper hand.

"I know what you're doing here," Roan said, breaking first. He'd stopped fiddling with the knife to give her his full attention. Though he kept it gripped in his hand, the wicked blade pointing in her direction.

Arden couldn't decide whether he was serious. "You should. You were there when Mina manipulated me into this farce. As a matter of fact, you probably know more about my situation than I do. So why don't *you* tell *me* what I'm doing here."

Roan snorted, looking unimpressed. "I mean, I know you're here to infiltrate us."

"I am?" Arden sighed. She didn't have the patience to deal with his entitled conspiracy theories. "Trust me, if I had planned this, I wouldn't be lying here right now. I'd be getting into your business."

Roan did have one point to his credit. She wouldn't have weakened her own hideout by bringing in strangers with whom she shared no loyalty. The fact that Mina had done exactly that confounded her. Roan should be questioning Mina, not her.

"You are not going to get away with tearing us apart. Mina's not like your last gang. You can't make us distrustful of one another."

"You think I did that?" Arden couldn't decide if it was a compliment. The fact that he thought she had so much power was flattering.

"Mina watched you." He paused. "*I* watched you. You weren't faithful to them. At the first opportunity, you bailed."

She thought of Dade. That she'd chosen him wasn't a stab in the back to Lasair. It was an effort to control her own destiny for once in her life. "They forced me to move on. I didn't leave."

"Just know that I'm watching you," he said, stabbing his knife forward as if to make a point.

"Okay, if that makes you feel better."

He scrunched his face, perplexed by her answer. "It doesn't."

Arden forced herself not to smirk at how easily he became confused. She glanced at the knife still leveled in her direction, though his hand was now lax. "Is that supposed to intimidate me?"

"What?"

"The knife." She pointed around her, sweeping the room. "This whole thing. Did you think you'd wait for me to wake up, and then I'd see you and suddenly be so overcome with fear that I'd tell you all my secrets?" Arden laughed, and moons, it hurt. She sucked in a breath, forcing her body to be still.

His lips thinned, and his eyes narrowed. She realized that he really had thought that. The boy was not a mastermind.

"Does Mina know you're here?" she asked. When he didn't answer, she added, "How about Nastasia?"

In the silence that followed, she pointed to the camera mounted in the corner of the ceiling. "Don't you think they'll find out?"

His eyebrows went up. "How did you know that was there?"

"I know where cameras are at all times. It's kind of in my job description."

Though he was clearly surprised that she'd properly read the room, Roan didn't seem concerned that anyone would find out about his information expedition. It was curious. Almost as if Mina was okay with her crew members doing anything they wanted. What kind of gang was this?

If he was just going to glare and threaten, she might as well ask the important questions. "Am I locked in?"

"No." The implied *You should be* was left unsaid.

"How much longer are they going to keep me hooked up in med bay?" And why wasn't Dade here instead of Roan? That had been the real question she wanted to ask.

Roan's lips pressed together. "For as long as Nastasia says."

Interesting. "So she's in charge?"

"Mina is. But Nastasia runs the compound."

As far as her experience went, she'd never met a head of anything who could properly delegate. Arden had a healthy skepticism that Roan was telling the truth. "Then get Nastasia so I can ask her."

"You're a pain in the ass, you know that, Sunshine?"

"I've been told that a time or two."

Roan snorted.

She bit back the other questions she wanted to ask him. They were all about Dade and would give too much away. Why wasn't he here? Had something happened to him? Pragmatism settled in. If he was hurt, Mina would have told her.

If anything, Dade's absence underscored their pulling apart. Instead of forcing him to open up sooner, she'd let this weird silence build between them. When she thought about it, it left a burning in her chest.

Unbidden, she reached up and rubbed it, the heel of her hand pressing against her sternum.

Why had he not told her about Mina? Dade had said he'd been rescued, and she'd all but pushed that aside. She was confident that they could worry about it later. Yet he had to have known how much trouble he was in. Did he not trust her?

She felt a little peeved too, truth be told. Dade should be here. She'd be waiting for him to wake up if the situation was reversed.

But she kept her thoughts to herself. She wouldn't display her weakness as far as Dade was concerned. It could be used against her. The last thing she wanted was to become his liability.

Realizing she'd slipped into a frown, Arden smoothed out her expression. She knew better than to let any of her internal turmoil slip. Now Roan probably thought he'd gotten into her head. That was a bit insufferable.

Roan's eyes narrowed. "Are you okay?"

She nodded. What could she say? That she was heartsick? Who'd believe that?

CHAPTER TEN

Dade followed Saben through the city. They both wore slimline packs stuffed with explosive toys and other gadgets from Mina's stash. They didn't speak, preferring to move the way they always did on jobs, with a natural rhythm that came from practice. Their mood was somber. Neither knew what they'd find when they reached their destination.

They'd slipped out in the middle of the night. It was the best time to travel unnoticed through the streets. The govies monitored curfew, but their presence in the Levels had thinned due to the daily rioting.

No one in the compound had stopped them. Mina seemed to ignore any activity not pertaining to her directives. It didn't mean she was unaware, though. They were most likely being tracked. Dade was okay with that as long as Mina allowed him to take care of his business.

He felt better. It was a wonder what a little sleep and some nano-tech could do. In addition to not having to worry about how to survive his day-to-day existence. He owed Mina for that, for this chance to figure out how to start the rest of his life.

While he'd been in the med bay, Saben had been out every night searching for his family. It had taken a while. With the city in chaos and having to remain covert, it meant that finding missing people took time.

Dade had just been released, his hands finally usable again, when Saben had informed Dade that he had a lead. There had been a moment of indecision: should he stay and watch over Arden's recovery, or should he find some answers? He knew there was nothing he could personally do for Arden. She was still being mended and would be down for another week. Her injuries had been worse than they'd feared.

Upon first taking her to the med bay, Nastasia had clicked her tongue and shaken her head. She'd said, "It's a wonder you're still alive."

Arden had given her a fierce glare. "This isn't going to kill me."

"Stubborn," Nastasia murmured. But she said it fondly.

Today, knowing that Arden would insist on coming even though she'd spent the last week unconscious in the med bay, Dade hadn't told her about their mission. He'd visited Arden a few times but had mostly avoided her for a reason. He couldn't keep his secrets to himself. Every time he saw her, he wanted to tell her everything. If she knew, she wouldn't allow him to do this without her even if she wasn't fully healed. Hiding information from her didn't feel right, and yet he didn't want to set back her health. If he could bring back answers, then it would be worth it.

Leaving provided him the first opportunity to see the city alone. Dade had been stuck in survival mode for weeks, his only news coming through the visicasts. Not only did he need facts, but he also needed that deeper, gut-level connection. Going into the streets would give him a good idea of what people were feeling. In order to make decisions moving forward, he needed to grasp what was happening now.

The stagnancy he'd experienced in the last few weeks had left him numb. Moreover, he missed his weekly runs. Missed having adventures.

"Have you seen them yet?" Dade worried that perhaps they were walking into a trap. The cityscape had changed greatly in the month since he'd roamed the streets. New gangs had popped up, and there was a general distrust among everyone.

"No," Saben answered tightly. Maybe he thought the same thing.

A gust of wind pulled at Dade's cloak. His hood did little to stop his hair from coming loose and trailing into his face. He wore a synth-mask as he was too recognizable. If anyone realized he was alive, then a price would be placed on his head. For now it was best to keep up the farce of his death.

"Where are we going?" Dade asked. He knew this area. Every step they took toward the remains of what had been the joint refinery made the heaviness inside grow a little more. From the news-vids, all that had been left was a blown-out mess.

"Don't blame yourself," Saben said. "It would have happened whether you were there or not."

That was true, but it didn't do anything to help Dade find absolution.

Seeing for himself the raw crater that had formed where there were once buildings pulled the breath from his body. The destruction was so horrible, it hurt to look at it. The area around it had been decimated. All that was left was the dried-up husk of what had once been the refinery and the apartments that had surrounded it, the steel cores that went all the way below to Undercity now visible.

The loss of life must have been astronomical. Worse than what the visicast had reported. The govies would have tried to keep how bad it had been from the citizens to help quell the riots and regain order.

As they neared the area, the smell in the air changed. The tang of burned material, mixed with the sulfur of the static cloud, left a thick residue in the back of his throat. He wished he had an air-breather, but they had planned to mix in with the displaced citizens.

This wasn't how he'd thought he'd meet Saben's family. For so long he'd wanted to know where Saben had come from. And now, because their home had been destroyed, Saben was finally letting him in.

In a way, he was happy that he was wearing a synth-mask. Saben's family members were staying with others who wouldn't be receptive to a Solizen in their midst. Anonymity would help him navigate the many layers of simmering anger that he needed to understand before he could help them.

On the other hand, he hated that he was hiding. It felt wrong, as if he were ashamed of himself. Dade was unsure how Saben's relatives would react to him. They knew that Saben had worked for Dade in Sky Tower Two. He hoped that Saben would have told them that he and Saben were friends more than they'd been employer and employee. He wanted to make a good impression but wondered if it was possible.

Dade knew very little about Saben's family. The only time he'd been allowed close was when he'd watched the boy he'd assumed to be Saben's brother die. But it could have easily been a younger cousin. Either way, the boy's death had given Saben a manic resolve that convinced him to help Dade escape the Towers.

It felt like Saben believed in Dade more than he believed in himself. That he was positive they'd figure out a way to help Saben's people. Dade wasn't sure if he deserved that trust. So far, he'd made a mess of things.

They entered a hollowed-out building that had previously stood connected to the joint refinery. A full city block had been destroyed, leaving behind empty skeleton structures. Some walls remained, the floors between what had been stories and exposed metal beams. Chunks of debris were everywhere. The larger pieces had been left in place, but some had been swept into piles to create a path to the center. Most of what they walked through from the skywalk to the middle of the building was deserted. The wind screeched as it wound its way through. And it was almost entirely dark in there, because the city lights couldn't penetrate into the gloom.

Saben snapped out a glo-wand, and Dade followed suit.

At first he heard the sounds of coughing. Then he started to see the faint glow of torchlight the farther they went. He realized the refugees had set up makeshift barriers from the debris, trying to insulate themselves from the elements as best they could. They were grouped around small fires, huddled together for warmth. They'd collected as many things as they could from the wreckage of the apartment buildings that had been adjacent to the refinery—anything that hadn't been destroyed beyond reason—and used it to make their spaces comfortable.

He estimated that there were hundreds of families here. No wonder Saben had trouble finding his family. Even if the data sensors implanted in their wrists could be checked on the city grid, it would only ping a location. He'd still have to search the encampments, one by one.

Dade broached the question he hadn't had the opportunity to ask. "I don't understand why you went to Crispin."

The whole thing hadn't made sense. Crispin had kept Saben in relative comfort, and when Dade had approached him, he'd been eager to make a deal. He needed to understand whether Crispin was an enemy. Saben had warned Dade many times to stay away from him, and yet Crispin had been the first person whom Saben had gone to for help. There was more going on here than Dade understood. He felt he needed to get to the bottom of it in order to know who his true enemies were.

"What else was I supposed to do?" Saben asked. "You were missing. I thought you'd died. I was hurt and wouldn't last on my own. I couldn't go back to Sky Tower Two, not after the govies shot you. I wasn't sure who to trust, and I needed medical attention."

Dade remembered what it felt like to be lost, alone, and without his connections. He didn't blame Saben for his choice. And Dade had obviously done the same thing, indenturing himself to Crispin.

"Sometimes there are only crappy choices," Saben said. "There's no reason to look back and regret them."

Dade grunted in agreement.

"I knew I had to get better before I went to find my family." Saben sighed. "I couldn't be more of a burden to them. They're in no position to help me."

Dade nodded. The pit in his gut that was always there, whispering his failings, grew deeper now. If he hadn't asked Saben to play the Ghost that fateful day, then Saben would still be safe in the Sky Towers. If

Saben hadn't been hurt trying to escape, they both wouldn't have been bound to Crispin.

Saben, unaware of Dade's inner turmoil, said, "Crispin is decent. He may not be ethical, but he keeps his promises. He was always fair to his fighters. Better than the other slavers. I was well fed and had access to a med pod, even years ago when I worked the pit."

"Right," Dade said in acknowledgment, though he didn't agree. Crispin had kept Saben in a cage. Dade would never forget or forgive that. "You were friends once?"

Saben made a negative sound. "Not friends. He's someone I knew I could count on to take care of me when I needed it. For a price."

A price that had been too high, for both of them. Arden was right. He should have thought it through a bit more before he'd struck the bargain. It would have turned out much the same, but at least he may have been able to put in some safeguards.

Saben's family turned out to be quite large. There were aunts, uncles, and numerous cousins who shared space around a fire. He had four brothers, all younger, and an older sister. They all looked like him. Without the muscles, of course. Skinnier versions with wiry dark hair and big eyes.

They seemed eager to meet Dade, welcoming him as one of their own. Generous even in the midst of the crisis they faced. It surprised him that Saben had kept them a secret. And not for the first time wondered at the reason Saben had kept his background private for the many years he'd worked in Sky Tower Two.

Dade and Saben didn't stay long. There was no place to sit. And it became increasingly uncomfortable to politely turn down the offer of their meager food rations.

"We can't just leave them," Dade said as they were walking away. "We have to do something."

Saben shook his head. "I needed to make sure they were settling in okay, but there's nothing we can do right now."

"Can't we help them find better shelter?" But even as Dade spoke, he had no idea where that would be. The city was crowded, space at a premium. The loss of a city block of apartments had only exacerbated the problem.

"They're on the waiting list for relocation," Saben said. "I'll keep checking on them and make sure they have current rations."

If they were scheduled for relocation, that meant they had work permits. They were lucky, probably luckier than most of the people they'd seen tonight. Saben's family would eventually get out.

"If we weren't going to do anything for them, why did you bring me here?" Dade asked in frustration that had been building all night. Now he couldn't contain it. He knew there was no upside to giving in to his anger, but he hated feeling helpless. Both feelings had been his constant companions for weeks.

Dade was not going to sit around. If he couldn't figure out what to do with his own situation, then he would use his excess energy to help these people. He wasn't without choices. Dade just needed to broaden the scope of what he thought he could do.

"For now I need help moving fresh water in here." Saben pointed at the metal drums the people squatting in the building were using as storage containers. "It's going to take some manpower, and most of them are too weak to move it."

Dade nodded, thinking. "And in the long term?"

"We have to get them VitD. Not just my family, all of them. Even if they manage to survive the cold and hunger, they'll die without VitD."

Dade nodded again. He'd figure out a way to get it done. He felt the change inside him. The rightness clicking in. The knowledge that this was where he was supposed to be, what he was supposed to be doing, and who he was supposed to fight for.

Chapter eleven

"Stretch it out one more time," Nastasia encouraged. She stood behind Arden and supported Arden's arm as she lifted the flex plate. It was flat, no wider than her palm, and strapped over the back of her hand. When turned off, it weighed less than an ounce. When it was turned on, it used airflow to push a weight against her stressed muscles.

Grunting, Arden followed Nastasia's instructions. The pull in her side made her breath catch. Her flesh was knitted together thanks to several sessions in a med pod, though the muscles underneath had not regained their strength.

She was still assigned to the medical bay. The med wires had been pulled from her body, and she was able to leave her room daily to walk on the light track in the gym. She'd been careful not to wander too far and hadn't explored Mina's compound at all beyond those two areas. While the confrontation with Roan hadn't scared her, it had served to remind her that she didn't want to look too eager to see the setup. Not appearing too curious would be the first key to earning their trust.

She felt better, almost herself. Her slow recovery hadn't improved her disposition, though. Every time Nastasia showed up to help with her physical therapy, Arden's mood tanked. Logically, she knew that she had to be in top shape in the field. That was a matter of life and death. Still, working toward full mobility did nothing to curb her frustration at not being perfectly healed.

Nastasia's voice was pleasant as she gave Arden instructions. That, along with the encouraging smile she always wore, rubbed Arden the wrong way. Arden wasn't buying the nice act. There was a reason Nastasia was being so amiable.

She kept waiting for Nastasia to pump her for information. Slyly, of course, because Nastasia had so far turned out to be everything she'd expected of Mina's second: whip-smart, with a sense of dry humor, and always silently calculating. And yet, not once had she asked Arden anything remotely pressing. The more Nastasia didn't ask, the more irritated Arden became.

Perhaps Arden was just grouchy and it was coloring the way she saw everything. That was a high possibility too.

She'd had a lot of visitors over the past couple of days. Roan, the idiot, kept coming. She might have even thought he worried about her, given how often he showed up. Coco and Annem had come as well, always together and always for a scant few minutes. Mina had dropped by several times. She'd take a seat and try to have a conversation, but as neither one of them wanted to speak about real issues, there had been very little to talk about. Even Saben had come to visit, though he was mostly silent. He'd fill her in on day-to-day activities so she felt like she knew what was happening beyond the walls she currently occupied.

And then there was Dade.

He'd come to visit as well. Except that every time he showed up, their conversation was strained. They were both aware of the camera. And knew that they couldn't share what they were thinking. Seeing Dade, and yet not being able to connect on an emotional level, only heightened the tension between them.

No wonder she was crabby.

She'd had too much time alone. It gave her ample opportunity to think and plan. Her head was filled with a million different scenarios. And yet she hadn't the ability to discuss them with anyone.

"Focus," Nastasia reminded her. "Physical therapy is an important component to regaining full mobility."

Arden grunted.

Nastasia turned off the flex plate and took it from Arden. Next, she had Arden do several stretches without any resistance. Then Nastasia gently put her hand against Arden's triceps and pushed.

Arden let out a little gasp of distress that she couldn't hold back.

The burn flared through her side. It moved along her body and into her chest. Making her feel as if her lungs had collapsed. Her mouth fell open as she began to pant in shallow bursts. Arden wanted to beg to relax her arm. Though she kept her mouth shut, she locked her jaw together, suffering through the pain.

Nastasia paused, her gaze assessing Arden. Then she released her, letting Arden's arm drop. "We need to work on your range of motion."

"It's fine."

"Sure, until you have to fight for your life. Stubbornness will get you killed."

Arden couldn't argue with that. Hearing the truth, though, poked at her anger. She rubbed at her side, in an ineffectual effort to loosen the skin there.

"How come you're so smart about this stuff?" Arden asked. Most of them knew how to do field patching, but this required specialized knowledge.

"I trained to be a doctor before I joined Mina."

Arden raised an eyebrow. "You wanted to be a doctor, and yet somehow you ended up in the gang of a weapons dealer. What did she have on you to get you to agree to that?"

Nastasia gave a bark of a laugh. "She didn't manipulate me if that's what you're implying. I'm an idealist. It just so happens that my job here fits into that nicely. Turns out I can get more done illegally than I could in the medical profession."

"I see." Arden continued to rub her aching side, thinking.

What had surprised her the most when coming here was how much Nastasia was involved with the operation. And how clearly she had been in charge for a long time.

"Tell me the endgame," Arden finally said.

Nastasia, who was putting away the equipment they used, paused and turned back to face Arden. "What are you talking about?"

"Mina. You. What the plan is for Dade and I." Arden crossed her arms. "I asked Roan, and he doesn't know. Or pretends not to know. I'm thinking maybe you'll tell me what's going on here."

Nastasia didn't say anything for a long time. And then when she did, her words were measured. "She's offering you a family."

Arden snorted.

"I'm not going to pretend she won't ask you to do things that maybe you won't like. That's a given. But she knows who you are, and she knows you're loyal to your core. It must have hurt when your gang turned against you."

It felt like she'd been stabbed straight in the chest. Arden didn't say anything. She couldn't. Her breath had disappeared when creeping white began to fill the sides of her vision.

"Why don't you give it time?" Nastasia asked. "See what happens. It's not like you've got much to do anyway."

Arden knew how that worked, though. That was how they sucked you in: fed you, gave you shelter, fixed your broken body. She wouldn't fall for it.

Nastasia seemed to know the direction of her thoughts, because she asked, "Have you ever thought about taking what you deserve?"

"What do you mean?"

"You were dealt a pretty crappy hand. But that doesn't mean that you have to live with it. You are perfectly capable of changing things."

Yeah, Arden had considered that. Had even followed through with it. And then it had all fallen apart. "Maybe I deserve this. I betrayed my family. Perhaps constantly fighting for a place in this world is the price I have to pay."

Nastasia looked her straight in the eye. "Do you really believe that?"

Most days she did. When the guilt was too much and it all felt so crushing.

Walking over to her, Nastasia placed a gentle hand on her arm. "Some people are your family because you're born with them. Some people become your family because you need them. These people are my family because I've chosen to be with them. And that's the best kind of family to have."

Was family a choice? Her cousin had said as much to her before his death. Had urged her to get out of Lasair and find a new path. She'd thought it meant either staying with her gang or leaving them completely. Yet more and more she was considering a third option.

Choose.

The thought was so simple, it left her bereft.

Chapter Twelve

Dade walked next to Arden. He fought his instinct to say something to get her to smile. But if he did that, they might talk about other things. He wasn't good at subterfuge. Avoiding anything that would require him to come clean seemed like the best course of action. "Are you happy to be out of the med bay?"

"I'm ready to escape the constant monitoring." She sounded tired but mostly herself. "Nastasia said she'd find me a bunk after the meeting."

Dade had swung by the med bay that morning to walk with her. He'd found her dressed, sitting on her bed waiting for him. He'd been surprised that she'd looked so well—perfectly put together again with no trace of her injury, including the closed-off expression he'd come to expect.

He'd kept tabs enough to know that she hadn't wandered the compound, so he'd thought that she was still too weak to do so. That had been a mistake. He obviously hadn't visited her enough to stay on top of her recovery status.

He knew he should say something to her. Tell her about finding Saben's family. Tell her about his decision to resurrect the Ghost. Tell her that he wanted to do something more to help people. The words ate at him from the inside, and still he kept his mouth shut.

While she watched their surroundings, he watched her. There was the occasional squint when she overextended the arm on her wounded side. It was miniscule, really. No one would notice unless they studied her. Arden was whole. Relief filled him. For the first time in weeks, he felt hopeful. That was, if he could find a way to come clean.

"Where have you been the last few days?" she asked.

Dade swallowed, trying not to take too much time to find his answer. He knew she was upset with him for being MIA. That much was obvious. She had a right to be, honestly. Though she hadn't treated him much differently from before, except maybe a little more coldly.

It might be best to tell her a partial truth. "I've been working out. Getting back into fighting shape. Doing some physical therapy with my hands."

She looked at him with narrowed eyes. He knew that she wanted to talk about things just as much as he did. And yet, she knew that they couldn't speak here. Not for hashing out future plans that might be at odds with one another. And wasn't that the crux of it? He didn't want her to tell him that she wanted something different.

Each time she looked away from him, tilting her chin up, his stomach tightened.

Dade would explain to her about Saben and his family eventually. He couldn't handle the rejection quite yet if she didn't agree. Plus, he wanted to figure things out first. And he was afraid that if he told her now, she'd tell him that his future was best served by focusing on how to get away from Mina.

Arden didn't press. Instead, she changed the subject entirely. "I'll probably end up bunking with Annem and Coco." She let out a breath. "It will be better than listening to the beeping machines in the med bay."

They entered the command center that Mina used to plan their missions. It was also where Venz spent his time. The room had an elaborate display of electronic gadgets. A desk and a data monitor set up for

Venz ran along one wall. He had multiple light boards and other tech to access all the feeds in the city. He watched screen after screen of current vid-feeds and seemed to take it all in. It looked like he was monitoring the entire city grid.

Multiple vid-projectors lined another wall, simultaneously showing several channels of visicast airing current news.

In the center was a long glass table with insets at each seat in which individual vid-projectors could switch between 2-D, 3-D, and 4-D with the flick of a control.

Coco, Annem, and Roan were already sitting at the table, talking to one another. Saben was there as well. He sat apart, quiet. But he didn't look uncomfortable.

Venz was at his desk with his back to the room. His hands worked over the various light boards as if he were playing an instrument. He hummed, his head bobbing, but there was no music. Small in stature and slight in weight, he appeared quiet and unassuming. Dade had found that while that assumption was partially true, Venz also thought on an entirely different plane of existence.

Dade directed Arden over since Venz was the only one she hadn't met yet.

Venz looked up, eyes blinking behind round goggles. He pushed them up onto his forehead, sliding his dark hair back.

After they were introduced, Arden pointed to the goggles. "Those are cool."

The lenses resembled halo-glasses, but while halo-glass was slim, this was set in a casing of metal and plastic that molded across his face. Dade could just make out the faint blue edge of the information as it was spread across the screen in front of his eyes.

Venz smiled, showing his crooked teeth. "Thanks. I modified them. Halo-glass can't process the information as fast as I need it."

"Venz," Coco snapped, "don't give away trade secrets."

Venz's face flushed.

Arden chose a seat not too far from the door, yet close enough to the others so it looked like she wasn't purposely keeping herself apart.

Sliding into the chair next to her, Dade gave Saben a nod. He needed to speak with Arden later to gauge her thoughts on this group. He was warming up to them, admittedly. But by the way she carried herself with stiff shoulders and a straight spine, he figured she hadn't thawed yet.

"You made it," Coco said. "We had bets going on how long it would take."

"Yeah, I had you down for next week," Roan said. "You sure you don't need more beauty sleep?"

Annem offered Arden a smile. "I'm glad you feel better."

Arden blinked. Her facial expression stayed placid. "I heal fast."

"Note to self: if you want to kill Arden, try harder," Roan snickered.

"Not funny, Roan." Annem glared at him.

It was evident that they'd worked as a group for some time. There were inside jokes, fighting, laughing, and they were free with one another's space. It felt oddly welcoming. He'd never been part of a group before. Not like this. He'd had Saben, and Clarissa, but they'd never worked together except for that one disastrous time.

Mina walked into the room, followed by Nastasia. She positioned herself at the head of the table. The group snapped to attention, instantly quieting, though not in a militaristic way. It felt more like respect, with leashed anticipation. As if they knew there was something exciting about to start.

Nastasia snagged the seat to Mina's right and took a moment to set out her things: a datapad that she plugged into the mainframe, a steamy cup of something that smelled like citrus, and an electro-pen that could be used to write on any surface and would save data to her digi-stream.

"Good, we're all here," Mina said.

Nastasia set to work typing into the light board to bring up the information from her datapad to the flash-feed so that they could all access it from their spots at the table.

Dade placed his hands flat on the table on either side of where the projection hovered. Then he flipped up his hands so that the projection was in front of him and spread his hands wide for a bigger visual. The projections were transparent, so they could still see and speak to each other across the table.

He stared at the schematics. It took him a second to realize what he was looking at. Dade blinked, not believing the truth of what he saw.

"She's got to be kidding," Arden said under her breath.

Mina leaned in and pulled up her own screen. "We have two items on the agenda. The first, as you can see from this visual, is that we're going to break into the CRC."

There were mixed reactions from around the room. Coco let out a barking laugh. Annem darted confused glances between Coco, Mina, and Nastasia, while Roan whistled and leaned back in his seat.

Across the room, Venz nervously chewed his bottom lip. He didn't look surprised. If he'd been the one who'd managed to get the floor plans, he was more tech savvy than anyone Dade had ever met. Dade didn't have a clue whom he'd stolen them from.

Beside him, Arden didn't make any sound, but her face looked thunderous. She gripped her hands into fists on the table and stared with cold fury at Mina.

Dade was numb. He heard the words, he saw the projection, and yet he still couldn't believe it. This was what she'd manipulated him here to do? It was a suicide mission.

No one had ever successfully broken into the City Reeducation Center, let alone broken out. It was a mind-conditioning location, where the govies took people to interrogate them, where they'd disappear. But it was also whispered to house some of the items too important to be kept in the city vault.

"You're joking," Coco said.

"Do I ever joke?" Mina asked. Yet Dade could tell that she enjoyed shocking them. There was an amused twist to her mouth and a lightness to her eyes.

"Why would we do that?" Annem asked. "Going into the CRC is suicide. Everyone knows that."

"The govies keep the recipe for VitD inside a CRC vault. We're going to figure out where exactly it is, and then we're going to steal it."

"Wait a second," Arden said, her voice low and intense. "We're going to *figure it out*? Are you saying you're not positive that it's there?"

Mina raised one eyebrow. "My sources say that it is."

Arden grunted. "No offense, but that's not good enough."

"I'm with Sunshine on this one." Roan ran his hands through his perfectly coiffed hair. "What if we break in and it's not there? Moons, we may not make it out again."

"We're going to make sure it's there before we go in, and we're going to have a plan for getting out." Mina's voice didn't waver, and her chin remained high. If it weren't the most insane thing he'd ever heard, Dade could have almost trusted that she knew what she was doing.

Annem did a little wave to get Mina's attention. "Why would the Solizen give the recipe to the govies?"

Roan crossed his arms. "The most important recipe on the entire planet and the Solizen didn't keep it? Why would they allow the govies to lock it up where they couldn't get to it?"

This Dade could answer. It made sense to him. "Because it keeps it safe. Information on the digi-stream could be stolen. There's a lot of infighting among the families. They all share ownership of the recipe, and it's programmed into the mainframe so that no one can see the actual dosage specifications. The machines mix it. By giving it to the govies, it keeps any individual family from making its own and under-cutting the market. The CRC would be the one place that no Solizen would be able to get their hands on it."

It was brilliant and reckless to trust the govies. To put it where it would be impossible for the Solizen to take it back. And if the Solizen couldn't get to it, Mina's crew had no chance. What awaited them if they tried was a mind wipe at the very least, and if they were really unlucky, experiments on them beforehand. There wasn't any other light to see it in. And yet, Mina looked cool, as if what she suggested would be easy.

"What are we going to do with the recipe if we manage to steal it?" Annem asked.

"One problem at a time," Mina said.

It was a naive question. Everyone at the table knew it, except for Annem. Mina wasn't going to make the VitD. She would sell the recipe. It would be worth hundreds of millions of credits on the open market.

Arden looked to Dade. Her eyes were hot and bright, and her mouth was pulled tight. She gave a single shake of her head before she looked away.

"That brings us to the second item on the agenda." Mina looked directly at Arden. "I need your brother."

Arden showed little reaction. "I don't even know if my brother is alive."

Very few had made it out when they'd blown up the joint refinery. Most of those who did had been rounded up by the govies. By and large, it was unknown how many people had died that day. The fire burned so hot that the bodies were turned to dust. With no body count, the people who were missing were presumed dead. It made sense that Arden had assumed that her brother was one of that number.

"We tagged him years ago," Mina said as if that weren't a bombshell. "Niall made it out."

"Does he know you tagged him?" Arden's voice was edged with venom.

Mina raised an eyebrow, her perpetual smirk a little wider. "Of course not."

Dade blinked. Today's information was one improbable thing after another. They'd managed to tag the leader of Lasair without his knowledge? If that was the case, what else was Mina capable of doing? As comfortable as he felt with them, maybe Arden was right to be wary.

It made him question whether Mina would keep her promise to let them go at the end of this—if they were even still alive. Mina sounded sincere when she offered to work together, but honestly, he didn't know anymore. She was also sincere about doing whatever needed to be done to get what she wanted.

"Would you have tagged me if I hadn't agreed to join you?" Arden asked.

"I've always wanted you as an ally, Arden. Subterfuge wouldn't have been my first choice."

Arden's lips thinned. "And if I don't fall into line?"

Mina stared but didn't bother to respond.

The tension in the room felt strangling. Everyone reacted to it. Venz turned back to his wall of data monitors. His body hunched as he tapped on his light boards, attempting to disappear. Coco, Roan, and Annem all avoided eye contact as well.

Dade wasn't sure what to say. He understood why Arden was upset. He was upset too. But he wasn't about to make a public point of it. Not with the new plans that had started to take form in his mind. He needed to use this to his own advantage, though he wasn't sure how to do that quite yet.

"It's best we focus forward," Mina said to Arden, but her gaze swept the room. "Maybe if I tell you some things, you'll feel less resistant."

"I doubt it," Arden said.

Mina nodded to Nastasia, who changed the projection feed to show several recorded vids of Undercity. The footage was grainy, obviously from a street cam, and focused on members of the Lasair gang. From the angles of the feed, it looked like they originated from the city grid. Most of the cams were nonfunctional in Undercity. Had Mina fixed them to spy? Or had the govies fixed the cams, and Venz had managed to piggyback the feed?

Each clip was from a different street with different gang members, and yet they all seemed to show the same thing: Lasair members running in groups of three or four, intimidating people. The first clips were of them targeting ordinary people on the street and taking them down, stealing anything of value before they wanded each victim's data sensor to mine credits. The later clips showed groups entering shops, presumably intimidating the owners to pay for protection. It seemed as if in the absence of new VitD, they'd focused their gang on running the streets. No more than bottom-of-the-barrel thugs.

Dade had never been a Lasair member, but even he could see how they'd changed. They'd become a lot more like an organized crime syndicate. Their movements were precise, casting their net of power wide and locking down more and more territory. They were more overt in the way they openly displayed their phasers and manned the streets of Undercity.

Arden watched intently. The furrow in her brow deepened, but she didn't comment.

When the clips ended, Mina said, "Lasair has been under surveillance for some time, before the joint refinery mess, by the govies and me as well."

"Why are you telling me this?" Arden asked.

"Because I know you don't trust me."

"You're right, I don't."

"Uri is in charge now," Mina said. "There is more going on in that gang than you realize. And has been for some time."

"Like what?" Arden's voice was flat and low.

Mina blew a breath. "I need Niall, both for the job and also because if I tell you what has happened right under your nose, you won't believe me. I need proof first. Trust me, getting your brother is in the best interest of us both."

CHAPTER THIRTEEN

Dade was sick of waiting. He sat on a bench outside of a café that he knew Clarissa preferred. It was located in an upscale mall near the skywalk. He'd been here for hours, and he couldn't stay much longer.

He wore a cloak that covered his head and a synth-mask that hid his face. They were expensive and hard to requisition, which made him thankful for Mina's supply. If he and Arden had been on their own, he'd have had to traverse the city with his own face. Maybe he could have changed his hair color, but even then people would know who he was. He'd been plastered on all the pap-feeds for years. It was far too dangerous.

From his position, he could remain innocuous while keeping an eye on the customers who strolled around him. The synth-mask didn't make him feel less vulnerable. Knowing there was only a thin layer of nanotech between himself and the rest of the city concerned him. Though he had to admit that he enjoyed the anonymity.

Dade shifted in his seat, unsettled and frustrated that Clarissa still hadn't shown up. It had been a long shot that she'd be here. More of a hope than a true plan. Clarissa was predictable with her shopping habits, or she had been. He hoped that eventually she'd appear, because he didn't have another means to reach her. At least one that wouldn't alert everyone in her Tower to his overstated demise.

He couldn't very well walk up to her on the skywalk. She was watched constantly. The gossip-vids had always been obsessed with her—with them. Clarissa was a wealthy Solizen socialite. Of course they'd want to document her every move. While he'd avoided that kind of attention as much as possible, she'd pose for mags or docu-stories in which they'd detail the lushness of her life.

Why any of these people would be fascinated with that life when they had no possibility of having it, he didn't understand. But they were. They liked seeing all the frivolous things she did, cataloging how she dressed, how she styled her hair, what she ate for lunch.

They liked even more when one of the Solizen fell from grace. Which was exactly what had happened. The news-vids had begun to give daily briefings of Clarissa's run-ins with the govies. Circling as they readied to feed from her bones.

After everything the govies had put her through and the nightly court of public opinion on the visicast, Dade knew she was stubborn enough to show her face in public simply to spite them. However, he hoped that "eventually" would be today, because he didn't have many more opportunities to come back.

Saben sat on a bench farther down the skywalk, pretending to read a datapad. They took turns strolling around the shopping area so that no one would notice them sitting in one place for too long.

Dade hadn't seen Clarissa since their last mission had imploded and he had "died." It was public knowledge that the govies had taken Clarissa in for questioning for working with both Dade and the Ghost. Every visicast had covered it. Vid of her coming out of the blown-up building, crouched behind the vehicle as they took incoming phase-fire, helping them to escape. The speculation had been rampant.

Clarissa had been cleared. She'd claimed that in the haze of the phase-fire that day, she'd been concerned only about Dade, her fiancé. It was enough of a logical truth that the govies couldn't charge her without more proof of collusion. And since her questioning had been so public and she was a Solizen with family power behind her, they couldn't hold her somewhere like the CRC. It hadn't made the suspicion go away, however. Wherever she went, all eyes were on her: those of the Solizen, the govies, bystanders in the street.

He felt guilty. She'd ruined her reputation because she'd helped him. Dade worried what it would cost her over the years. Her own people might turn against her. He wanted to see for himself that she was okay, even though Clarissa was more than capable of landing on her feet. If anything, today was a chance for a sincere apology. He never should have gotten her mixed up in the Ghost stuff in the first place.

However, even though he felt remorse, it didn't change the fact that he was still making choices that would affect other people. Arden would be pissed when she found out he met with Clarissa. He'd not even told Mina that he was doing this for her plan, afraid that it wouldn't work out. She wanted into Sky Tower Two, his former home, and he no longer had access to it.

There were personal reasons as well. He wanted to talk to Clarissa about helping him get new Ghost gear. The only way to repair the damage he'd done was by taking a stand. This was the only way he knew how.

Twitters of gossip rose loud enough that Dade raised his head to follow the murmurs that moved from one table to another. They spread like a blanket rippling out. Small punctuated whispers that became excited gasps. He couldn't hear what they said, yet he straightened, knowing only Clarissa would attract that much attention.

She walked through the tables of moonglass like a queen. Her steps were affected with such grace that it looked as if she floated on her four-inch heels. Her back was straight, and she held her head high. She wore a white dress that dipped across her body and swept the ground, appearing both regal and lush. Clarissa did not seem like someone who'd endured interrogation for weeks.

Though the guests gossiped, a wall of silence surrounded Clarissa as the waiter pulled out her chair. But they stared. Eyes wide and mouths half-parted.

She sat with a graceful dip into the seat.

Moons, he'd missed her. Dade couldn't help the grin that spread across his face. For a moment, he remembered the person he had been, when they'd had an easy friendship. When everything was easy, and she'd teased him about taking some risks.

They'd seated her at a table in the center of the open café. This was a place to be seen. She'd come here with a purpose. He had no doubt that she'd asked for that table. It was Clarissa's way of letting the city know that she wouldn't be cowed by rumor and innuendo.

The visicasts repeatedly played commentary that she was devastated by her fiancé's death—by Dade's death. She looked the part: serene, confident, a little sad, but fully a Solizen who would take no crap. Jewels encased her ears and throat. She wore her hair in a high faux hawk—her usual style when she wanted to give a public middle finger to the govies by appearing both vicious and refined. Blush had been applied in streaks to her cheekbones, giving her color. Her lips were painted red, outlined like a doll. And her lashes were dark lined to set off the amber of her almond-shaped eyes.

To be fair, he realized that she *was* mourning his death. He was the idiot who had forgotten to tell her that he'd survived. It added to his nervousness about approaching her.

Dade waited until the waiter left the table before he stood and entered the café. He weaved his way through the tables. Glad that they were still too focused on her to pay him any attention. That would change as soon as he sat down. The mysteriousness of Clarissa's table companion would stir up the gossip all over again. But that couldn't be helped.

He kept the hood of his cloak pulled low over his face even though he wore the synth-mask. His hair hung loose to further obscure his masked features in case a pap-drone cam was pointed their way. It was best not to give away his borrowed features too easily. He didn't want to be linked to other activities. Mina would be pissed if he blew a synth-mask that fast.

Clarissa didn't look up as he slid into the seat across from her. She continued to flick through the menu projected on the halo in front of her. When she did finally raise her eyes, they were hard, and Dade realized that she'd pulled out a palm-sized phaser. She pointed it at him from across the table, low enough so that others might not see.

Dade hadn't even seen her reach for it. Though admittedly, his focus had been on other guests and not her. He'd never considered her a threat.

"I don't know who you are, but get up and leave this table at once." Her eyes became slits, and her glossed mouth twisted into a dangerous snarl.

"It's me, Clarissa." He hadn't put on a voice modulator, hoping that the cadence of his speech would be enough to convince her it was him. He couldn't very well unmask himself. At least he knew his disguise worked.

"Dade?" She squinted with disbelief. "You're alive?"

Then her face went blank before it hardened and became thunderous. "I should shoot you."

"But you're not going to." He *hoped*.

Her mouth flattened, making her vowels stick when she whispered, "Trust me, I'm thinking about it."

"Put away the phaser, Clarissa, please." He laid his hands flat on the table. Tried to look nonthreatening. He knew she really didn't see him as the enemy. She needed to process what she saw. He gave her time, though it killed him not to yell at her to get a grip.

They were in public, and he had to keep things as quiet as possible. Even now, those at the nearest table looked with curiosity. He didn't think they could see Clarissa's phaser from where she hid it with her hand and the table.

"How are you not dead?" she asked while sliding the phaser away. One minute it was there, and the next minute it was gone. If he hadn't seen it and known Clarissa so well, he would have second-guessed that it had been there. It was a neat trick. He'd always been impressed by Clarissa, and she continued to surprise him.

"So?" she pressed.

Dade exhaled. He stretched his fingers out on the table. They were still tight at times after being nano-healed so fast. Then he pulled his hands close and leaned forward. "It's a long story."

"I've got the time." She raised an eyebrow, her glossed lips pursing.

"Right."

Up close, he could see what the makeup hid. There was a dark bruising around her eyes from lack of sleep. And her sparkle was gone, as if all the joy and fire had drained out of her. The business she'd been through had taken its toll. But when she looked at him, he could still see the core of steel she had at her center.

"How are you?" Dade asked, concerned. He worried now that he'd caused more of a mess than he'd originally thought.

"Stop deflecting. I had to deal with the fallout you left me." Her words caught. Clarissa swallowed, letting the seconds pass. Then she looked straight at him and continued, her voice hard and sour. "I saw you fall off the skyway. You'd better tell me how you managed to not be dead, or I'll gut you right here and make the news of your demise real."

He said under his breath, "What's with the women in my life threatening to kill me?"

Yet he understood her frustration, the anger that seeped through her words, and the hurt that underlay it all. He knew he should have gotten word to her. But the upheaval happened so fast that time had slipped by with frightening speed.

Dade didn't lie as he told her about Mina's rescue and about everything that had happened to him since he'd fallen off the skyway, including the disaster at the joint refinery. How injured they'd been. How he'd gone to work for Crispin to help Saben. How eventually Mina had come for her favor.

Clarissa listened with a serious expression on her face. She asked a few questions here and there for clarification. But mostly she let him talk. And it felt good. Cathartic, as if he needed this release to feel centered again.

He left out Mina's plan to break into the CRC. Telling anyone might put him, Arden, and Saben at risk. Plus, he'd thought a lot about the VitD recipe. If Clarissa knew that was the prize, she might manipulate the situation so that she'd somehow end up with it. And if he was going to risk his life, he wasn't letting someone else take it. Not even a friend he was about to ask for a favor. Dade had enough people manipulating his life at the moment. He was determined not to give Clarissa a chance.

Dade finished his explanation with an apology. "I should have gotten you word. It's just been intense. I'm sorry."

Her eyebrow rose. "I also know what it feels like to lose track of time. I was grilled and kept prisoner for days."

Swallowing, he forced himself to maintain eye contact with her. It was difficult. If not for him and his harebrained ideas, she wouldn't have been interrogated. "Thanks for not outing me as the Ghost." Clarissa could have easily given over whatever knowledge she had of his secrets in order to keep the govies far away from her own affairs. But she hadn't.

"Why would I do that?" she asked. "We're friends. I don't betray friends."

"Because you thought I was dead. What harm would it have done?"

"It would have shown them that I knew what you were up to and didn't report you." She shook her head. Then she stared at him intently. Her face softened. "I'm happy you're alive."

Dade nodded. Words didn't seem to be enough to thank her. "How are your parents taking my death? Your inquiry?"

She rolled her eyes. "Well, they're not happy. But seriously, they're angrier at Nakomzer."

The govie leader, Nakomzer, was a friend—or had been a friend—of his father's. They'd worked together often. Though now he wondered if that was still true, considering Nakomzer had given the govies the okay to kill Dade.

"Because the govies shot me?" Dade asked.

"Yes, but your family isn't doing anything to avenge you." She raised an eyebrow. "Don't you find that interesting?"

"Immensely." Which was why he needed to get into the Sky Tower. Mina's request for him to find a way in was only an excuse to make it happen. He had to figure out what had led to the call for his death. "Speaking of that, I need your help."

"I knew there'd be a catch. You couldn't suddenly rise from the dead and not need my help, right?"

Dade let her irritated comment go. "I need to get into Sky Tower Two."

She sighed. "Of course you do. I suppose you're aware they completely revamped their security protocol?"

"Yes. Does that mean you can't get me in?"

Her smile was indulgent and crafty. "I can get you in. But then you owe me."

Dade didn't even hesitate. "Agreed."

"And there's one more thing." She propped her elbows on the table and leaned in closer. "You're playing a dangerous game."

"I know."

"No," she said, drawing the word out long and hard, "I don't think you do. Be careful of both Mina and Crispin—but perhaps, more especially Crispin. He works toward his own ends, as do we all, but unlike us, he has nothing to lose."

"What do you mean?" Dade knew he couldn't hide the surprise that slid over him. Clarissa knew who Crispin was?

Her eyes clouded. "It's not my story to tell."

Dade wondered at that. She didn't often refuse to divulge information to him, but when she did, Clarissa was impossible to crack. If he was in danger, she'd tell. But this seemed like something else. As if telling him Crispin's secrets would be a betrayal. It felt the same when she'd said that she had kept Dade's secrets from the govies.

He found himself agreeing. "All right, let's talk about pleasant things before I go."

She smiled at him, the sensuous Clarissa smile he'd missed, and began to tell him about her day.

CHAPTER FOURTEEN

Arden was dressed for sin. Tonight they were heading to the Den, a club in Undercity. It sat three blocks and a subtrain stop away from any sort of neighborhood that would complain about the noise and drug use that spilled out into the streets.

Her dress shimmered, sending rainbows skittering over the floor. Inside the club with the strobes, it would glitter like a star. The fabric clung to her every curve. She'd never worn anything so soft.

She'd styled her hair loose, one side gathered up and pinned so the rest fell to her opposite shoulder. Along the clip that held her hair were faux flowers of the dilly plant made from tissue striated in orange, gold, and red.

A touch of blush, red lipstick, and dark mascara completed her look.

Excitement stirred in her, making her feel alive. She finally felt like herself after long weeks of recuperation, of being someone that she didn't recognize. She was usually in charge, strong. And the hits that she'd taken had shaken her in a fundamental way.

Roan whistled when she came into the rec room. "Look at you, Sunshine."

"Don't call me that," she growled, her satisfaction over her appearance falling away.

Dade stood up from the couch and walked over. He smiled at her as if she were the only person he saw. He looked edible dressed in club clothes: tight synth-leather pants and a thin tunic cut to show off his frame rather than to hide it. She had to stop herself from sighing out loud, swallowing against the need that rose inside her.

He moved in front of her. His hands came up to grip her hips as he leaned into her and brushed his lips against her cheek. He breathed her in, his nose against her temple. Then said softly, "You look beautiful."

Her heart fluttered. "Thank you."

She'd had to dress up for the club anyway. However, she might have put a little more thought into it than strictly necessary. She wanted to look amazing. She'd known Dade had gone to see Clarissa. He'd told them after he'd returned that Clarissa had agreed to help get them inside Sky Tower Two. The fact that Arden hadn't been aware that meeting was happening had pissed her off. Underscored by Roan's snotty smirk to her as if he could read her thoughts. That was when she'd determined to show Dade she was not to be forgotten.

It appeared to have worked, though perhaps a bit unexpectedly and in the completely opposite way. Her breath shuddered out of her. The point wasn't to get in her own head.

Roan gagged, a loud retching sound that broke the moment. He rolled his eyes and muttered, "I don't get it. He's not that amazing."

But he was.

Dade pulled away so that they faced each other, his hands still on her. They felt as if they branded her, linking her to this place and time. She wanted to kiss him. A real kiss, not just the brush of skin that barely put a dent in her desire.

Not here, though. She took a deep breath. Not where everyone could see and gawk. She wanted to run away with him and have things be like they should have been when they'd left their families. To have the freedom to indulge in all sorts of things she shouldn't and to promise him things she couldn't.

His hands slipped away, and he stepped to her side. Dade kept their connection, though, touching her back with the tips of his fingers.

Arden leaned into him.

The others were dressed up as well. Roan was suited similarly to Dade, only the fabric of his tunic had a translucent quality so that the dips of his muscles were visible. Arden kept herself from rolling her eyes, barely.

Annem had chosen red. The dress she wore was short and flirty, with a swing skirt and lots of skin on display. A pair of silver boots came up to midthigh.

Standing beside her, Coco was more sedate, wearing pants, boots, and a tunic, all in black. Her only deference to their going into a club was that the collar of the tunic had subtle embroidery decorating it.

Nastasia swept into the room. She appeared softer tonight, of all of them looking the most unlike herself. Her hair was down, and she wore a peekaboo dress with sheer sleeves that billowed and gathered at the wrist. It made Nastasia look both sexy and formidable, not at all the coolly calculated girl who'd nursed Arden.

Seeing her reminded Arden that Mina's crew members were dangerous, including, and maybe most especially, Nastasia. Mina had picked them for a reason. It was foolish of Arden to rely on first impressions. She knew better. This change into something different shouldn't have surprised her.

Mina stood in the room watching them. She had turned over her duties to Nastasia for the night, so she wasn't dressed to go out. She had been shifty on her reasons, but it was obvious she had something else to do. Arden was curious about what that something else was, but she couldn't blatantly ask. And if she did, Mina wouldn't tell her anyway. All Arden knew was that Mina was using Saben for some hush-hush op.

"Everyone, strap up," Nastasia said, taking charge from the moment she stepped into the room.

Arden made her way over to the weapons wall. She studied the various phasers and charge sticks. Out of everything available, she'd only be able to conceal knives under her dress.

Coco snickered as she took a larger phaser off the wall and strapped it to her waist, pulling down her tunic for full coverage. "This is why you need to wear pants and a tunic."

"Or wear boots," Annem said. She took two small phasers and tucked them into her thigh boots, then looked at Arden. "I like the dress."

"I like yours too," Arden said. Not having phasers would be frustrating but not problematic. It just meant she had to be stealthier and get up close to take someone out if she needed to.

She selected a pair of blades off the wall. The knives had a wicked curve. The metal had been crafted so thin that it could have almost been see-through, with a sharp edge she knew wouldn't take any pressure to carve into skin. It would require only the barest tip of her wrist.

The handles fit in her palms with a nice weight to them. Their tangs were made from bone that had been polished to a shine. They felt cool to the touch, but she knew they would warm when she used them.

Arden slid each knife into a synth-leather sheath and strapped them to her thigh. She made sure they wouldn't peek out beneath the hemline of her dress and yet were strategically placed so that she could slip them out if necessary.

These blades might get drafted into her personal collection easily enough. Mina didn't seem too territorial about her weapons.

"The goal for tonight is intel," Mina said, standing at the edge of the group as they geared up. "You watch and follow. We need to figure out where Lasair's new headquarters are. Do not engage."

Arden agreed that finding Lasair was important. Figuring out why Uri was in charge even more so. If Niall was alive, why hadn't he taken back control of the group? That was her biggest question. Because if they'd somehow demoted him, his life was forfeit. The fact that Mina could no longer trace his tag signal was a huge issue.

Or Niall could still be running things and had figured out he'd been tagged. Maybe Uri's being in charge was a front. They couldn't have dismantled the tag. But maybe he'd figured out a way to block the signal. She held out hope, because as many problems as she had with her brother, she did not wish him dead.

Mina looked pointedly at Arden. "Don't go rogue."

Arden wondered how well Mina could read her. She was a master at keeping thought-revealing expressions off her face. It was scary to think that Mina could somehow guess her feelings.

"Don't worry, I'll keep a close eye on Sunshine," Roan said.

Arden glared.

Once done with their preparations, they swung on their cloaks, pulling their hoods up over their heads.

"We won't be late," Nastasia said in singsong. "Don't wait up."

Mina smirked. "Have fun."

They took the sloping pathway up and out of the mine. The tunnel contracted into a narrow walkway the closer they came to the surface and into Undercity. Orbs of poloosh, the indigenous stone that glowed, had been installed along the apex of the tunnel. Their dull shine created just enough light to see by, but not enough to cut the shadows that crept up the walls. The sound of water dripping from the ceiling echoed loudly.

The temperature dipped the closer they got to the surface. All traces of modification that Mina had implemented fell away as they walked the last few yards in total darkness.

Exiting the tunnel, they took out their glo-wands to light their way across the stretch of wasteland that bordered the city. They were in the last piece of land before the containment filter met the Wilds. The soft hum of the biometric field gave off a pink haze as it cut the city off from the dangerous animals beyond.

Undercity had no natural light source, entrenched as it was within the walled dome. There was no light in the Wilds either, just unending black pitch. And they were too far away from the city for public lights.

Far in the distance, they could see the glow from the sunfields on the horizon where the govies raised food. Not for all the citizens, though. It would be shipped to Above, while the citizens of Undercity subsisted on meta-grains.

They walked to the nearest subtrain station. Hovercars and speeders were banned in Undercity because there wasn't open sky. Everyone used public transport. Though most commuters also had personal transports, hoverboards or speedpacks for shorter distances.

It was late by the time they entered the city. The others moved forward ahead of Arden. Roan in the front. Coco and Annem talking to Dade. Arden hung back, walking next to Nastasia.

Nastasia, it seemed, wanted to speak with her too. "Are you ready for this?"

"I'm always ready." Arden needed to get out of the compound, so she would have said that anyway. Though she knew that she'd have no problem pulling her weight on this job.

They walked a few minutes before Nastasia cleared her throat. "I know that the transition to working for Mina has been difficult for you. But I just wanted to say that you should give her a chance. I know she seems intense and often secretive, but she always has a reason."

"I'm sure she does," Arden said, "and maybe if she explained what her reasons were, I could get on board."

Nastasia grinned. "Would you? Admit it, if the situation were reversed, you wouldn't explain anything to her or us."

Arden certainly couldn't deny that. Still, it wasn't like she would have coerced Mina to work for her either.

"Mina is trustworthy," Nastasia said.

"Simply saying that isn't going to convince me. Besides, I'm not thrilled that she's had Niall tagged for months, perhaps years. If she wants me to have some faith in her, she's got to show me more than her puppet-master routine."

"You are both so stubborn," Nastasia said. "All I'm asking is that you give her a chance. I know that sometimes it can be difficult to see her schemes for what they truly are."

Arden snorted in response. Oh, she knew Mina had underhanded schemes. That was what she worried about. Still, she allowed silence to fall between them as they made their way into the crowd flowing into the center of Undercity.

CHAPTER FIFTEEN

Dade shifted as he watched the club entrance. He'd put on his mask, as had everyone in the group. The masks were plain black and covered their eyes and upper cheeks. Nanotech woven into the fabric was keyed to their DNA and would stay affixed to their face.

The six of them stood in the shadows at the far side of the street. Waiting cautiously, they surveyed the lay of the land to make sure the govies weren't monitoring the area in front of the club. They couldn't afford a raid tonight, not here. There was no escape plan if that happened.

"How does it look?" Nastasia spoke into the comm.

Venz immediately came back with the all-clear from where he was positioned back in the command center. "I haven't picked up any chatter, and the streets look unmonitored. There's no movement at the station."

"If I'd had access to the govie cams, my job would have been a lot less dangerous," Arden muttered.

"You like danger," Dade pointed out.

She grinned and leaned into him. "You're right, I do."

Roan cracked his neck. "You were just running with the wrong gang."

Arden narrowed her eyes at Roan, and the corner of her mouth lifted in a snarl. "Shut up. You know nothing about my life or about Lasair."

"He's not kidding," Nastasia said. "Though we don't have to convince you, eventually you'll understand."

Dade wondered what they had to gain from saying that to Arden. All it did was piss her off. She was sensitive about her former family. And even though he tended to agree with Roan and Nastasia that Lasair hadn't been worth her loyalty, Dade kept it to himself.

Before an argument could truly break out, Nastasia was already moving forward. She slunk out of the shadows, then glanced back. "Let's go."

From the outside, the club looked like an abandoned building. Half the lights on the street were dead. Trash littered the sidewalk. The windows were bricked up like most of the buildings in Undercity. It kept the noise that beat inside somewhat muted, though the low boom from the bass would hit every so often, sending sound vibrations into the street. Whenever the front door opened, bursts of the higher wail of instruments would flood the street.

No one from Lasair was outside the club. No one was dealing at all. That didn't stop Shine users from smoking in groups, passing the disks between them. The vapor curled above them, mixing with the smoggy air. Their skin looked thin and bruised. Most had sunken eyes peeking out from behind masks. They wore skimpy club clothes and shivered with their arms around one another.

Most would stay high and addicted, dying on the streets. What would happen when the Shine supply ran out? If there was no VitD, there would be no Shine because the street drug was made from changing the molecular structure of VitD. Shine did the same thing as VitD, helped the body survive without the sun, but it would also give the user a high. The drug would surely be replaced with something else. Maybe a harsher chemical that would do greater damage.

No one paid them any attention as they approached the club. Roan stepped forward, pulling the door open for the group. Music blared with a crashing sound at decibels far above comfortable. The noise felt like a wall, battering against Dade with its overpowering sensory assault.

There was a tiny vestibule inside with a guest check counter. They left their cloaks there and were supposed to leave all their weapons as well according to club rules, but that didn't happen. Nastasia slipped extra credits to the girl behind the counter to keep their cloaks near the front in case they had to leave quickly.

The girl looked at them suspiciously but did as they asked. She wore a ring that ran through her bottom lip. Her tongue kept touching the metal, wetting purple-colored lips. Her head was shaved, and her face was hidden behind a dark purple mask with whiskers that danced against her cheeks.

Roan leaned in, his body maneuvering half over the counter. "We're looking for a Shine dealer." He didn't add "from Lasair," because this was their territory, so that information was redundant.

"Isn't everyone?" she said, and then her look turned calculating. "If you're looking for Shine, the price has gone sky-high. Not much available, you know?"

Roan slipped into a charming caricature of himself. He blinked slowly with eyes that promised something more in a dark corner if she was willing. He pushed his body even closer to her.

The girl mimicked him, leaning over the counter the rest of the way so that they were separated by less than an inch. Her tongue peeked out once more, licking her lips and leaving them shiny.

Roan ran a finger over the back of her hand. "Is anyone working the floor tonight?"

"He's not here yet."

"What does he look like?" Roan asked.

"He's fifteen, maybe. Dark hair."

"That could be anyone."

She shrugged, the bones of her shoulders dipped and ridged under her skin.

Roan closed the last bit of space between them. His lips brushed hers, lightly. It was just a touch before he pulled way. "Anything else?"

Her eyes blinked open at the loss of contact. She stared at Roan. Then looked to the rest of them before she moved back to her side of the counter. Her tongue came out to worry at the lip ring again while her fingertips slipped to the edge of the counter, pressing the skin white. "Would you like me to tell him you're looking for him?"

"No, we'll find him, thank you," Nastasia said, already pulling Roan away.

Before he left, the girl snaked her arm out and clutched Roan's hand. "Are you going to be around later?"

Roan smiled. "Thank you, you've been very helpful."

The girl sniffed, then turned away. It was obvious that she'd hesitated for some reason in giving them information. They needed to lose themselves in the wildness of the club before anyone looked too close.

A new group had entered the vestibule. Half had started taking off their weapons, while the other half pushed forward toward the doorman to wand them. Nastasia grabbed the opportunity for distraction, engaging them and the doorman in a discussion while the rest of their group slipped past into the club.

Once free of the doorman and with all her weapons still on her, Nastasia caught up to them. She rounded on Roan. "What were you doing? Any longer and someone would have started asking questions about why we're here."

"Now they know we're looking for him," Arden said. "She'll tell the dealer. I doubt we'll see him tonight."

Roan looked less than pleased that either girl was questioning him. A scowl replaced his usually teasing expression. "We paid her. She can give better information than that."

Nastasia huffed. "We're not trying to make an impression. Pushing will make us easier for her to recall. And for sun's sake, stop flirting with women as if they're naive enough to give you what you want if you just look pretty."

Arden snorted.

Roan shrugged, a distinct non-apology in the movement. "Flirting is how I do business."

"Maybe you should start using your brain instead," Coco offered.

"C'mon, let's find the guy before she tips him off." Nastasia straightened and led them deeper into the room.

The Undercity club looked much the same as any Dade had been to in Above. It was awash with lights, sounds, and bodies moving in communal rhythm. Though it was a little muted. This area was poor. They didn't have the money for the tech that usually brightened the clubs in Above. Not that it mattered. The kids were just as intoxicated and just as willing to look for a good time.

"Split up," Nastasia said. She used her fingers to indicate the directions she wanted them to go.

Dade tucked his arm around Arden. They were working as a team tonight. Coco would go with Annem, and Nastasia had to put up with Roan.

Arden melted against him. This was a mission, so he'd half expected that she'd demand distance and for them to remain professional even if they were supposed to play the part of lovers.

Roan crossed his arms. "I still don't think it's smart that Sunshine and siskin go off on their own."

"I swear, the next time you call me that, I'm going to stab you," Arden said with a growl.

Dade suppressed a chuckle.

"Good thing I'm in charge, then," Nastasia said to Roan.

"They're tagged. Where are they going to go?" Coco asked.

The reminder was like a splash of cold water to the face. Dade sucked in a breath, but Arden had already turned away. Taking his arm, she pulled him with her. Her head was high, and she walked like she owned the room.

He heard Nastasia through the comm. "Signal as soon as you spot someone."

Arden led him straight to the dance floor. She slipped her arms around him and tucked herself close. Over his shoulder, she scanned the room.

Dade tried to concentrate. The warmth of her body against him nearly made him groan aloud. He forced his gaze to sweep for action instead of focusing on her. No one stood out as their mark. But Arden continued to distract him. She was everything, sucking up all his thoughts of job and duty, until there was only her.

Arden's body pressed closer. He felt her chest, her hips, her legs, all brushing him with a siren's song. Her scent was a warm spice that always smelled fresh. He closed his eyes, trying to get a grip. It didn't work—her feel, her scent, they became overwhelming.

He needed to smooth out things between them. Wanted to have it all out in the open. Yet he couldn't let go of the fear that she'd react badly if he told her that he was going to become the Ghost once again. She'd been fine with it before, back when their futures weren't intertwined. Maybe she wouldn't be as supportive now.

However she reacted, he couldn't see her wanting to help him. That was the best-case scenario. If she decided to move on, said that they should take separate paths—well, he didn't know what he'd do.

It forced him to stay silent. Having her in his arms was everything he'd remembered. Dade wanted this moment. It was simple and felt right. The last thing he wanted to do was ruin it.

He opened his eyes and realized that she was staring at him.

"What?" he asked, both hating and loving that she could make him breathless with a look.

Arden smiled. Her head was tilted as she studied him. "I love dancing with you. We should do it more."

He agreed. Dade didn't want to do it for a job. Wanted to have these quiet moments simply to spend time with her and relish them for as long as they lasted. He could visualize an easy relationship where they could just be themselves and spend time with each other because it brought them pleasure to do so. Not because they were bait or watching for marks.

How would they ever make this thing between them real? Because it felt like they were putting things off until life worked itself out. Their circumstances weren't easy, and they didn't have many quiet moments like this. Maybe they should. Perhaps he could make an effort to stop their spinning world and just breathe with her.

He loved holding her in his arms. It was like holding starlight. The feeling of warmth as the sun hit the Sky Towers. He didn't miss the sun because with her he always had that burning light. She made him feel as if he could do anything. Perhaps even fly if she told him he could.

Dade leaned forward. He brushed her lips in a kiss while his body continued to sway with hers to the music. She tasted like sugared cherries. His hands slid down her back, and her head tilted to allow him closer.

She moaned into his kiss, gripping the back of his head with her fingers. Anchoring him to her so that she could take what she wanted. It was always heat, and need, and fire with her. He loved this connection, craved it like these club kids craved a fix.

The kiss ended with a lingering of their lips and a shared breath. He couldn't tear his gaze away to watch the dancers or scan the area. She consumed too much of his attention.

He leaned close to her ear. Nuzzled it. Bit her lobe. And then breathed, "You look amazing tonight, have I told you that?"

She turned her face into the side of his neck. He felt the smile rather than saw it. It was small, secret. "Yes."

"You're always beautiful, though. I can't decide if I like you more when you're dressed for vengeance or when you're so bright that it almost hurts to look at you."

She laughed. "I have a feeling you enjoy my knife skills more."

"Perhaps you're right." He ran his lips across her cheek and then pulled away to study her again.

The strobes from the club and the mask she wore made her brown eyes seem deeper, pools of emotion that he might never be able to read. She kept most of herself locked away. He knew that he'd only begun to scrape the surface of who Arden was, that there was so much more to know of her, to understand.

And that was okay. It was a pleasure to learn new things each day. There was no reason to rush a discovery that brought him so much joy; they had plenty of time ahead. That was, if the secrets they kept from each other didn't rip what they had apart.

Dade swallowed, not allowing that thought to fix inside his head.

Arden's lips skimmed the side of his neck. "The last time we danced, it ended terribly."

"Shush, don't jinx us." He felt his laughter bubble up as he thought back to the night she'd first taken him to Undercity to avoid a govie raid. He remembered the joy of being there with her and not worrying about survival or who might stab them in the back next.

He hated that they hadn't had any time for these simple pleasures. If they were different people, perhaps they could have made a life together. Not always fighting for their existence. Let someone else take their city's burdens and figure out how to fix the problems their families had caused.

"We're supposed to be working," she reminded him. And yet she made no attempt to pull away or scan the area again. Her gaze remained solely on him.

He felt the weight of her focus, sensing how much he meant to her. The softness of these moments were few and far between. Arden rarely let down her guard.

Dade kissed her again. He couldn't help himself. He worshipped her mouth, letting his need for her become expressed through his touch. He wanted her to remember this when they were separated.

She gave a little mewl of pleasure, grasping for him.

But then, as always, the kiss had to end.

They both panted as they continued to dance and stare at each other.

This moment couldn't last. Reality crept in and filled his chest with heaviness. It wiped away the warmth of her. Left him feeling only cold regret.

Arden sensed the change in him. She pulled out of his arms enough so that she could properly see him and then reached up and clicked off her comm. She'd still be able to hear the others, but they couldn't hear her. "What's wrong?"

He also shut off his comm before answering. "You don't owe Mina. You should leave."

Not that he wanted her to go. He'd be devastated not seeing her every day. But he'd make it work. And if that was what it would take for her to be happy and safe, he'd manage to go it alone. Because he didn't want her to be a part of this plan with the CRC. He was the one who'd indebted himself. He wasn't going to allow her to die because of that.

"I'm tagged too, remember?"

"But not bound. If you asked, she'd let you go."

Her eyes flashed and narrowed, sparking behind her mask. "I'm not going anywhere."

"But, Arden—"

She cut him off, enunciating each word, her voice harder. "I will not leave you."

He nodded slowly while gulping back his overwhelming frustration. Dade was all mixed up inside. Elated that she wouldn't go, and sick that he was so selfish that he wanted her with him. Devastated she might be caught and tortured. He could not live with that.

Under her breath she asked, "Why does everyone ask me to leave? As if I'd abandon them."

He wondered whom she meant by "them." Though it didn't matter. "I didn't intend for this to happen."

"Of course you didn't." She rolled her eyes. "We can't second-guess our path. Looking back and wondering 'what if' makes us weak."

"You're so sure about everything." Maybe that was his problem. Maybe he needed to learn to accept fate.

"I'm not." Arden shrugged. It was an elegant movement that made her dress glitter. "But worrying about it hurts me inside—so I don't."

He wasn't sure that was the healthiest way to deal with life. Dade opened his mouth to say so, but he realized that he'd lost her attention.

Her eyes had narrowed at something over his shoulder.

Chapter sixteen

Dade knew better than to turn his head. Instead, he tried to steer them around so he could see. But she stubbornly planted her feet in place.

"Stop," she hissed. Arden gripped his shoulders harder, her stare not wavering from beyond him. "Move with me, to the right."

He loved a whole lot of things about her. Yet the one thing that irritated him was how her usual instinct was to take control and shut him out in the process. He could help her if she'd let him.

"Do you see the dealer?" he asked.

She made a humming noise. "I think I see the Twins."

"What?" He glanced to the side, but she jerked his shoulders back into place.

Arden gave him a look that told him to stop struggling. He pressed his lips together and forced himself to not protest as she maneuvered him backward, using his body to push their way through the crowd. They were working as two separate people, not as a team. Each of her demands reminded him that they weren't in sync. Irritation flicked to life in the ever-present frustration that lived inside him.

They edged along the dance floor closer to the tables. "I can't be sure . . . It has to be them."

"Why would they be here?" The Twins certainly didn't fit the demographic for this place. If it was them, they were here on Crispin's business. Was Crispin after Lasair too? Or had he assigned the Twins to keep track of Dade and Arden?

Dade knew they should let Nastasia and the others know, even if this was only a hunch. It was their op, and Nastasia was the point of contact. Yet he didn't move to turn his comm back on. Mostly because he was too focused on trying to make Arden listen.

If she would just slow down and talk to him, they could figure this out.

He pushed out a frustrated breath.

"If it is the Twins, I doubt you'll get another shot at seeing them," Dade said. "That you managed it once is quite impressive."

Her mouth pursed as she thought. "Unless, of course, that was the point. And if Crispin does want me to see them . . ." Her thought trailed off as she stared at Dade. "What kind of game are we all playing? I feel like everyone knows the rules but us. And I have to tell you, it's ticking me off that we're being manipulated."

Dade agreed. Crispin was crafty, and Mina just as much. If the Twins' being here was a deliberate ploy by Crispin, it made Dade even more cautious. Perhaps they should get the others involved after all.

"The Twins could be here to kidnap us," he suggested.

"If that was the case, we wouldn't have seen them. They would have come from the shadows and either grabbed us or stabbed us already."

"True."

Arden gave up any pretense of dancing. Her hands slipped from his shoulders, and she stepped around him. Taking his hand, she led him off the dance floor.

Dade squeezed her palm to keep them together as they wended through the maze of dancers. "They'll see you."

"I want them to," she said as they kept walking. Her gaze stayed razor-focused on the dark edge of the club.

She moved fast.

He let go of her hand as he followed behind her. Keeping her in sight while giving her a few feet of space. He wanted to stop her and demand to know exactly what her plan was. At least she had mentioned seeing the Twins and not simply disappeared without a word. He half expected her to do so at this point.

"What's going on?" Nastasia asked over the comm.

Dade didn't stop moving. He couldn't see Arden anymore. His senses screamed at him to stay alert. His muscles tensed even though he told himself to calm down, breathe, and assess the situation.

He growled. Where had she gone? They were working together for a reason. He couldn't watch her back if she didn't allow him to.

Turning his comm back on, he said, "I'll tell you in a moment."

He didn't want to warn them until he figured out Arden's plan and was positive she'd seen the Twins. And he certainly didn't want them to know that Arden had ditched him. His pride was taking a serious beating.

"Venz?" Nastasia asked.

"I'm locked on their coordinates. They haven't left the building," Venz said.

Dade exhaled in frustration. He would have informed them if they'd left the club. He hated to be micromanaged. They said they wanted him to feel like part of the team. Yet they made no effort to hide that they were tracking his every move. It was hard to see the truth in their offer of partnership.

Between the tight leash they kept on him and his detachment from Arden, he felt like screaming.

The sea of people suddenly parted, and he caught sight of Arden. The sparkle of her dress drew his eye. She had paused, stepping behind a large group. Not hiding, but not being obvious that she was prowling either.

Dade slid into the space beside her. They stood in the shadows at the edge of the room. He scanned the area where she was focused, trying to find any glimpse of the Twins. Instead, he realized that she'd latched on to something different—their original target.

The boy wasn't doing much to blend in. He had dressed like the clubbers, with his skimpy clothes and mask, though the look wasn't quite right. There wasn't the same ease about him. He stood steady, too alert, and he wasn't holding a drink. His gaze tracked the dancers, darting here and there. He acted as if he knew he was being hunted.

Then the boy moved. He interacted with those in the crowd as he slipped through them toward the door. His hand would press against another in what looked like a greeting. And though Dade never saw the drugs exchange hands, he knew better. The boy was getting farther from them, closing in on the door at a rapid pace.

They needed to move. Adrenaline hit him, focusing him. They needed to trap the boy and make him talk.

Arden's hand reached out to snatch his wrist, stopping him. Her eyes were narrowed, and her mouth had flattened into a frown. She'd picked up a drink from somewhere. Tipping it up, she pretended to sip it and waited.

She didn't watch the boy leave, though Dade knew she'd seen him go. She'd tracked him when he'd started walking, but then her gaze had returned to the dark corner.

Time became an issue. He felt pressure to pursue the boy. Noted each second as it slipped by. And yet she still hung on to his wrist. Dade forced himself to relax, to trust. When she felt his body respond to her request, she released him.

Not knowing what they were doing, Dade stepped behind her and wrapped his hands around her waist. He selfishly wanted to hold her. Touching her calmed him. Allowed him to let go of his growing resentment. It kept him from following his instinct to tell the others and leave anyway, even though she'd requested that he not.

Arden didn't seem to mind. She brushed back against him. Tipping her head to the side so that it rested against his shoulder. A quirky smile pulled on her lips when she glanced back.

He leaned forward to brush his lips against her hair. He kept himself there, filling himself with her scent.

She let out a sigh. It was inaudible, no more than a puff of breath. But she closed her eyes briefly, then stiffened, pulling away slightly to watch the shadows their target had left.

Roan interrupted over the comm, asking, "Does anyone see anything?"

Dade knew Arden hadn't turned her comm back on and therefore wouldn't answer. He got the feeling that she wasn't ready to point out the boy's location quite yet. Even though he had to be at least to the door or out of the club by now.

He said into his comm, keeping his other hand around her, "Nothing yet."

Arden shifted. It was slight, barely perceptible. His only warning as her body subtly communicated things to him that would have otherwise been lost.

Separating from the shadows were the Twins.

Shock coursed through Dade. She'd been right.

The Twins made their way to the front of the club after the Lasair boy. They moved as if they were smoke and night. The androgyny of the two from this far away made them appear to be copies. Girls, boys—either and both, their gender fluid.

They were hunting the boy too.

"We should find out what the evil Wonder Twins want from Lasair," Arden said. She tossed the cup away and followed them.

"That's not our mission." Dade stepped after her, staying beside her even though it caused the clubbers to yell at him when they were shoved out of the way. His chest was tight with annoyance. Of course she might take off without any backup and ignore every safety precaution. Even when he was working with her, she didn't spare a moment to discuss her plan.

Yet he followed her, not wanting her to leave unprotected. They were partners. She might not treat him like one, but he wasn't about to leave her back exposed. Plus, he was very concerned about what the Twins wanted. Chasing after them without a plan wasn't smart. This could be a double cross.

He reached out to pull her to a stop. "Tell me exactly what we're doing."

"The Twins are following the boy. If we follow the Twins, not only are we still following the boy, we can also figure out how Crispin fits into this and ultimately what he wants from us." Arden gave him a flat stare. "It's important to know what everyone wants so we can we figure out a way out of this mess when it all goes to hell."

Arden didn't wait for him to agree. She twisted out of his hand, this time moving with a speed he hadn't seen in weeks.

Dade cursed under his breath while reaching for his comm as he started running. "We've found the Lasair dealer. We're following him out of the club."

Chapter seventeen

"Arden, wait," she heard Dade call to her through her comm as she left the club. Then they were all yelling in her ear, scrambling to meet up with her. But she was already striding down the street, turning the corner in pursuit of the Twins.

She'd lost track of the dealer some time back. Had to trust that the Twins were still tracking him.

Following the Twins proved challenging. They were competent trackers, aware of everything. If she got too close, they'd notice. It forced her to hang back farther than she was comfortable and allowed them to slip in and out of her view.

Noise continued to crackle in her ear, chatter that she didn't latch onto. Distantly she knew that it was the team talking. They followed her, as she knew they would. Venz gave directions to her location, tracking her with the tag.

Arden let that all fall away. She stayed focused on the prize. If she wasn't going to be given answers, then she'd find them herself.

Her feet pounded the pavement, and she felt the tattoo of that movement reverberating in her chest. She breathed through it, only a small hitch as it expanded her lungs. She'd kicked her shoes off some time ago. The gravel from the street bit into her soles. Yet even that kept her focused. It honed and cleared her as pain often did.

Arden barely remembered to grab her cloak on the way out. Her focus was completely on the chase, but that didn't mean that she would leave the club without some kind of camouflage. Her dress was too showy. The Twins would see it straight off.

As she ran, she swung her cloak around her shoulders, fastening the toggles to hide the shine of her dress. Next she pulled out the gauze flowers, letting them flutter to the ground, and began to braid her hair back with swift fingers. She kept her mask on, pulling the hood up over her so that the edge rested low over her forehead. At once she was someone else. Not the fun-loving club girl she'd been moments before. She was now a weapon looking for revenge, a girl on the hunt, blending with the night.

It was the unknown that lent her caution. Whispered to her to watch her every step and focus her moves several paces ahead. She couldn't ignore that there was a price on her head. It only took the right person to see her in the wrong circumstance and she could be caught. Her life would be forfeit.

She was in enough trouble. No need to add avoiding death to the mix.

But there was also that need, the pulse under her skin she couldn't ignore, to kick some ass and take names. The combination of excitement and fear was potent and addicting.

The warm burn in her legs made her feel alive. She pushed faster. Hearing the beating of her heart as it pumped and the harshness of her breath as she gulped air.

She turned everything to white noise. Used it to focus.

Arden almost smiled. It was ridiculous how happy she was. This was who she was meant to be: a warrior, not a person to be sidelined. She had a choice.

Red lights blinked in the darkness. Cameras that had never worked during Arden's entire life in Undercity had been switched on. The cameras monitored the area using infrared.

It was the question of who watched the other side of the feed that concerned her. Was it the govies? Or the Lasair? Or maybe even Mina? Someone had taken control of large chunks of Undercity.

Dade came up beside her. He kept pace, running silently. For once, they were in sync—their movements, their breath—both focused on keeping up with the Twins. They navigated over trash piles and turned into sections almost too dark to see. Eventually entering a residential neighborhood in front of a section of row houses.

The Twins slowed.

Arden and Dade slowed as well, keeping several paces behind. They were close to wherever Lasair was holed up. Her heartbeat felt like it had taken over the space under her ribs. Swallowing, she pulled herself back and reined in her excitement. She tasted the thick, wet mineral tang of the air as she breathed heavily from exertion. It was the unique taste of Undercity, and it held the memories of her childhood.

She didn't know of a Lasair hideout in this section of Undercity. It had to be new or stolen from another gang, which confirmed Mina's statement that they had switched up their hideouts. Just how many other things had changed and why? She'd been gone only a few weeks. This level of transition shocked her. It made Mina's warning that something more sinister was happening in Lasair sound more reliable.

Secretly she'd harbored hope that she could reconcile with Lasair. That maybe she could change their seeing her as a threat. Now she wondered if finding a way to go back to Lasair was the best option.

Arden stopped at the mouth of an alley. She shivered as she pressed her chest to the cool dampness of the brick and leaned out to peek at the street where she'd last seen the Twins.

She took stock of where they were, at the desolation of this part of Undercity. Poverty had grown like a cancer on these streets. The housing block in front of her looked like the one she'd lived in with her parents. The brick expanse crossing several blocks with domes where the streets cut through. Above the street, along which there had once been separate buildings, more housing had been created, connecting the original structures together. Several sections of the building had crumbled away. In front, the trash hadn't been hauled away for weeks. The rotting garbage emitted a strong odor.

Logically she assessed the location. This wasn't the best place for the Lasair to hide. It was too quiet here. Empty streets meant watchful eyes. If Uri had picked it, he'd done a terrible job.

Dade stood behind her, close enough to touch. He placed his hand against her but didn't make a move to look around the wall. Instead, he watched behind them in case the Twins had doubled back.

Voices still squawked in her ear. Distantly, she heard Dade updating their position even though Venz was already tracking them. "We're at the corner of—"

"We know where you're at," Roan snapped. He sounded pissed.

It was Venz's voice that Arden locked on to. He was calm and reassuring as he spoke. He made a good comm leader. Probably the best she'd worked with other than Colin.

She ignored the twist in her gut at the thought of her deceased cousin.

Venz said, "Do not go inside any of those buildings. Every one within the next block has active cams. Backup in five."

"Think you can last that long without getting into trouble?" Roan sniped.

The Lasair boy stepped into the light just ahead at the stoop of the old building. A thick mist had settled in the street. It wove around the boy, parting as he moved. His shadowed features came into finer detail the closer he got to the light of the doorway. He shivered and looked back into the darkness, rubbing his arms, as if he felt the weight of her stare.

The Twins were gone.

Her pulse beat. Where were they?

Worry over the Twins calmed her. If she expected trouble, she could plan for it. Calculate every angle they could attack, what she could do to prevent it, and how they'd escape. She had several scenarios running through her head even now.

The boy looked around once more before he opened the door and disappeared inside.

Her gut twisted. Time was short, and she needed to decide if answers were truly what she wanted. If she didn't move now, before the cavalry arrived, this part of the plan would go to shit.

Arden pulled back and then signaled to Dade. Pointed two fingers at herself and him, and then signed that they were going to leave.

Dade nodded. He didn't look surprised. And really, he'd anticipated her moves more often as of late. As if he'd made it his mission to study her.

She didn't know how she felt about that. It was sweet and disconcerting. How could she hide the darkest parts of herself if he insisted on knowing everything? She didn't think it was healthy to know a person that well.

Arden flipped on her comm. "The boy's moving. We're going to follow." Then she turned and ran, leading them west. Eventually she'd "lose" her quarry and double back later.

Dade followed right behind her.

CHAPTER EIGHTEEN

Dade stood in the skytram station in Level Four, Above. It was one of the larger stations in the city. Three lines intersected at this hub.

Thirteen disks stretched across the open sky between one skywalk and the next. Each circle was a different diameter and placed at a different height. The larger platforms were the main embarkation zones for the three lines. They were cushioned by smaller platforms, allowing for further access to the skytrams. Around the outside were medium circles with ticket dispensers and projection screens that showed the routes.

Connecting all the disks were bridges that stretched across the expanse. They arched to allow the trams to pass through the sky beneath. Passengers teemed across them, the bridges' clear sides making them appear to walk on air.

A tram was about to dock in the station. People were queued on one of the larger disks and trailed off onto the two surrounding it. It was a well-chosen meeting spot, central to the city and with enough crowd movement that they'd not likely be noticed. Not even Clarissa.

Clarissa's ping had said she'd find him. And he knew she would. If he didn't know better, he would swear she'd implanted a tracker in him. They were friends, and he knew she wouldn't do that to him, though she'd be tempted. Clarissa was much like Arden that way: she straddled ethical lines if it meant that her agenda could be furthered.

He was conscious of everything: each person who swept by him, the annoying gaggle of teens on the next platform, the old lady who kept shooting him looks. Awareness prickled, right down to his breathing. He kept his body calm and loose.

Dade knew they were there before he saw them. He anticipated the reaching slide of the hand. When it came with no more than a whisper of displaced air, he was ready. He snatched the hand, pivoting his body as he twisted the arm. He kept the phaser that the attacker was holding pointed away from him while he continued to press her body forward and down.

The girl was light and small. He couldn't see her properly. But he could feel the thinness of her bones. She was dressed similarly to him. Swathed against the cold with a flowing cloak. Her hood slipped down as she fought against his hold, letting out a spill of hair that had come loose from her braid.

He continued to grip her wrist and squeeze.

She gave a little yelp.

"Let the phaser go," he said. And then twisted her hand a little more, putting maximum strain on her wrist. He contained their interaction, keeping his voice low.

The phaser she'd held clattered to the floor. She remained defiant, though, straining against him in an attempt to gain her freedom.

Another person came up behind Dade, the second of the team. But whatever action the individual intended was cut off with a sharp cry.

By the time Dade turned, Saben had ahold of the other girl, not much older than the first. They looked similar, sisters perhaps. These two might be part of a gang, but Dade didn't think so. They were gaunt, half-starved. Their clothing was stained and ragged, inadequate for the temperature. Most likely they were opportunists. And they were hungry, by the look of it.

He turned the girl he held around to face him. She wiggled, but he kept his grip tight. Making sure to exert the right amount of pressure to keep her pinned without hurting her. As he looked at her now, she appeared even younger than he'd thought.

The other struggled against Saben's hold as well.

Saben looked almost bored. "We can't do this here."

He was right. They didn't need the attention. So far they'd garnered a look or two. The thwarting of a pickpocket was common enough, though.

"Are you going to kill us?" The girl Saben held spat the words too loudly.

Dade sighed. Placing his foot on the phaser the first had dropped, he said, "Go," and pushed her away.

Saben had taken the other phaser. He let his quarry go as well.

Neither kid made a grab for their lost weapons. They both raced away, disappearing into the crowd.

Dade reached down to snag the phaser from the ground and handed it over to Saben. "Clarissa will be here any minute."

Nodding, Saben pocketed both weapons. "I'm watching your back."

"I've never doubted that."

"Stay alert," Saben said, and then he turned and disappeared. He'd wait out of sight for the meet. Ready in case anything else happened.

Air popped as the protective barrier dematerialized when a tram left the station. Whooshing, the current moved Dade's hood. The barriers blocked the skytram when it docked and departed, keeping commuters from being sucked into the air wash.

At the far dock, another tram pulled close to the station. A second pop sounded as the protective barrier again snapped into place. The platform he stood on began to fill with commuters in the ensuing chaos as people exited the skytram and made their way either to another disk for a connection or into the buildings beyond.

Suddenly, Clarissa appeared in front of him like a whisper of light. She wore pale orange, reminding him of the sunshine he hadn't seen in what seemed like forever. The hood of her cloak had fabric that billowed out about her face. Stylish and yet not obtrusive enough to be picked out by the cams and remarked upon.

Up close, he could see the stress on her face. Her painted red mouth quirked as she smiled at him in spite of it, and she tried to give him a cheery greeting. "Still wearing the synth-mask, I see."

Dade grunted. "I wish I could go out as myself, but you know how it is."

"I do." She looked pointedly at a pap-drone that hadn't caught sight of her yet. "Someday, though, you'll want to use your real face."

"I doubt that." So many things had to change for that to happen. He had to be not dead for one, and two, the gossip-vids needed to not care about him.

"We'll see." There was an enigmatic quality to her statement. It made Dade's gut clench low in his stomach. She was up to something.

"I thought you'd never get here," he grumbled.

She shrugged and slipped her arm through his. "Walk. We only have a moment before the next tram comes in. I need to be on it."

"As if you were never here?"

"Exactly."

He figured that meant she'd planned this little tête-à-tête while she was en route somewhere else. It was smart and daring and totally Clarissa. They were surrounded by people and crowded into the center of the bridge as they crossed it. Knowing Clarissa, he assumed she had some kind of noise dampener on her so that their conversation would not be overheard.

He'd worn his own disrupter as well. Had taken to wearing one regularly after he'd found a supply within Mina's stash. The disrupter didn't have a long range, creating a bubble around him so that the cams couldn't get a lock on his voice.

"They're watching me all the time." She let out a little sigh. "I'm virtually locked in Sky Tower One. My parents—well, let's just say we have differing opinions on how to navigate the social disaster my life has become since your death."

Dade could imagine.

"Anyway, enough of my grumbling," she said. "We're here about you."

"Did you find us a way in?" he asked.

"I did. And let me tell you, it was not fun. Even I can't get into the other Sky Towers. And not just because I'm persona non grata." She made a sour face. "The families are fracturing. No one trusts anyone anymore. The Sky Towers have locked themselves up into mini units."

It was the opposite of what Hernim, Dade's father, had planned. And because of that, Dade liked the outcome. His father wanted to be in control of all the families, to rule the Solizen and eventually the city.

The families had always been wary of one another. But they'd been forced to get along to hold sway over the govies. Without the glue of the VitD manufacturing to hold them together, their natural distrust and competition would have kicked in.

"This stunt of yours is going to cost me. I'm blowing one of my lines for you." Clarissa's words were dark.

He couldn't see her face as she walked beside him. The billowing fabric kept her hidden. He wondered if this was on purpose. If she didn't want him to have a full picture of the pressure she was under.

"Thank you for helping me," he said, meaning it sincerely. They were friends, had been his whole life. He wished he could bring her with him now. Hated that they had to be separated from each other by time and space and civil unrest.

Though Dade knew he needed to focus on himself. He had his own things to deal with, and staying alive was priority number one.

"I managed to get these at great personal cost." She held out her hand.

He extended his palm, and she dropped items into it. They were patches, about a quarter of an inch wide, with wires of tech inside. He pressed his thumb into one, feeling the slightly raised center.

"What is it?" Dade closed his hand around them and stuck them into his pocket.

"The patches are part of the upgraded security in Sky Tower Two. They're no longer relying on the global ID system. Your father is extremely paranoid."

The working relationship between Hernim and Chief Nakomzer had indeed broken down if his father was no longer using the implanted data sensor to keep track of those inside the Tower.

"Anyone inside the Tower is required to cover their data sensors so that the govies can't monitor who's in the building. Even guests are asked to put on a blackout band prior to entering." She gave him a flat stare. "They don't care that it's against the law. Honestly, I think that's a big part of it, seeing how far they can push Nakomzer before he pushes back."

"Not too much farther, I would think. Nakomzer is as power hungry as the rest of them."

"Agreed," she said. "The patches are issued at the beginning of every shift and changed once between. They're single use. As far as I can tell, they last four hours. After that, an alert is sent to the central hub. Get yourself programmed into the system, and only turn them online when you're inside."

He nodded.

Her gaze flicked to the rotation of govies who lined the skyway above looking down on them, studying the crowd. They had large phase-blasters in their hands. "That's not the worst of the problem."

Dade looked in the direction in which she stared. Assessing the tactical team. "They're mobilizing."

Clarissa made a noise of derision. "The govies are making a power play, yes. But they're not the ones taking over the streets."

"What do you mean?" He'd been underground too long. If he'd even done some reconnaissance in Undercity, maybe he'd hear grumblings of who was moving to the top of the pile. Because he didn't doubt that she spoke the truth, that someone was taking advantage of the situation.

She bit her lip, and then turned to him and gave him a smile. "We'll see how it eventually plays out. Can't very well fight if they don't come out of the shadows."

They were almost at the next platform. The skytram's countdown was projected into the darkness of the static cloud above it. They had two minutes until it left the station.

He knew Clarissa was getting on it.

Reaching out, he grabbed her hand. "We can have a better world."

Her eyes glinted. "I always did like that you were such an optimist."

Dade winked.

Chapter Nineteen

Arden snuck down the street, staying out of the streetlights and blending in with the shadows. She moved fast, knowing she had only a small amount of time before Venz became suspicious and raised the alarm. She could only imagine that Roan—and probably Coco and Annem—would realize what her presence here meant, and converge to stop her. They'd ruin her plans.

Her destination loomed ahead. The very building the Lasair boy went into the day before. She paused at the opposite corner to contemplate her options. Arden couldn't use the front entrance. There were too many lights, and she would be seen. Neither did she have the time to circle around the building. This would have to be quick and dirty.

She decided that using a window would be her best bet. Arden chose one far enough away from the spill of light, though still close enough to the front that she'd be able to backtrack to the lobby and hopefully pick up the boy's trail. The window she approached was missing the moonglass that had once fit into the casing. Instead of using brick to seal it, someone had stretched synth-board across the opening.

The board had warped in the dampness, the synth swelled with condensation. Sections had disintegrated, pulling away from the sill. As a result, there was enough room in the gap between the board and the sill for her to slip her fingers underneath. The wood was damp enough for her to pull the corners loose, though it took some effort.

Her muscles strained. Eventually the board buckled with a groan. The space she'd opened was only large enough to shimmy her body through, but it was enough.

Arden placed her hands on the sill and hoisted herself in. She used her toes to notch into the brick to give her a little help up. She was dressed in her synth-suit and boots with the grip soles. Her gloves had suction grips that could be turned on if she needed them. It made climbing into the building easy.

She'd had the entire day to plan. How many phasers she'd take, which weapons she needed for close contact. It kept her mind focused while she waited for the others to go about their business.

Arden had decided not to take Dade with her. A disconnect, a barrier, had grown between them. She didn't think he was lying to her. But he was hiding something. It irritated her. They only had each other. There shouldn't be secrets between them. Still, she was doing the exact same thing. Too many secrets flitted through her head, and she had a difficult time trusting anyone, even Dade.

He'd stuck with her and her lies, though, the night before. Mina had looked at her suspiciously when she'd spun tales about losing the Lasair boy. She'd managed to distract Mina by mentioning seeing the Twins, telling her that they'd been after the boy as well.

When Dade and Saben had taken off that afternoon and then Mina had left the compound with Nastasia, Arden knew the time had come. She'd suited up and bolted.

The window she crawled through entered into a bathroom. She landed with a soft thud on the tiled floor. The light was off, and the door to the hallway was open. A leaky faucet dripped in the sink, staining the bowl yellow. Mold crept up the shower stall. It stank of stale wetness.

There were people in the apartment. The sound of daily living muted through the walls. Arden went to the door, using the wall to partially shield her body while getting the lay of the apartment.

Someone was in the kitchen. She could hear the clink of cookware against a hard surface. To her right, another door was open, and a loud snore filled the hall like off-key music.

Arden slid out of the bathroom and headed toward what she'd thought would be the main hall and front door. Her booted feet were soundless on the threadbare carpet. It was dark in the hall, though enough light spilled from the living room and the kitchen for her to see.

She was exposed as she disengaged the locks on the front door. The thrum of adrenaline had settled into her gut like a low-churning warmth. It heated her chest and made her breaths staccato. She hit the pad for the door to open.

The apartment complex hallway was empty when she slipped into it. There was some light coming from overhead, but most of the bulbs had burned out, which allowed her plenty of dark spaces to use as cover.

Arden headed toward the front of the building. With Lasair's hideout here, there would be some sort of lookout standing duty for her to take out.

In the entrance hall, she found a dark corner beneath the stairs. She tucked herself into it, her body primed to move. Arden withdrew a single blade. Knives were the best when she needed to keep things quiet, though it required her getting close. Using her phaser would make too much noise. The flash of the phase-fire would be too bright in the darkness, and it had too much potential for her to lose control of the situation.

She didn't have to wait long.

A girl came out of the opposite hall and into the entrance vestibule. She didn't bother to look around, careless with her assigned security detail. If Arden was in charge, that kind of negligence would not be tolerated.

The girl opened the front doorway and took out a vape-disk. She opened the pipe and dragged on the mouthpiece. There was a moment of silence before she exhaled. A curl of smoke wound its lazy way to the ceiling of the vestibule. It smelled of sweetness, with a tang of wildflowers.

Arden snuck from her hiding place. She moved with a swift lightness, a specter at the girl's back. One hand coming up to snatch at the girl's hair, angling her head back, as her other pressed the knife into the girl's throat.

She pulled the girl out of the lit doorway with a swift jerk that sent the girl stumbling. Arden made sure to direct their bodies into the darkness. Spinning the girl around, she slammed her into the wall and pushed the knife back into her neck. The girl was smaller than Arden, slower. Her instincts were not as honed. It didn't take much work to get her into a position to be interrogated.

The girl and Arden stood face-to-face. She kept the point of the knife on her. Arden would kill her if she stepped out of line.

The girl knew it too. Fear flared in her eyes, and her breath quickened.

Arden felt satisfaction at seeing it. That meant that this would go fast, then. Good, because the stubborn, macho ones were irritating. It took many wasted minutes to break them, and she didn't have the time.

"I need to know which apartment Lasair is using." Arden made her voice quiet enough so it wouldn't carry into the rest of the building. But she made sure to add a menacing undertone.

The girl blinked. "Who?"

She twisted the girl's hair till she winced and then cracked her head hard against the wall.

The girl let out a cry.

"Where?" Arden repeated.

The girl's eyes were large. "They'll kill me."

"So will I." Arden raised an eyebrow. "Make a decision: die now, or die later. But at least you'll have time to prepare if you choose later. Who knows, you might even make it." Doubtful, once the Lasair learned the girl had betrayed them. Still, Arden thought it was a fair offer.

The girl swallowed. "I . . ." Fear made her voice squeaky.

Enough. Arden's internal clock blared not having time for this. She dug the point of the knife into the girl's skin. Twisted it so there would be extreme pain but not much damage. Arden didn't want to kill her if she could help it. Her offer had been sincere.

The girl winced. "Don't kill me, please."

"Talk."

"Second floor, fourth door. Number two fifty-six."

"Excellent." Arden shifted her hand quickly so that the knife's hard bone handle hit the girl in the temple. It landed with a solid thunk. Arden could feel the push and give, as the pommel connected with the girl's skull.

The girl went down like a sack.

Arden pulled the girl into a dark corner and slid away her knife.

She then pulled out a pair of micron pads for her gloves. The material was not yet coded. It was see-through and thin. Arden worked delicately as she unfolded the pads and attached them to the palms of her gloves. Then she removed the covering layer, exposing the gel.

Next she pulled out a tiny wand that looked like a silver tube about an inch tall. She expanded it to its full six inches, running it over the girl's palm. The wand beeped, and Arden then ran it over the micron pads to embed the scan. The gel heated and began to dip and pivot, recreating the girl's palm print. When the nanotech hardened, it would feel like skin. It had the same texture and heat signature, and would fool typical scanners.

When both gloves were done, Arden collapsed the wand and stuck it back into the tool belt at her waist.

She was cautious as she climbed the stairs. The hallway was deserted. Arden put her palm to the scanner at the door the girl had indicated and waited for it to run its diagnostic. The door slid open, and Arden crept inside.

As the door slid shut behind her, Arden forced away the feeling of being trapped. She let out her breath, taking a moment to steady herself before she crept forward toward the voices.

Chapter twenty

Arden crouched low and peered around the corner into the living room. She needed to know how many people were in the room and where they were positioned. It was risky to expose herself, but she needed to get the lay of the apartment and know whom she'd have to fight if things went badly before she searched for Niall.

Her vantage point was not all that good because it was obstructed by couches and chairs. But she could hear perfectly. Arden began to count how many people were in the room by their different voices. There were at least nine, maybe as many as eleven. Too many to take on her own.

She pulled out both knives, just in case she needed to throw one. Balancing on the balls of her feet, she tucked her knives close to her chest and then leaned farther into the room. She kept her back to the door frame, using it to steady her body.

Arden caught sight of Uri. The first thing she noticed was that he had shaved his head. It made him look meaner and somehow bigger, though Uri had always been a behemoth. It emphasized his blocky face and a deformed nose that was wide and squat from one too many breaks. His face was littered with fading bruises turning greenish yellow.

Arden replayed the last time they'd spoken at the refinery. How he threatened to kill her if he ever saw her again. She believed him. He wouldn't greet her with friendship.

As she listened, she realized Uri was truly in charge as Mina had said. He stood at the head of the room, and the others deferred to him, though not exactly with respect.

Arden couldn't work out how Uri had ended up as the head of Lasair. He'd been high in the food chain and well regarded, sure. But that didn't automatically mean that he'd be next in line for the leadership position. Their gang was way more mercenary than that. Usually the biggest backstabber got the prize. And there would be quite a few deaths before the matter would be settled. Including former leaders, which in this case would be her brother, Niall.

The others she was able to see in the room concerned her. She recognized a few of them, not because they'd been her former gang family, but because they'd been high-ranking members of the other local gangs of Undercity. These were not the leaders—or former leaders—of those gangs. They were the muscle who carried out orders. Several she'd tussled with in the past. It worried her that not all of these gangs just cashed in on Shine. Some of them peddled things more sinister, things that even Arden had a difficult time justifying.

They didn't appear comfortable as they sat together. Their gazes were shifty, as they looked at one another with suspicion. They'd separated themselves into subgroups within the room. It was obvious they distrusted one another. Yet it was clear from the conversation that they were now operating as a single group.

What had happened to their leaders? Arden supposed they had died in the joint refinery explosion. If the other gangs were as decimated in numbers as Lasair had been, it made sense that they'd band together for protection.

Uri had never struck her as particularly charismatic. His evident ability to join together various factions of broken gangs didn't make sense to her. And why had he chosen so many outsiders for his inner circle? She couldn't fathom how they could be trusted. A gang was family, and these people weren't part of that family. What was Uri thinking?

The others began to buzz in her ear. They'd finally noticed she was gone. She'd taken the comm only because if she got in over her head and needed backup, she knew they'd come.

Still, Arden was glad she'd made it all the way inside before they'd started to annoy her.

It was Roan who yelled and screamed in her ear now, questioning where she was. He was insistent that she come back immediately. As if his bullying could get her to do what he wanted.

Arden ignored him.

She didn't worry that he would derail her operation at this point. They might follow her into the building, but they wouldn't come into Lasair's apartment. Not without getting a set of prints themselves or breaking down the door. And Mina and Nastasia weren't around to approve that.

Still, she wished she could tell Roan to shut up so she could concentrate. He had to know she couldn't verbally respond. And he seemed to take advantage of her inability to cuss him out, conducting a one-sided tirade about what an idiot she was. Arden could take the comm out, but it seemed the easiest way to monitor their progress.

Roan's yelling in her ear while she was simultaneously hiding from members of her former gang brought home with clarity the fact that she was friendless. A vulnerability crept up inside her. It wasn't nervousness or even panic. It was closer to a pain of longing, coloring everything. It made her extra conscious about checking each decision she made because she knew she was emotionally compromised.

Being here, around Lasair, brought up bitter memories. While she'd been friends with Uri once, their friendship paled in comparison to the memories of Colin. Arden drew in a deep breath, holding it and letting the burn center her. This was not the place to fall apart. Her cousin was gone. Mourning him and the memories that were suddenly as real as the day he died had to be ignored for another hour.

Before she pulled back, she caught sight of Mariah. Her former friend sat in the back of the room, set deep in her chair as if wanting the cushions to swallow her and allow her to disappear. Her knees were pulled up to her chin, and her feet rested on the seat. But she tracked the movement of the room.

Mariah had fought beside Arden inside the refinery. Had saved Arden's life. She hadn't been there when Uri told Arden they were now enemies.

Arden was happy that Mariah had escaped. Though she wondered what had transpired since. Mariah looked haunted. Her lips were chapped and cracked. She bit at them, apparently unaware that they bled.

The room exploded with sound as an argument broke out, reinforcing the tension she'd felt. There were threats, and bullying, and a whole lot of posturing—all the typical stuff but with more of an edge than she was used to. The words had no seeds of friendship to temper them. Arden looked away from Mariah to Uri, who was speaking louder than everyone else.

He didn't look pleased at being questioned. His shoulders tightened, and his eyes narrowed. "I want Nakomzer."

Arden blinked. Uri wanted the chief of the govies?

A voice yelled back, "We can't go to war with them. Didn't the refinery teach you that?"

Uri growled. "We're already at war with them."

"Why do you want Nakomzer?" another voice yelled out.

Yes, why exactly? But the answer never came. Uri deflected, and there was more argument. It was precisely the cover she needed to move farther into the apartment and search for Niall.

"Arden, I know you can hear me," Roan yelled. "We're outside. Give us an update stat."

Backing out of the doorway, she slunk down the hall. She paused at what was designed to be a dining room but now served as the center hub. Two people were monitoring various electronics that lay on the table. Neither of them noticed her, and, not recognizing the individuals, she moved on.

The last room on this side of the apartment was a storage room. Boxes crowded the space. Various logos emblazoned on the side told her they were stolen.

Arden retraced her steps. She crossed past the room where Uri was currently trying to calm the assembled group, to a kitchen. Peeking inside, Arden was surprised to find Mariah at the stove.

Mariah stared at the teakettle, her sight unfocused. An empty mug hung loosely in her hand. In the several seconds it took Arden to check the rest of the room, Mariah didn't move or blink.

Sliding her knives away, Arden made a sudden decision. She stepped into the kitchen on silent feet. Rounding the room, she stayed out of Mariah's peripheral vision and slipped in behind her. Quickly, she reached forward and grabbed Mariah. One hand cupped her mouth hard, and the other moved across her chest to pull Mariah back against her.

Mariah instantly snapped to life. She fought the hands that held her, bringing up her mug to hit Arden in the head while simultaneously kicking out with her foot.

"Stop," Arden hissed in her ear. "It's Arden."

Though she wasn't sure if that was helpful. Arden was the enemy. It was a fact she couldn't forget.

It took time for Arden's words to sink in, but when they did, Mariah paused.

Arden waited a heartbeat before she slowly released her hold. She kept her arms up, ready to subdue Mariah again if necessary. But allowed Mariah enough room to turn her head and see that Arden spoke the truth. She waited for a tiny nod from Mariah before she fully stepped back.

She put distance between them. Stepping back more, out of fighting distance, yet close enough to get control again.

This was the problem with trusting her instincts and not taking a moment to assess the situation. Her instincts usually ran true. Yet Arden had given in to nostalgia. She hadn't given a thought to approaching Mariah before she'd done that very thing. Now she realized that she'd trapped herself in the center of the building. Mariah could easily yell and bring everyone running. There was no way Arden could fight them all.

Tension tightened Arden's chest. She forced herself to stay calm, to plant her feet and keep her hands ready to move. To grab a knife or a phaser and fight her way out should she need to escape.

Yet Mariah said nothing. She didn't scream or move. Instead, she stared as if seeing a ghost, her eyes a little too wide and mouth slightly parted. The mug in her hand almost slipped, but she gripped it at the last second. Her surprise melted into frantic movements. With shaking hands, she set down the mug and turned off the teakettle. Then her hands fluttered as she signaled Arden to follow and darted out of the kitchen.

Mariah led her into a sparse bedroom. Four pallets lined the floor on either side. There was not much else, only a few personal items, but no furniture or cubbies to tuck things into.

Mariah shut the door to the hall and leaned against it. Her voice was quiet, stressed. "Are you insane?"

Arden shrugged. She was a fugitive with no friends. "It's debatable."

"This isn't a joke. How did you find us? How did you get in here?" She made a cutting gesture with her hand, swift and blunt. "Never mind. You're you. Of course you'd be here."

Arden rolled her eyes but took the words as a compliment. She couldn't help the smirk that formed on her mouth.

Mariah shook her head. "Things are really, really bad. You can't be here."

The smirk died. "How bad?"

"The other gangs—the members who didn't join us, they're trying to run us out of Undercity. They're forming new groups, so it's difficult to tell who's working with whom. It's war. Three of our members were stabbed on the street tonight. Another two got into a phase-fight with the govies, and they were taken."

Arden nodded her head back toward the room she had spied on. "How many has Lasair swallowed up from the other gangs?"

"The number changes almost daily."

Interesting that Uri was having a difficult time keeping a core group together. It affirmed her assessment that he was the worst person to lead. He didn't have a personality that inspired people. But she couldn't worry about Lasair. It wasn't the family she was here for.

She pressed on with her questions because Mina would want to know. And that might get her out of trouble for lying. "And the other gang leaders?"

"Most of them were lost at the refinery." Her voice threaded. "I thought you were gone too."

Arden swallowed back a twist of guilt.

"What's Uri's plan to stop the gang fights?" It was bad for everyone if that continued. There would be deaths, and innocent people would get hurt. The govies would swarm Undercity, making it impossible for anyone to move about without notice. It was bad business for everyone. If Uri was the head of Lasair, it fell to him to figure out a way to stop it.

Mariah looked away. She bit her lip. It was obvious she didn't want to answer.

"Mariah," Arden said, using the voice that bled authority, "that shouldn't be a difficult question. What is his plan?"

"He hasn't said."

147

That wasn't too surprising. Sometimes plans were kept secret until they were ready to be implemented. Though she doubted Uri had a plan. Her gut told her he was flying blind. It was obvious how much of a mess he was making by the lack of control he had in the meeting. And if he had a plan, wouldn't he tell his girlfriend?

Mariah licked her lips. "Since I was taken, Uri's been . . . strange."

"Strange how?"

"Secretive, not telling me things. Maybe it's to protect me. But he's acting sketchy. Lying all the time. And then he gets angry."

That sounded familiar. Arden had spent far too many years in Niall's shadow not to know the signs of corrupting power. It had scared her too. Perhaps that was the reason Mariah was being so open with her.

Or maybe she was willing to talk because they had been friends. She'd helped to break Mariah out of govie custody. Arden didn't mind using that connection.

"What about Lasair's inner circle? Where are they?" They couldn't have all died in the refinery. Someone had to have made it out.

"They're all missing."

"Every single one?" She couldn't believe they'd all perished.

Her suspicion traced back to how Uri had ended up leading Lasair as well as what had remained of the other gangs. He was consolidating power within Undercity. Grasping larger portions than Lasair originally controlled. She wondered why. Whatever was happening here was a dangerous and deadly game.

"Some are dead, but most are missing. The govies got a few. And there were others who joined the remnants of the other gangs to fight against us."

Questions swirled in her mind. Gang members did not just switch allegiances so quickly. But she knew these questions would have to wait for another time. Staying too long here put her in danger of being caught. Roan's squawking in her ear had become more insistent. She needed to get what she came for.

"Where's my brother?" Arden would not lose any more family. Not even one who wouldn't care to see her and might even try to gut Arden himself.

Mariah looked away, refusing to meet Arden's gaze. "I don't know."

"I know Uri has him." It was a bluff, Arden suspected, but she didn't know any such thing. Piecing together Mina's intel, which had been correct until now, Arden was positive they had custody of Niall. The proof was everything she'd seen that day. It only stood to reason that if Niall was alive, Uri would have him.

How did Niall fit into Uri's plans? It was difficult to understand why they'd kept him alive. If the power had already shifted within the gang, they should have killed him. It was the only way to keep his loyal followers from fracturing into an internal war. Unless Uri and Mariah were the only two original Lasair members who knew he was here. Perhaps this was why they were in a hideout Arden knew nothing about.

Mariah's distress screamed from across the room. The other girl refused to lift her chin to connect her gaze with Arden's.

"I know he's alive," Arden insisted when the silence became too much. "You might as well tell me where."

Eyes shining, Mariah bit her lower lip. She began to shake her head. It wasn't a "no." It was a more violent denial, as if she were afraid to say.

"Where is he?" Arden pressed again, sensing that the other girl would break with a little more prodding. It was easy to inflect the frustration she felt into her voice. She had very little time left here. Needed to get out as soon as possible before she was discovered.

Mariah's gaze met hers. "He's not here anymore."

That stopped her cold. "What do you mean?"

"He was here, Uri had him beaten." Mariah wouldn't meet her eyes. "He was in bad shape, no one was allowed to help him. And Uri made sure that no one Niall knew was in the room with him. I wasn't sure how much longer they were going to keep him alive. Then last night—" She shook her head. "He's gone now."

"He's dead?" Arden's mouth went dry.

Mariah looked up, her eyes wide, and her voice wobbled, her words barely audible. "No, someone took him."

"Who?"

"I don't know," Mariah said. "Uri's been furious all day. Questioning everyone."

Like a bright light in her head, realization set in. Arden had been shortsighted. She'd seen the Twins last night. They took Niall. That was why they'd been following the boy. There was no other explanation as to why they'd followed him out of the club. Niall was what they'd wanted with Lasair.

She should have asked herself what the Twins wanted last night. Or perhaps should have said something to Mina and the crew instead of thinking she could handle this on her own. Arden had been so close to Niall and she'd failed. And it was all her fault.

She reminded herself that Niall knew the consequences of his actions and was ultimately responsible for his own life. He'd gotten himself caught, had made his own decisions. Still, she felt that cloying sense of regret creep into her consciousness again, mostly because she'd left him in the refinery. He was her brother. Family had to count for something.

At least now she knew where he probably was. If the Twins did take Niall, that meant that Crispin had him. What sorts of secrets did Niall have that not only spared him with Uri but also gained him Crispin's attention? He was always up to something, and it looked like his schemes had finally caught up with him.

It was only a matter of time until Uri figured out who had taken Niall. Which meant the clock was ticking. She had to get back to Mina and her crew and let them know. They had to figure out a new plan that matched a much slicker opponent.

But Arden's instincts were driving her crazy. Mariah was still acting strange even after admitting that Niall was gone. She chewed on her lip and kept opening her mouth, only to immediately close it again.

"What else are you not telling me?" Arden asked.

Mariah shook her head.

Arden waited. Mariah obviously wanted to say something. She'd wait Mariah out even if she felt the pressing need to leave. Each second it became more dangerous to stay. They stared at each other. The weighted silence dragged on for what felt like minutes. Whatever Mariah was holding back was significant.

Finally Mariah let out a breath. "I didn't know. I want you to believe that. If I had, I would have told you."

"What?"

"I found something out, and I—" Her eyes filled with tears. "Uri was the one who betrayed us. He sold us out to the govies, and the Solizen, and who knows who else. He's the reason they were ready for us at the joint refinery. Why we lost so many people."

Uri was the mole . . . Uri was the mole . . . Uri was the mole . . . The words played through her head in a taunt. A blistering headache formed. How could she not have seen it? It was one thing to backstab the leader in order to wrest control. That was accepted. But they never betrayed the gang. Never sold themselves out to outsiders. Gaining control of Lasair didn't mean fracturing their lives, or restructuring the power in Undercity. It was beyond comprehension.

Arden felt like she'd been shot full of phase-fire. She gasped a breath. Her chest burned. She'd never known that a betrayal could hurt worse than an open wound to her side. It was too much to process.

The plan had to have been in motion for a while. He'd worked so subtly that no one had realized. This move had to be about more than control over just Lasair. Otherwise Uri could have done that in any number of ways that wouldn't have caused this much internal destruction.

She remembered the moments before they stormed the joint refinery, wondering why they were working in tandem with the other gangs. Had he meant to devastate the other gangs in Undercity so he could seize a larger territory to control? If that was true, Uri wanted control of everything, perhaps all of Undercity.

Who else had known? Niall had been there. He'd talked with the other gang leaders. Had Uri tricked him too? Perhaps Niall somehow suspected an inside betrayal and set in motion things to hinder it. Maybe even that was the reason Uri had kept him alive.

She'd stupidly played into Uri's hands by leaving Lasair on her own. Arden thought back to when Uri had threatened her. He'd told her never to return or he'd kill her. At the time she'd thought his threat was about Dade, yet now she realized that it was about much more. Arden was yet another piece he'd had to remove in his climb to grab power.

Now that she knew, she wasn't going to let him win. There was no backing away from this. Uri would pay for his betrayal.

"How did he do it?" Arden could barely make the words audible past her clenched teeth.

"I don't know." Mariah's mouth twisted. "But I'm going to find out."

She'd been played. Arden wanted to walk up to Uri and smash his face in before she gutted him with her knives. It was by the thinnest thread of control that she held herself back. This was not the time. She knew that. She'd make her move eventually, but she needed time to properly pay Uri back for all his duplicity.

Of all those who could have been the mole, she hadn't expected it to be him. Kimber maybe. Arden sucked in a breath as she remembered the girl. "Where's Kimber?"

"She's missing too."

Of course she was. And that was just as suspicious, especially when all these "dead" people were turning out to be still breathing. "Did she work with Uri?"

"I have no idea. I don't think so."

Roan yelled in her comm again, jolting Arden. She had to go. "Come with me. We can find a place for you."

Tears were thickly falling down Mariah's face. "I can't leave."

"You're going to stay with a traitor?" Arden didn't understand.

"It's complicated," Mariah argued.

Arden was aghast. "After knowing what he's done? You'd choose him over your family?"

"Didn't you?" Mariah asked.

The question hit like a knife plunged to the gut. Arden wanted to deny the accusation. It wasn't the same thing at all. Dade hadn't tried to have them killed. He was trustworthy.

Uri was a piece of shit.

Yet she understood Mariah's dilemma. Would Arden give up Lasair for Dade if she had to do it over? She knew she'd choose Dade again, but maybe she'd manipulate the situation a bit differently.

This was something Mariah had to come to terms with on her own. Arden couldn't help her. "You'll always have a place with me. But know, if you choose him, then you'll be my enemy."

Mariah closed her eyes as if the words pained her. "We're already enemies."

Maybe, but today had proven that Mariah still had loyalty to Arden. Maybe someday they could make this right.

Chapter twenty-one

Dade had gone with Saben to help construct his family's temporary residence and to see what else they could collect—albeit illegally—to help ease the struggle of the other displaced families.

They hadn't been gone all that long. A couple of hours at most. Not long enough for all hell to break loose.

He'd meant to sneak into the compound even though Mina knew where they had gone. She'd helped them acquire building supplies. Still, he'd wanted to avoid any pointed questions about their disappearance from the others. Saben wasn't ready to share about his family, and Dade respected that.

They'd just stepped into the living area when the yelling stopped Dade short. He focused all his attention on trying to figure out what was going on, trying to decide whether to investigate or avoid it. Mina's crew members bickered as much as they joked. Usually, it wasn't too bad, even though Dade had made a pointed effort so far to stay out of it. But now their voices were loud and harsh, carrying down the halls. This wasn't the usual skirmish.

Dade and Saben looked at each other. Saben's eyebrows shot up, and he shook his head. In response, Dade shrugged before he jerked his head toward the direction of the noise, indicating that he thought they should check it out.

They slunk down the hall, not wanting anyone to know they were there. It sounded as if the yelling originated from the command center. They'd already made it halfway down the hall before Dade heard Arden's voice. It was at full tilt and raging.

His body locked up at the sound. He had never heard her yell, not like that. There was a wobble to the sound that indicated she was beyond furious but not out of control. She knew exactly what she was doing.

Then he began to run the rest of the distance, desperate to see what was going on. Heart pounding, he stopped at the threshold to the command center. Dade didn't bother to hide his presence. Everyone was too caught up in the argument to notice him anyway. The anger in the room instantly put Dade on alert. His hand strayed to the phaser at his hip.

His gaze darted as he took in the scene as fast as he could, trying to process what was happening. The fight looked to be between Roan and Arden. Though Venz, Coco, and Annem were there too.

Roan gestured to the wall of visiscreens behind where Venz sat. He was in Arden's face, yelling, "Didn't you think you were being monitored?"

Clenching her jaw, Arden yelled back, "Of course I knew, and I didn't care."

Venz looked distinctly uncomfortable. He slumped in his chair, trying to make himself appear as small as possible as he watched Roan and Arden with wary eyes. His hair was all over the place, as if the night had been particularly troublesome and his hair had suffered from the wrath of his hands.

Coco and Annem stood by the door. They hadn't turned when Dade and Saben arrived. Annem's arms were folded, and she looked contemplative. Coco stood beside her, her shoulders hunched and her head tilted forward, ready to charge. She hadn't inserted herself in the fight yet. Though it looked like it might happen at any moment.

Annem must have sensed that too. She reached forward to grab Coco's forearm. It seemed to be enough to hold Coco in place.

Mina and Nastasia must still be gone. If they had been here, this would have been stopped by now. Or at least the argument would have been somewhat civil.

Roan and Arden moved closer to each other. Stood toe to toe, each snarling. Their faces were flushed, and their hands were clenched, brought halfway up their bodies, looking close to blows. They both were posturing, neither one taking the first shot with their fists.

Tension had crackled under the surface for days between Arden and the rest of the crew, but most especially between her and Roan. It had only gotten worse when they'd "lost" the Lasair boy they were supposed to tail. Dade had expected it to come to a head, though not in quite so dramatic a fashion. He'd only been gone a few hours. The hideout looked intact. Everyone was alive. What could have possibly happened while he was out to cause this?

Roan's face was a mask of rage. "You put everyone in danger with your stupid antics."

"You didn't have to come for me," she yelled back.

Dade's gut twisted. He'd known she was up to something last night. She'd lied to Mina and made it clear to him that she was running her own agenda. He had known that as soon as he left her alone, she'd do her own thing even if she hadn't said as much to him. Dade should have pushed her to tell him what her plans were, and maybe he could have helped. But once again she'd left him out as if his opinion didn't matter. Only this time, whatever she'd done had caused the cautious working accord of the group to crack.

Not that he was any better. They were both running their own agendas without helping the other. Obviously, that wasn't working. One of them had to give.

Frustration nearly overwhelmed him. He reminded himself that she was alive, so whatever she had done couldn't have been too bad.

Still, he'd unwittingly helped her accomplish it by willfully keeping his mouth shut about the Lasair boy. He only had himself to blame.

Arden threw up her hands. "I'm not going to sit on my ass when I can get information."

Roan wasn't having it. "That's because you didn't let us know Lasair was there. You can't just unilaterally decide to run an op."

"I made it clear that I was here on my own. I don't have to wait for Mina to give her okay. That's not how I work. I don't have to ask you or anyone else for permission."

"You are a part of a group," Roan said. "When you do something, it affects us all. We were tailing that dealer for the group, not for you."

"I don't want to run with your group at all."

Roan spread his hands wide. "You can leave at any time."

"Who died and made you the de facto leader? You can't kick me out of here. Last I checked, you followed orders, not gave them."

Roan growled and squeezed his hands into fists. He leaned forward, using his body to get into her space, to intimidate.

"You gonna hit me?" she taunted. "Go ahead and try. I'll lay you out."

Her eyes heated with passion. Dade found her glorious. This was the most dangerous girl he'd ever met, the Arden that had attracted him in the first place. The power inside her had been stoked to life again. It had been slumbering, recovering from loss and pain.

Now she was back, more badass than ever. Dade hadn't realized how much he'd missed her fire. The strength that he knew couldn't be broken.

He loved her. It had started out small at first, that potential well of feeling that had the possibility to grow. Seeing her every day and knowing how hard she worked to keep her focus caused that love to deepen. It had become something staggering in strength. It grew daily as she displayed her grit and determination.

She was everything to him. That she always fought so hard. That she questioned everything. The way her mind worked was stunning. Arden was both beautiful and fierce, but what made her special was the dichotomy between the softness of her heart and the steel of her will.

Coco stepped forward to interrupt. Despite her small stature, she got their attention. It might have had to do with the fact that she'd unstrapped the blast-phaser that had been across her back. She held it cradled in her arms, her finger on the trigger, with the barrel still pointed away. Then she gave an ear-piercing whistle and yelled, "Everyone shut the hell up."

In the resulting silence, Dade asked, "What happened?"

Roan turned to him, snarl still in place. "Sunshine here decided that she was going to visit Lasair on her own."

Okay, Dade should have expected that. She'd known where the hideout was. Of course she would head back the first chance she got.

"She lied about losing the dealer," Roan continued. "Then she decided to go rogue."

"I was looking for Niall."

"Who wasn't there," Roan yelled.

"But we know where he is now," Arden said. "We know Crispin has him. So stop having a temper tantrum, and let's go get him."

Roan grabbed at his hair. "We can't just go off looking for your brother without a plan, Sunshine."

Arden bared her teeth. "Stop calling me that."

Saben leaned in and whispered to Dade, "You need to de-escalate this. She's looking for a fight."

Dade found himself nodding. Arden was calculating above all. Her steady interpretation of events was something he counted on. Though he wasn't so sure that a fistfight with Roan would do either of their agendas much good.

"Are we finished here?" Dade asked. "If you have a problem with what Arden did, bring it up with Mina."

"Shut it, siskin, no one asked you," Roan snarled.

Dade expected the epithet, letting it roll right off him. The last thing he needed was to become mired in this brawl. It was better to ignore it and extricate Arden, otherwise the goodwill he'd worked on with Mina would be blown.

"Roan," Annem chided.

"Why are we protecting him?" Roan asked. "He's one of them."

"He's one of us, dumbass." Coco stepped back and rested against the tabletop. Obviously she shared Saben's view that this was getting out of hand. She adopted a casual pose, but she kept her phaser at the ready.

Roan was too far gone, though, to be so easily calmed. He narrowed his gaze on Arden. "You like being kept by a siskin, don't you?"

Annem sucked in a loud breath.

Coco grumbled, "Here we go."

"That's not fair, Roan. He's not a Solizen anymore," Annem said. A last-ditch effort to stop the apocalypse.

"He looks like a Solizen to me," Roan said. "He still has the sunstar tattoo."

Arden turned away. She started pacing in a short circuit. Her hands shook, and she loosened her limbs. It was an admirable effort to gain control.

Venz looked scared. He'd rolled his chair even closer to the visiscreen wall, putting as much space between himself and the other two as possible.

"You can take them out of the sky, but—" Roan's words were cut off by Arden's fist connecting with his mouth. Blood sprayed.

Roan shifted to return the punch, but she ducked and kicked her booted foot into his stomach. He flew back into the wall with a loud grunt.

Arden pulled her knife and threw it. The metal thunked into the wall, missing Roan's head by a hairbreadth.

Coco let out a whistle that sounded like admiration.

Roan was slow to react. He turned to look at the knife, his eyes wide.

But Arden was already on him. She flipped Roan around and pushed him against the wall so that his face smashed into the unforgiving surface. Holding him with one hand, she pulled the knife from the wall.

As she held his arms taut behind him, she brought the knife to his throat. Arden leaned in and exhaled heavily in his ear. Her chest moved with each breath.

Still, like a complete fool, Roan didn't back down. His eyes shone with a manic glee, and his lip curled when he taunted, "Do it, Sunshine. Go on, slit my throat."

Dade thought she might actually do just that.

He immediately strode over. He couldn't allow her to murder Roan. He wasn't sure how they'd explain it to Mina. Though he admitted that he wouldn't be that broken up about it if it happened. It just couldn't happen now.

"Arden, *enough*." He let his frustration leak into his voice. It made her pause. Then he said more softly, "Let him go."

She took a deep breath. It was loud and rattled. A long moment passed before she stepped back. She said to Roan, "Watch yourself."

CHAPTER TWENTY-TWO

Arden left the room with the knife still gripped in her hand. Anger burned in her gut. It felt good to hold the knife, reminding her that she was capable of taking care of herself. That she was not a victim of circumstance. She carefully didn't look back at Dade. Didn't want to see his expression and read any disappointment there.

It was probably best that Dade had pulled her away. Her anger wasn't really about Roan, even if he'd made himself easy to lash out at. Roan had every right to question her decisions that put Mina's crew in jeopardy. If he called her Sunshine, it wasn't the end of the world. She could have brushed if off.

Every emotion she'd struggled to contain for the last few months seemed to explode from her now. Arden couldn't pretend anymore that she was fine. She hadn't dealt with any of it: Colin's death, Uri's being a lying, backstabbing piece of crap, her brother's death wish, or even working with Mina or her crew. It was no wonder she'd lost it.

Arden slid the knife back into its sheath, forcing herself to let go of her aggression. Pushed it down and sought out her calm center. She needed time to collect herself. To find a place where no one would bother her. But she knew Dade followed her, and she couldn't continue to put him off.

He walked up beside her and reached out to slide his hand against hers.

She let her fingers run through his, but then let go. She didn't want the comfort he offered. Didn't want anyone to "talk sense into her." She didn't think she deserved his understanding because she knew she'd overreacted, and that sucked.

Dade wasn't dissuaded. He stepped quickly in front of her. And while he didn't stand directly in her path, it was enough to make her stop.

They looked at each other.

He was steady, calm. His face was clear of judgment. She saw only concern and acceptance. It offered her a moment to reset.

She took a deeper breath.

He was her compass. He made her world click into place. She needed to learn to trust in that.

Dade must have felt her relax incrementally. He stepped in, closing the distance, and lowered his face to hers. He brushed her temple with a light kiss. "It's okay." The whispered words were like an endearment or maybe a promise of something better.

His body covered hers like a blanket as he leaned her into the wall. She shivered against his heat, wanting more.

Arden exhaled. She let herself sink into him. Her head dropped forward so that they rested forehead to forehead.

Dade ran his hand through her hair, his other hand on her cheek. His thumb brushed her jawline. "It's not a big deal. It will blow over tomorrow."

"I know," she said, even though she doubted her own words. She could almost believe him when he spoke with such conviction. The truth was, Mina's crew were right not to trust her.

Dade brushed his lips against hers. "Whatever is wrong, baby, we're going to be okay."

"How do you know that?"

"Well, it can't get much worse." He grinned and winked.

Arden strangled the snort of amusement she felt. Why couldn't she stop worrying and let her life be this easy?

She liked Dade close. He was tangible, real. She liked when he pressed his body against hers. Her hands slipped up to his hips and held them there.

Dade pulled back to look into her eyes. "It's not your fault we're here. You don't control everything. If anything, I got us into this mess."

The words made a knot in her belly. She had guilt about a lot of things. But Arden didn't want to talk about the issues she struggled with.

"Roan annoys me," she said. "He expects me to take his crap."

Dade frowned. "He's jealous. It's how he deals with it."

"Why?" Arden didn't think that jealousy was likely. "He's got the life he wants. His crew respects him."

"Because I have you, and because he wants something like that. He needs to feel wanted in a different way than as just another team member."

That she did understand because she felt the need for connection too. It made her feel a little more lenient, though Roan was still an idiot.

"You and I are not like that. I'm not your 'Sunshine.'" She rolled her eyes, completely disgusted with the whole thing.

Instead of arguing, he leaned forward and brushed his mouth against hers.

Honestly, she was okay with that kind of answer. It was what she'd rather do anyway. Not worry about Roan, or Mina, or her brother. Not think about Uri the backstabber.

He smiled when he pulled away. "You're not my Sunshine?"

She grunted. "No."

"What if I want you to be?" He kissed her again, light and playful.

She laughed, teasingly biting his lip. When she opened her eyes, she asked, "Why did you meet with Clarissa without me?"

Dade paused.

For a moment she thought he wouldn't answer. Then he said, "I asked her if she'd be able to have a new Ghost mask made for me. I didn't bring you with me because I wasn't sure if you'd be okay with my returning to being the masked vigilante."

She raised an eyebrow. "You're going to resurrect the Ghost?"

He was selfless, so that didn't surprise her. It was only a matter of time before he'd get back into the game. He was right, though. She didn't know how she felt about it. Not that she really cared. There were just other pressing concerns.

"Why her?" Arden asked. "You could have told me, and we could have figured it out together."

"Because she's my friend, and she has the resources to make it happen."

"She's also a Solizen."

"So am I." Dade hissed out a breath. "You sound like Roan."

Arden startled back. "I'm just trying to say that we don't know who we can trust. Old friends could be enemies now. We have to be careful."

The thought cut through her, making her remember her own emotional wounds. She knew all about betrayal firsthand.

"I trust her," he said. "You want me to support your decisions, then you need to back mine as well. I promise I won't do anything that compromises you."

She nodded slowly. "Okay."

His words rang true. Trust was not a one-way street. It was unfair to ask him to give her what she was not willing to reciprocate.

"We're still going to figure out how to make a life together, right?" She needed reassurance they were still a team, even if they sucked at it.

Dade nodded.

"I feel like I'm losing you," she said. "All we wanted was to be left alone, and they keep sucking us back in. I don't know who to trust anymore."

Defeat made her tired. Made her limbs feel like lead. Arden couldn't figure out that next step. Or even if it was worth pushing for freedom when someone was inevitably going to pull them back into the fighting.

"I'm here, Arden. I will never cut and run. I'm by your side for the long haul."

He was too good a person, and she adored him for it. Others would take advantage of that softness. They would never see that inside, Dade had a core of strength, and that core was probably stronger than hers for all her prickly shell.

She felt remorse that she had dirtied him with her world. He would always be heroic no matter what situation they were in, yet now he was forced to make messier choices. She wanted to keep him from that darkness as long as she could.

Arden needed to do something for him. To stop being so selfish when he was clearly thinking about them both. She needed to help him too. He was right. A relationship needed to work both ways.

If this was what it took to make Dade feel like he was whole, then she would do everything in her power to help him. She wanted to be a part of it. "I want to help you resurrect the Ghost."

His eyebrows rose, but he didn't argue. "We need to figure out who has a supply of VitD that we don't mind pissing off when we steal it."

"I can help you with that. I found out today that I need to deliver some favors." She practically ground her teeth flat as she said it. Her anger at Uri flared. The rawness in the pit of her stomach got impossibly wider.

Dade reached out and cupped her face. "Tell me."

She took a deep breath and said, "I found out who betrayed Lasair. It was Uri." The words nearly stole her breath, stabbing deep. She forced herself to continue. "I don't know if Mina knows, but she's dropped hints. This whole situation—Uri, Mina, my brother—is interconnected, and I'm not clear how. I don't trust anyone."

"Eventually you're going to have to have faith other people besides me. We can't navigate this city alone. And Mina isn't that bad."

"She's the one who warned me that there was a mole in Lasair. If she knew that person was Uri and didn't tell me—" She let that thought go. It was pointless to think of the "what ifs." How she could have stopped the mess if she'd been better prepared. She had to move forward with what she knew now. "I don't want this disconnection to continue to grow between us."

"You know you're the thing that means the most to me," he said.

The words burrowed themselves straight into her heart. "I know."

"And I meant it when I told you I love you."

She nodded. "You and I."

"Forever."

They moved at the same time. Their bodies pressed tighter against each other. She felt his heat against her skin, his lips a scant breath from hers. Her thoughts skittered away. She closed her eyes and breathed deeply, willing herself this moment of peace.

His breath caressed her face as he said, "Arden, please."

She didn't know what he was asking for. And honestly, at that point she didn't care. She tilted her face up, and her mouth met his.

Their need flared to life. It was hot and desperate. Her hands grabbed at his shoulders while his gripped her hips.

She jumped up, wrapping her legs around his middle. Moving herself closer to take the kiss deeper. Wanting him with a consuming need.

He pinned her to the wall. Leveraging her so that he could kiss her harder, make her feel wanted and special. She needed this connection to ground her. To remember there were other things to fight for.

A throat cleared.

No, no, no. Arden kept kissing Dade, refusing to let this end. Forget whoever it was. They could leave and come back later when she was much less busy.

The throat cleared again.

Dade pulled away first. Arden almost chased his lips. But instead, she growled and turned to glare at the jerk who thought this was the perfect time to interrupt her.

Mina stood in the center of the hall, her hands on her hips. She looked angry.

Arden groaned and banged her head back against the wall. *Why now?*

Dade set her on her feet.

"Arden, can I speak with you?"

She wanted to say no. There was nothing she wanted to talk about anyway. Still, it was probably best to get it over with. Arden looked to Dade, who nodded once before turning away.

Arden waited until the hall was clear before she asked, "When did you get back?"

"Just now. I heard you're causing problems."

Arden grunted.

"I know you don't want to be a part of our team," Mina said.

That was an understatement. "If you're here to yell at me, save it. I should have let you know what I was doing."

Mina frowned. "I want you to know that no matter what happens, you can come to me for help."

Arden raised an eyebrow. "That sounds like you think I'm gonna take off as soon as possible."

The corner of Mina's lip twitched. "The statistical possibility is high."

That made Arden chuckle. But still, why was Mina seeking her out to tell her this? Mina was a mystery Arden felt sure she'd never understand.

"I just want to make sure you know that," Mina said.

Arden was silent for a moment—staring at her. And then eventually she nodded. "Okay."

CHAPTER TWENTY-THREE

Arden stood to the side of the room, leaning against the wall with her arms folded. It was the middle of the night. Not much time had passed between getting Mina caught up on who had snatched Niall and the decision to go get him.

There wasn't a plan. That alone made Arden anxious. She liked a well-organized op. Going in blind was the best way to get killed. She ignored the feeling of doom because she wanted this. Knowing that she'd missed her opportunity to rescue Niall the night before only made the need to go in with phasers blazing that much more powerful. In spite of knowing it probably wasn't the best course of action.

Arden and Saben were dressed in black running suits. Saben worked through the evening's logistics with Venz, Nastasia, and Mina while Arden watched. They discussed which tech supplies might be needed most to break in, and then packed them into slimline backpacks. Various items were strewn all over the table. Since they couldn't carry in everything, each item became a protracted negotiation.

Mina looked over to where Venz sat at the computers. "Pull up all the schematics we have on Crispin's business. Let's go over the most likely areas they'll hold Niall."

A loud shout from Roan interrupted the otherwise productive work they were doing. He'd been sent from the room about fifteen minutes before because he could not stop himself from arguing with Mina, much to Arden's amusement. Now he was in the kitchen, doing who knew what. The yelling was then followed by loud banging and then a crash. It sounded as if he'd knocked down the entire shelf of pots.

"Can you calm him down?" Mina asked Annem. "I don't need my kitchen destroyed."

"Sure thing." Annem slid off the table where she was perched.

"I'll help," Coco said, following her out.

Arden's gaze went to Dade when he stepped past the girls and into the room all suited up. The synth-suit fit him like a glove. She bit back a sigh. He looked so good, and she wished they had more time to continue what they'd started in the hall. But for now, she'd have to make do with the eye candy.

Dade looked over to her. He seemed to sense what she was thinking, because he gave her a wicked grin.

"If Crispin has Niall, we need to act on that intel before he moves him to a different location." Mina stared at the three of them, Arden, Dade, and Saben. "I don't like sending you in alone, and if I had a choice, I'd take more time and figure out something else. But with the time crunch, it's our only option."

Arden wasn't upset that they were going in with a small group. Mina couldn't invade Crispin's business without declaring war. Which meant the three of them would be on their own, just the way Arden wanted it. She'd much rather do a job with a smaller group she could trust than with people she was still unsure of.

She pushed herself away from the wall. "We don't need you to babysit. We'll be fine."

After last night, Arden felt determination knot inside her. There was a job to do, and she was going to execute it with precision.

"It's not babysitting. It's called working as a team," Mina said.

"We can't monitor you," Venz said to Arden. "Crispin will have anti-tracking in his building. If we use a comm signal, he'll be able to pick it up."

"If anything goes wrong, get the hell out of there," Mina said. "If you get in trouble, we won't be there to bail you out. I'd rather lose Niall and figure out something else than lose the three of you."

"Don't worry, we've been in worse scrapes." Arden was excited to go and vent her frustration into this plan. She couldn't help but feel like this was a big game of chess. Except Arden not only didn't know the rules, she didn't know the players. That had to change.

It didn't take long for them to jack three speeders. It was simple, and easy and exhilarating. Arden missed this. She needed the constant adrenaline rush to feel alive. Driving a speeder after so long was a thrill. The wind pulled at her hair as she darted through the static cloud to their destination.

Across the city, they ditched the speeders. They needed to go up. Entering one of the many buildings, they used the internal lift to reach Level Seven, and then exited a block from their destination.

Crispin's building looked like it had been retrofitted with reinforced steel and moonglass. It appeared newer than the others, enough to draw attention and to caution anyone targeting it. Signs out front proclaimed it private property. Crispin's symbol was on the center of all of them. That alone was enough to turn even the stickiest thief away.

It was both a place of business and residential apartments. Mina assured them that Crispin had his private quarters here. If he had Niall, this was where he would most likely be holding him.

There were a lot of people moving about. The building was surprisingly busy for this time of night. Not to mention the guards they could see through the moonglass doors.

They stood across the street, weighing their options.

"I say we go in from below," Arden said. "There has to be a way inside. Someone like Crispin would have at least five emergency exits in case things went bad. We have to be able to find at least one of them."

Saben studied the other buildings surrounding Crispin's. "It's a solid plan."

"He's going to have safety measures," Dade said.

"I'm not worried. I made it into the Sky Tower to visit you. No locked or manned building is going to keep me out." Her thoughts immediately went to Mina's proposed job of breaking into the CRC, and she hoped that remained true.

"Such arrogance," Saben said dryly.

Arden laughed. She moved to give him a fist bump, and he obliged her. He wasn't a bad guy. Maybe a little growly and stoic, but the big goon was growing on her. Plus, he always had Dade's back, so that had to count for something.

They consulted the schematic Venz had provided one last time before suiting up by pulling the hoods over their heads, tucking their hair inside. Masks were next, followed by their air-breathers that would modulate their voices and keep them from breathing the gas they'd set off. Mina had requested they not kill anyone unless it was necessary.

Arden double-checked her weapons, making sure they were all in working order and strapped where she needed them. She raised a hand, pointing her finger and circling. The signal they should head out.

It had taken them a full fifteen minutes to figure out how to get inside and another twenty minutes to work their way through the lock system without detection. This job was taking way too long. They'd be caught if it took much longer.

Arden was on edge. Her body thrummed, and her skin felt itchy. She cracked her neck and pulled out her phaser, going in first. She rounded the doorway, moving her phaser up to shoulder level and scanning the area.

After making sure the room was empty, she signaled that they were clear, and the other two came in. Saben made sure to close and lock the door, but not rearm it.

Arden stayed on alert. She knew the penalty for taking things at face value and letting her guard down. People she cared about could die. Anything could happen. And she would not let these two down. Not on her watch.

The focus made her head ache. She was holding her back so stiffly that pain flashed across her shoulders. She took a breath and forced her muscles to relax. A mantra whispered through her mind: *Stay alert, stay limber, breathe.*

They checked and cleared the lower floors and all the business offices. They tried to sneak through and not engage. Stealth was key. It was important to delay setting off the alarms for as long as possible. When they had to, they used sleeping gas. For the most part, it was pretty easy to slip through. The people they ran into were workers, not muscle.

Niall wasn't there, not that they'd expected him to be, because that would have been too easy. Nothing was ever easy. She pushed out a frustrated breath and set aside her twinge of frustration. Each place they checked meant time off their clock.

Arden would find him.

They finished off a floor of offices. Dade took up position at the exit on the far side of the corridor. He checked out the last two doors, leaning into both with his phaser pointed out. Then turned back. "We've been here too long. Either we finish searching this floor, or call it and move on."

He was right. Time was running on fumes. They'd looked over two of the possible five locations Venz and Nastasia had pointed out. But now they had to make some choices. They couldn't clear them all.

Arden hated indecision, considered it a weak character trait. So when she was faced with it, there was a lot of added self-loathing attached. She looked at Saben, who was a pretty valuable statistician. "Ideas?"

"Maybe Crispin is keeping him close," Saben said.

Dade nodded once. "We work our way up to the luxury wing." He referred to the heavily secured area where Mina had said that Crispin's private rooms were located.

Arden frowned, but she was willing to go along with them. She didn't think it would be smart for Crispin to keep Niall near him. It spoke to friendship, or at least social ties. And she couldn't remember ever meeting Crispin before she'd gone to the boxing club with Dade.

Still, she agreed. If she couldn't make up her own mind, it was best to listen to the majority. Saben had some history with Crispin. It made sense to follow his lead.

She knew they were in the right area of the building when they reached a corridor with reinforced doors. The halls were empty, and the hum of the air filtration was the only sound. It looked upscale, though not quite as posh as the Sky Towers.

There were a lot of rooms. A camera was mounted on each end of the main hall facing in. As soon as they stepped past the doorway, it would catch them and the countdown would begin. Then they wouldn't be able to come back since their cover would be blown. Arden hoped that Niall was here, or they'd come all this way for nothing.

She looked at the others. After they both nodded back that they were ready, she held up three fingers and then counted down.

Arden shot out both cams.

They moved quickly, checking the doors on both sides. They skipped the ones that were locked and sleep-gassed those people in rooms that were open. It took almost forty-five seconds to clear the hall. They ended up with two locked doors.

Arden looked between them. She could feel her heart pump. Niall was here. Intuition whispered to her. He was behind one of these doors. She knew it. Nothing but the beating of her heart and the trust of her instincts held her in check.

"These locks will take almost a minute to crack each," Saben said, pulling out his datapad and a set of connectors. "We'll only have time for one."

Arden felt her frustration well up. It pulsed in her head. Not now, not when she was so close.

"Where are you, Niall?" she mumbled to herself. She could hear the weird echo of the voice modulator bounce her words back at her in a fragmented translation.

They both looked at her. Waiting to see which door she'd pick.

She took a deep breath and pointed. "That one."

Saben didn't hesitate. Just walked over and hooked his datapad to the scanner outside the door. His fingers flew on his pad.

Dade turned to man the door they'd come through that led to the next hall. He blew out the sensor pad to disengage the door. Then pointed his phaser at the closed door in anticipation of it opening. Anyone who came through at this point would be someone here to kill them.

Arden took up position behind Saben, watching the hall on the other side. There could be other entrances. Or they could have missed someone with their sweep. Stress, anxiety, anticipation, adrenaline—it all flooded her. Her body spinning on overloaded stimulus.

Behind her the sensor pad beeped, and she heard the door slide open.

Saben disengaged his datapad and walked into the room. Dade turned from his position and then followed Saben. And Arden made another quick sweep before turning into the room as well.

She hit the button on the other side, sealing in the door. And then used her phaser to blast the scanner. It wouldn't keep anyone out, but it would slow them down.

The room was small, but nice. It looked normal: a bed, a side table, a chair. The window faced the outside of the skyway. The dark static cloud swirled beyond the moonglass. It was nice if one didn't count that there was a lock outside the door instead of on the inside.

The first thing she saw was a lump on the bed.

"Is it him?" she asked. She could barely get the words past the thickness that had lodged itself in her throat.

Dade was already there, moving the covers back and rolling the person over. "Yes."

Relief made her legs shaky. Arden slipped her phaser away. She ran over, edging herself past Dade.

Niall looked sick. His eyes were red and unfocused. His lips were cracked and bleeding. His skin was bleached a deathly white except for the purple bruises that seemed to cover 70 percent of him. He'd been beaten, badly.

Rage filled the space that adrenaline had vacated. She had to remember who had done this to him. Crispin had him for less than a day, and these bruises looked older. Crispin had put him in a decent bed, with clean sheets. There was a full water cup on the side table. The damage was all Lasair's doing. Uri's fault. And he'd pay.

Between Arden and Dade, they got Niall up. They held him still while Saben stood behind Niall and began to strap Niall's back to Saben's chest. For as thin as Niall was, his dead weight was heavy and unwieldy. It didn't help that his body shook with unchecked spasms.

Words tumbled from his mouth in what sounded like mumbled protest. They were difficult to understand, just strings of punctuated sounds. Until she made out one word he kept repeating, "Help."

It broke her heart. She loved him even though he frustrated the crap out of her. They disagreed on almost everything. Though she saw his point of view, even if she didn't like the decisions he made.

At one time, they'd been close. But that had been long ago. She could remember wanting his approval even if she couldn't pinpoint when that had changed. It was a slow progression with each little decision that snowballed into bigger and bigger things, and eventually it had ended in hurt and distrust.

In spite of that, they were still family. Raised together in poverty and taught to claw their way out. At an early age, they had to make decisions that were morally gray. She understood why he'd chosen the path he did. It was a little darker than hers, a little more dirtied by anger and revenge. She couldn't blame him for that.

But she also knew that she couldn't support Niall's placing the blame for his problem on others. Everyone could choose better paths no matter where they came from. Niall included. That was a truth she carried in her heart. And maybe someday she could convince Niall of the same.

The door opened behind them. It was silent, but she felt the push of air as the door retracted.

Arden swung around, her heart in her throat.

The Twins slunk in. They gave identical smiles, full of teeth and mirth and deadly promise.

She felt that sinking free fall in her belly. Fear knotted in her throat. But she locked herself into place. Finding that center of calm peace and instinct.

"What do—"

"We have—"

"Here?" the Twins said in singsong. Their eyes scanned back and forth, seeming to glow in the darkness.

"We have been looking forward to this—"

"For quite some time."

There was a gleefulness about them that set Arden on edge. They wanted a fight. And a fight they'd get. Arden was thankful that the Twins didn't carry phasers, or this would turn out to be a different kind of fight than she needed it to be.

She immediately sprang into action, pulling her knives from her hips. Perhaps she should have just pulled a phaser and shot them, but her goal wasn't to kill them. If that happened, there would be an all-out war with Crispin. And Arden knew it would be with her, not Mina. Which wasn't the sort of muck she wanted to wade into just then.

She needed to keep control of the situation. The knives would allow that. Forcing the Twins to get close to her, so that she could keep them on the far side of the room, focused on her, and away from Saben, Dade, and Niall.

She yelled at Dade, "Get us out of here."

Then she rushed the Twins.

It turned out that the Twins were nearly impossible to handle on her own. One would have been an even match. Both of them together had Arden's body groaning within seconds. They forced her to react quicker, move faster. She struggled, trying to minimize the damage they inflicted on her while she guessed at their next moves.

She felt the pull and release of her muscles, and the grinding of her bones as she took hits. Arden could feel herself slowing. She needed to do something soon to disable them, or this would all go to hell.

A knife swiped her forearm. The cut seared, the burning blazing through her body. It was agony. Yet it cleared her head. Focused her.

Dade worked on the window of thick moonglass behind her. She could see his reflection every time she turned to fend off another swipe of a knife from the devil Twins. He worked quickly, though it felt like much longer.

Saben, with Niall strapped to his chest, moved away from both the fighting and the window. He kept his phaser pointed at the Twins, but he didn't shoot, allowing Arden to keep them busy her way.

"Fire," Dade yelled.

Arden had just seconds to duck away before the explosives he'd placed blew the window apart. Shards of moonglass rained down on them like tiny stars. They cut into the Twins' exposed flesh and lodged themselves in her synth-suit.

Saben was the first to move. He fell backward out the window with Niall.

One of the Twins landed a blow to the back of her right arm while Arden was distracted. She hissed, nearly losing her grip on the knife in that hand.

"Go," she yelled at Dade as she spun and kicked the Twin in the face. She felt the satisfying crunch as her boot hit bone. Hopefully she'd broken something and they wouldn't look so perfectly similar anymore.

Arden didn't see Dade leave. Just trusted that he'd obeyed before she pivoted and ran. She took a flying leap, jumping out of the window and into the empty space beyond.

There was the rush of wind as it blew by her, sounding like a tunnel inside her hood. The floors zoomed by in a blur. She fell Level by Level, gaining speed.

Arden let go of the knives. She struggled to reach the cuffs latched onto her wrists. The air current fought against her. She couldn't bring her hands together. She let out a sound of rage and pushed hard, feeling the strain in her arms and back.

Her finger flicked the switch, illuminating the gold wristlets with a white glow. Inside the slimline pack, her light wings unfolded. They caught the air, working to glide her to a slow descent. Her cuffs tethered her to the light so that she could steer her wings where she wanted to go.

Now in control, she twisted her body downward into a dive. Folding the wings back so that she sped up and darted through the deepness of the static cloud. Then she opened the wings just slightly so that there would be drag as she guided herself to their meeting spot.

CHAPTER TWENTY-FOUR

Dade leaned back, avoiding the others. Roan, Coco, Annem, and he were sitting in the cargo hold of a stolen electro-van, as old and nondescript as they could find. He was uncomfortable, which didn't help his focus. Still, a numbing calm that didn't seem quite real stole over him. He wasn't ready for this. But really, when would he be? Going home had never been in his plans.

Mina was in the front, driving. And Venz was on comm. However, at the moment he wasn't speaking to them over the live feed as they weren't to their destination point yet. The plan was to get in and out of the Sky Tower before the sensors expired. Hopefully, when they left, it would be difficult to figure out exactly how they'd let themselves in. To pull it off, they had to get into the subbasement of the building to hook up into the electrical operation so that Venz could then piggyback into the security system.

They'd created the need for the electro-services. A strategic blast on the power grid had taken out service to Sky Tower Two, forcing the Tower to run on auxiliary power. There were so many things that could go wrong before they even made their way inside. It was the most expedient plan, even if it was a gamble.

Dade didn't like how parts of this plan left them vulnerable. If anyone looked inside the van, they'd be in trouble, caught in this metal tube without any escape, ready to be picked off.

The interior of the electro-van was filled with equipment, most of it useless to them. It had taken Venz ten minutes to circumvent the circuitry and make it into a large-scale deadener. One that would keep communication from exiting the Tower, and if it became necessary, cut off communication inside Tower Two as well.

All four of them barely had room to sit.

Coco and Annem placed themselves near the front of the cargo hold where a little window in the wall separated them from the cab where Mina drove. They sat close, their bodies touching and heads turned together, whispering. He couldn't hear what they said, but there was something going on between the two of them. Their whispers were getting louder, punctuated with exclamations.

Dade leaned against the side of the van between panels of circuit boards. His legs were spread, knees folded up to his chest. The butt of his blast-phaser rested on the ground, the barrel gripped in front of him. He swayed as the van soared through the sky, the metal hard on his rear.

Yet no matter how badly his body ached, sitting across from Roan was more uncomfortable. They were positioned near the sealed back door. Roan's intense glare expressed a deep anger at Dade. He suspected it was because Dade had disarmed the altercation between Arden and Roan. And Roan was still spoiling for a fight. Roan's gaze never turned away.

Dade wasn't intimidated. He stared right back. They'd have it out eventually. And he was looking forward to it more and more. Perhaps he should have let Arden pummel Roan. The dude got under his skin.

It was warm inside the enclosed area. There was a little air shifting through the space to keep the equipment from getting too warm. Even with it, the machines still gave off massive amounts of heat. Dade felt like he was suffocating, like he was baking from the inside out. He shifted once more and pulled at the collar of his running suit.

Those in the group grew silent as they approached the loading dock below Sky Tower Two. Mina drove inside and stopped at the plasma guard wall, then spoke with the guard through the milky electro-discharge of the plasma guard wall. Dade could hear a voice, though the conversation was muted. This was the most dangerous part of the mission, when they were locked inside without an escape. Dade held himself coiled with the tip of his blast-phaser leaning toward the back door.

Inside the van, the glow from the panels lit their faces. Roan appeared as stressed as Dade, though his gaze remained on Dade and not on the door. Coco leaned heavily on the wall between them and the front, clearly listening to Mina's conversation. Beside her, Annem's eyes were wide. Her mouth moved, but there was no sound.

It was taking too long.

Just as Dade let the worry fill him that they were about to be detained, the electro-van was moving again. The breath left Dade's body with a hiss, burning his lungs. The tightness in his stomach didn't lessen. Instead, it sat heavy, making him feel cold and sick.

Several moments later, the van stopped again. Mina didn't turn to look at them, but she spoke loud enough that they could all hear her. "Be right back, stay alive."

She left the electro-van dressed in a utilities uniform. Her absence seemed to pull the quick-seal off the bubbling tension. Roan cracked his neck, and the girls began to argue with each other.

The feeling of being trapped overwhelmed Dade. He couldn't see outside of the electro-van to make sure they weren't attracting attention. There were voices beyond, reminding him that very little stood between him and the inevitable assault. Meanwhile, the girls' disagreement aggressively became louder.

"Stop it," Annem said to Coco, frustration laced in her words. "I know what I'm doing."

"I'm just saying—"

"You're telling me what to do," Annem said.

Coco rolled her eyes. "I'm not."

"Yeah, you are," Roan said.

Both Coco and Annem looked at him and said in unison, "Shut up."

"Keep it down," Dade hissed. What idiots. Did they normally fight like this during a mission?

Roan, of course, didn't listen to either girl. He held up his free hand. "Hey, don't take out your anger on me. I'm the voice of reason."

Coco snorted. "Reason, right."

There was movement outside the electro-van. Dade tensed. This was not the place or time for an argument. He needed to stop them. If Arden were here, she'd probably blast them all center mass—better they die than her. And being in this situation, he wouldn't fault her. Already his fingers twitched, wanting to deliver the charge.

"You're going to get us caught," Dade said, his voice no more than a hiss of air.

"Just because you lived in the Towers, don't think you're in charge." Roan sneered at him, his lip curling.

Dade ground his teeth and gripped the barrel of the blast-phaser tighter. "I don't. I just want you to shut up so we don't die."

Coco said to Roan, "Don't act like you're in charge either."

"You're one to talk," Annem said under her breath.

Coco sent Annem a glare full of frustration. "I worry."

"Well, stop it."

The three of them continued to argue. Dade closed his eyes, his head pounding. His grip tightened on his phaser, becoming painful.

Mina opened the back of the van. The doors dissolved, going opaque before disappearing altogether. "We're hooked in. Let's go."

She stripped off her work shirt, throwing it inside the van. Underneath, she wore a running suit like the rest of them. With Mina returning, all the idiots snapped back into shape. As if Mina were the only one who held them together.

CHAPTER TWENTY-FIVE

Dade silently entered the office in Sky Tower Two. His phaser raised to waist level in case guards were stationed inside. Adrenaline pumped a steady beat through him. He could almost hear it. And gut-clenching nervousness kept him alert.

His nervousness was not about the job. No, its sole focus was on the man sitting behind the desk.

Hernim Croix, his father and head of Croix Industries, sat with his head down. He worked over a light board and vid-projector, fully immersed in his task. Not even when the door swished open and closed did he notice Dade's presence.

It was ironic that this was how Dade had spent most of his life: ignored and unobserved.

He walked to the front of the desk and stood waiting for his father's attention. For some acknowledgment that he stood there with a phaser pointed at his father's head. That Dade held his father's life in his hands.

His father's office looked exactly like the last time Dade had been here. The only change was in himself. The difference struck him hard. He knew he looked the same on the outside even though every thought, feeling, and emotion had jumbled and twisted inside him into something new, something bolder and a lot more calculating.

Honestly, he couldn't believe he was here. When he'd left, his plan had been to never come back to the Sky Towers. Yet he now stood in his father's office, facing the one person he hadn't wanted to deal with ever again.

His father looked up.

A beat passed, a thunderous moment of time in which each of them simply stared at the other. Dade could hear his heart thump nearly out of his chest. His lungs burned with his held breath. Then Dade raised his hand and swiped off his mask and pulled down his hood. If he were going to do this, then there would be no doubt to his identity. He wanted to look his father in the eyes, to judge the truth of his words.

The intensity with which his father glared threatened to shake Dade's bones. Dade felt his hairline dampen and his hands become slick. Yet Dade remained stiff. He kept himself together, knowing he could do this.

His father didn't say anything at first, allowing the silence to stretch. It felt as vicious as the words could have been. That stare was the one he'd faced time and time again. His father never yelled, but there was always the heavy weight of accusation and disappointment. It felt as if he looked straight into Dade's soul and knew everything about him, could read every secret he had.

Dade wished he could interpret his father's expression, but he'd never been good at that. It was one of the things that would have served him well in the past.

Instead he relied on the coping skills he'd learned here, in Sky Tower Two. He didn't move a muscle. To do so would signal to his father that he was weak. Most of his concentration he kept on breathing evenly and projecting a confidence he didn't feel.

Hernim steepled his fingers to his lips, his elbows on the desk as he considered Dade. There was a long moment where Dade felt the full brunt of his judgment before his father finally snarled, "I knew you'd show."

He exhibited no surprise that Dade was suddenly there—alive. Dade had assumed his family had thought him dead. If his father had known he'd survived, why hadn't he bothered to find him?

"How'd you get past security?" Hernim asked.

Dade forced himself to answer with a nonchalance he didn't feel. "I have friends."

His father scowled. "That remains to be seen."

Dade held his tongue in the best interests of this mission. Arguing with his father was not what he'd come here for. Their final days together were a blur of disputes. They didn't see eye to eye and never had. Over the years, those disagreements had only gotten worse. Dade had never been motivated by money or power. Nor had he ever been the son his father wanted. Had failed his father in every way. He'd felt lost. Not fitting the mold his family expected had created a loathing that Dade nurtured within himself.

Until Saben had been hired as his bodyguard. Things had begun to change then. Dade had realized there could be more to his empty life. And Saben had suggested ways in which to give back to others, as a way to fill that hollow part of his soul. It had helped to soothe that ache of being different.

Perhaps it had always been inevitable that he and his father would be here now on opposite ends of the table. The trajectory of their relationship was always going to come to a head. Even if Dade had done his best to avoid launching a full-scale conflict.

Dade cleared his throat. "Why did the govies try to kill me?"

At the point when the govies had attacked him, neither Dade nor his father had made a move against the other. Hadn't yet crossed the line where they could no longer go back. For Dade, he hadn't felt ready. He still didn't have the necessary leverage or the plans to make his rebellion work out. And wasn't sure that he could wage a war against his father.

That had changed. Ready or not, his father had declared war on him.

The govies couldn't have known Dade would be rescued. The one thing that never had made sense was that the govies acted against a Solizen and risked outright war. The Solizen were too powerful.

Someone must have given permission to shoot at Dade. Nakomzer wouldn't have ordered the hit unless his father somehow knew and approved of it.

This was the one thing that he still had a hard time accepting. It gutted him to think this was the case. His father had always been a cold bastard. Dade had known that when the time came, his father would cut him out, regardless of familial relations. Yet he'd never considered the possibility he'd order Dade's death.

As much as he turned it over in his mind, he couldn't come up with another viable scenario. He wanted denial. Wanted it more than he could put into words.

Dade waited.

No denial came.

"You were in the way," his father said, confirming what Dade knew to be true, that power was more important to his father than his own son.

The hope that he'd been wrong died instantly. There was a moment of pure heartbreak inside Dade. It sliced through the center of his chest. The heavy shroud of betrayal clouded his mind.

His father really, truly wanted him dead. It wasn't just a supposition. He hadn't read the situation wrong. How much cruelty could be trapped inside a person to decide to end his son's life?

The physical manifestation of Dade's emotional pain was so intense that it nearly brought him to his knees. He found it difficult to breathe. Everything misted over suddenly, as if a sheen covered his senses, as if he watched this whole scene from far away, as if it were happening to someone else.

Dade's mind spun. He forced himself to stop and reassess. Deep down, he'd known his father would react to minimize him. Had prepared himself for this. It was why he'd agreed to be here today. His father did not deserve his loyalty.

"You wouldn't listen." His father made a sweeping gesture around his office. The cruel expression never left his face. "This was all yours. I built this for you, and yet you betrayed me."

"I didn't betray you," Dade said. At least he hadn't before he'd agreed to help Mina mount a break-in at the Sky Tower. And now, he had no guilt over the current situation. This had happened because his father had pushed Dade to this point.

"Every time you broke into my facilities and stole VitD was a betrayal of everything we have, of our family. Did you think I would just sit by and allow you to ruin the empire I've built?"

Dade couldn't deny that he'd worked against his father and the other Solizen. Though it wasn't with the intention of crushing them. He'd made sure that while he'd stolen from them, his actions wouldn't cause lasting damage. Could his father say the same? It cost his father nothing but loss of credits, yet Dade had saved people's lives. He'd make the same choice over again.

He was proud of the work he'd done. The fact that he'd helped the poor, given access to life-saving meds to children. If he had died that day, his life would have had meaning. No matter how his father twisted his sacrifice, Dade knew it had value, and he would never regret that.

After he'd fallen off the building, in the moments before he'd blacked out, he realized that the only thing that would do differently if he had a chance to live life over was that he'd work harder for change. Increase his influence to upset the power structure.

The person who'd really betrayed their connection had been his father. Dade had never sought harm for anyone. He wanted love and hope. Not this anger and resentment that festered between them. He couldn't be loyal to this man. When he'd woken up and realized he'd been saved, it had lit a fire under him. There was no doubt about his life's calling. There would be no guilt about what steps he took to guarantee it.

"I gave you an opportunity to make it right, to sacrifice for your family. You were supposed to marry Clarissa and ensure our family's power. Yet you planned to run out on that."

"I didn't do what you wanted, so your solution was to kill me?" Dade asked. He was grateful that his voice didn't shake. Dade wasn't afraid of him, but Hernim was still his father. There was always going to be the link of birth, the connection that sometimes meant everything but in this case clearly meant nothing.

How had his father known what they were up to that day? Dade would stake his life that Saben and Clarissa hadn't betrayed him. Were his rooms bugged? Did his father have spies?

"I can't allow anyone who harms the family to live. You've made your choice, and I can't save you from that." His father was so furious that spittle flew from his lips as he spoke. "Uniting the families would have served us best, but your death helps equally as much. The families will be brought together for a united purpose to punish those who've killed you. Things are working out better than I'd planned. Now I just have to make your death real."

Dade thought of the protesters outside. What his father said wasn't strictly true. The Solizen were slowly losing power, their grip weakening. The world was closing in on his father and his cronies. He might not accept the truth of that yet, but he would in time. And Dade would do anything to help that noose tighten.

He also realized that by using the govies, his father had made sure they'd take the fall. Nakomzer had played right into his father's hands. What that meant to the shift in the power balance, where it ended up, was yet to be seen. Dade just hoped that when things tipped, he'd be on the right side.

All this, and yet he felt he needed to try one more time to dissuade his father from this course of action. He needed to be sure that there was no hope for reconciliation. He swallowed, rewetting his now-dry throat. "Dad."

"No, if you were truly my son, you would not have betrayed me." Hernim made a cutting motion with his hand. "You will pay, and so will Clarissa. The two of you will not ruin my plans."

At Clarissa's name, Dade felt both fear for her and relief that he'd been right. If she had betrayed Dade, his father wouldn't want her dead. Over the last few weeks, she'd been hounded by visits from the govies. The visinews had suggested that they were looking into collusion charges. But she was also making waves within the Solizen community. Obviously, she was causing problems for his father.

The threat to Clarissa made Dade's blood thrum, jump-starting his adrenaline again. There was a surging anger that was difficult to keep in check. He would not let his father destroy any more lives.

"You were unwise to come alone," Hernim said. "Pride led you right into my hands. You should have never left, we could have ruled together."

Dade refused to let the words hurt. His back remained straight, accepting that he hadn't chosen this rift. There was nothing he could do to make it better. He would be okay. They were all going to be okay.

"He's not alone," Mina said as she stepped into the room. She and the others filed in with quick and silent movements. Working as a cohesive unit, they'd gone from the crew he nearly wanted to strangle back in the electro-van to the people who had his back. All held long blast-phasers pointed at his father. The butts of the phasers rested against their shoulders. They were all looking decidedly twitchy, needing to shoot something.

In spite of all the revelations of the day, Dade didn't want his father to die. Take down his empire? Certainly. Have him face some kind of consequence for his cruelty? Absolutely. But death would do nothing to right his father's wrongs. Dade wanted justice above all else.

Once the others were there, Dade lowered his phaser to his side and took a step forward.

Mina had gifted him this time to confront his father. Somehow she'd known that he needed to face this broken piece of his life in order to make a permanent break. Otherwise, hope would have always been there. It would have kept him from moving forward, from making decisions that needed to be made. For this, he'd always be grateful to her.

Roan rounded the desk on one side of Hernim while Coco came around the other. When they reached his father, Coco gave a nod and motioned with her hand. Roan lowered his weapon and slung it across his back. Then he took out a pair of electro-cuffs and secured Hernim, all while Coco kept her weapon trained on him.

Annem had stayed by the door, her back to the wall. She kept her attention trained on the room, but also was turned slightly so that she could simultaneously keep an eye on the hallway beyond.

"We're in," Mina said into the comm to Venz.

"Affirmative," Venz replied. "You have three minutes until the guard rotation."

Mina looked over at Dade. Her gaze was intense, and she was clearly checking to make sure he was okay.

He nodded.

Surprisingly, he felt relief. As if facing his demons had given him the assurance he needed to go on and make different choices. He let out a breath that he hadn't realized he'd been holding. Feeling free for the first time in weeks as his purpose locked back into place. Things were going to be different from now on.

This situation with Mina and her forcing him to work with her crew had opened his eyes to the other options available. There were other groups who, while they might have different agendas, could be used to get the things he wanted done.

Mina walked over to his father's data log. She pushed the chair that Hernim sat in out of the way so that she could get at his light board and into his digi-stream. She extracted her datapad from her pocket and hard-linked it so that it would bypass all the control protocols, and then set about following the instructions that Venz relayed to her.

"The information is encoded," Hernim taunted. "You're never going to crack it. If you get out of here alive, you'll have nothing to show for it."

Mina ignored him and continued to download. She said to Venz, "Upload coming through." Making the transmission now was a guarantee that if they didn't make it out, the data would.

They didn't know quite where the information they wanted was stored, so they took it all. Venz would be able to decode it, he was sure. Dade was also sure that Mina had other uses for what she collected. As far as he was concerned, whatever data she managed to collect, Dade had every intention of retrieving it later. He'd use everything at his disposal to bring his father down.

When she was done working the datapad and while it uploaded, Mina turned to Hernim. She leaned the side of her body on the desk and crossed her arms. "Thank you, Hernim, for being such an admirable host. In gratitude, I'd like to give you a present."

Roan reached from behind his father and sank the injector into Hernim's neck, delivering the tag.

"I like to know where the players are at all times," Mina said. "So I guess we won't leave here with 'nothing' after all."

His father's face turned red, and his eyes bulged with anger. It looked like he was going to explode.

Hernim would need the help of Nakomzer and the govies, or even perhaps that of another Solizen with better tech ties, to get the tag removed. It was likely that he'd manage it, but not before he'd burn through a favor or two. Dade couldn't help the smile that formed.

CHAPTER TWENTY-SIX

The room was dark when Arden walked in. Niall sat in a chair in one corner, his body turned away from the lamp beside it. When she'd knocked, Niall hadn't answered. She intruded anyway, under the impression that he was avoiding her rather than sleeping.

Niall didn't acknowledge her even when the door slid shut, locking them in together.

Not much had changed since his stay with Crispin. They'd given Niall a room alone for his recovery. It was a smaller room than the bunkrooms the others stayed in, but clean and with a decent bed. As with Crispin's suite, Mina had changed the coding on the door scanner and locked it from the outside. He was as much a prisoner here as he had been there. And yet they'd treated him with respect. Nastasia had seen to his injuries, offering him medication and making sure he was fed.

It was very different than the way she, Dade, and Saben had been taken in. Arden hadn't realized how much Mina meant her overtures of friendship. She'd let Arden have the run of the hideout, access to all the weapons, and had barely blinked an eye when Arden had gone on her own to Lasair. It was almost as if she'd expected it and had offered as much help as she could by providing an open source of weapons and intel.

The others were gone on their op to the Sky Tower. She'd stayed behind to do this. Needing the illusion of being alone for this conversation even though her every word would be recorded and would no doubt be watched later. Still, Arden knew that unless she confronted him now, it might never happen.

She didn't know what to say to him. There were so many things, so much locked away inside her because she'd never thought she'd have the opportunity to say the words. It had left those thoughts and feelings stuck deep within, festering.

He stared into space and didn't so much as turn his head. "Go away."

No, they were going to talk. This conversation had been put off for way too long. Arden was going to stop being a coward. She blamed him for things that were perhaps not his fault, and things that could most definitely be traced straight back to him. His decisions had brought them to this point. She didn't understand most of them, and wanted to. Wanted to make sense of exactly what had led them here.

Thinking about those things—the loss of Colin, the loss of her connections to Lasair, the feeling of resentment that she was only now starting to realize she'd been nurturing—made frustration curl inside her.

Niall looked at her then. His face was sallow under the bruising, and his bones protruded from his paper-thin skin. His eye sockets looked like dark pits, and the whites were striated with red. The skin around his mouth and nose was purple, the rest of him a giant painting of bruises. He hadn't washed his hair in weeks. Its lank greasiness was tied back.

But his gaze was the worst, defeated and grief-stricken. Feelings she knew firsthand.

"I made it clear I had nothing to say to you," he said, his voice scratchy.

"And I made it clear I'm not going away."

It was difficult to separate the Niall she grew up with and was close to from the broken drug addict sitting before her. She could tell that he struggled, his Shine habit not yet kicked. Arden wondered if when Lasair had held him, they'd given him small amounts of the drug so he wouldn't go into full-blown withdrawal.

Mina had taken one look at him and told him he'd have to suck it up. That she wasn't wasting precious resources on him. Arden silently thanked her for it. Perhaps a sober Niall could be a friend and ally to her once more.

He snorted. "Not going away? You're the queen of disappearing."

"What is that supposed to mean?" She was lost. He sounded so angry with her. Which ticked her off, because she was the one who should be angry. He had no right to question her loyalty. "I was always faithful to you and Lasair."

"What about Mom and Dad? Have you seen them? Have you gone back since the explosion to make sure they're okay?"

Arden was silent. She hadn't. She'd thought about it early on when she was hurt. But then life had progressed so fast and she'd been distracted.

"No, I didn't think so," Niall said snidely.

"I was worried about you." Her words came out as more of a hiss than she intended. But how dare he question her intentions. It wasn't as if she meant to forget about them. Arden loved her parents.

"They're helpless," he said.

She knew that. The knife in her gut twisted a little more. Couldn't he see that she'd had to pick her battles? Survival had been her first priority. "It's only been a few weeks since we've seen them. Mom has Shine and enough credits. I'll go next week."

Niall's stare was blank.

How dare he criticize her? He was the one who'd made stupid decisions. Who'd put their family in danger. If it wasn't for him, they'd still be taking care of their mom and dad and running Lasair. He was the one who'd wanted to start a war with the Solizen. If Niall had gotten his way, they'd be dead by now. He hadn't seemed that concerned then.

Which made her ask, "Tell me what happened. How did you make it out of the refinery?"

His jaw clenched before he responded, "Why don't you tell me why you're playing nice with Mina?"

After he'd skewered her about their parents—rightfully so—she couldn't very well demand answers without giving any in return. Plus, what she wanted was their brother-sister relationship back, and that meant talking to him. Perversely, it reminded her of the times they had gotten along. Niall had watched out for her like he'd always done with their parents. He'd gone into Lasair originally because there'd been no credits or Govie Buy Certificates with which to purchase them food. He'd dropped out of school solely so that they could eat and keep the roof over their heads. He'd even fought Arden when she'd wanted to join. Eventually he'd given in. And he'd treated her like any other member of the gang while both giving her responsibility and keeping her from knowing too much of his underhanded dealings.

That last part frustrated her even now. She didn't need secrets to be kept from her. She needed the truth.

Arden found herself admitting to meeting Dade and their relationship. How she'd gone to the refinery, had gotten hurt, and then had left with Dade. She told him of how she'd come to be here with Mina, stopping just short of her knowledge of Uri and Lasair.

He didn't seem any more welcoming after hearing the explanation but simply getting it off her chest helped. It released some of the tension that had built inside her. Almost like the confession itself, it was what she needed to gain some perspective to heal.

Niall was quiet through it all. Eventually he said, "You're a fool."

"Perhaps," she said. "But what specifically are you referring to?"

"Mina manipulated you. How else did you think she was going to get me here? You did exactly what she wanted you to do."

Arden considered his censure. Mina and her crew were capable of getting Niall here on their own. Though she had to concede that in the end it hadn't been Mina's crew who'd gone into Crispin's territory. She'd understood that Mina didn't want to start a war. Which was reasonable. But so was Niall's theory that this outcome was exactly what Mina had planned.

She wondered if it was true, and the possibility made her feel naive and frustrated all over again. How many times was she going to trust in people and get manipulated into doing their bidding?

Still, she shook her head. "No, she needed Dade to get into the Sky Tower and—"

"I'm not saying she doesn't have other motives. Mina always has twenty plans going at once. What I'm saying is, you did exactly what she wanted. Now we're both her prisoners. She tagged me, Arden. She tagged you." He let out a dry, mirthless laugh. "She owns you now. Do you really believe she's going to let you go?"

"But if I didn't help to rescue you, you would have been at Crispin's mercy."

He just shook his head, repeating over and over, "You don't understand."

"Then tell me." She spoke with frustration. Perhaps her voice was a little harder than it should have been. She was sick of all this posturing, the evasive talk. He was her brother. And if he was going to take her to task, then he certainly could trust her as well.

"If you want to start running your own agenda, you need to start thinking farther ahead than you do," he said. "Stop being a pawn."

That brought Arden up short. She'd always considered herself a good statistician. She knew how to watch a series of events and guess the probable outcomes, how to manipulate them to her advantage. It was one of the very first things she learned growing up on the street.

Granted, maybe she hadn't been doing that great a job of it lately. She hadn't really considered her own agenda or what she'd do if she were in charge of things. Maybe she should. Maybe the risks were worth a bit of freedom.

"You are so worried about yourself," Niall said. "The truth is, you're selfish. I've only made decisions that take care of you, of Mom and Dad, of Lasair. Can you say the same?"

She couldn't. The truth of his accusation sunk in, bringing forth an awareness to which she hadn't given thought. And because of that she stayed silent. Perhaps she deserved his condemnation.

Niall shook his head. "I know that you hate me for the things I've done. But that's what a leader has to do, make the hard decisions. If you want to stay alive without a gang, you need to pull your head out of your ass and start making some hard decisions too."

Arden didn't know what to say to that. Instead she asked, "What happened to you?"

"They jumped me in the refinery. Took me out of there before it was blasted. Then the bastards locked me up."

"Who?" she asked. Arden knew it was Uri, but it was important for her to understand whether he knew. Or whether, like her, Niall had been kept in the dark about Uri's double-crossing too.

"I'm not sure. I was in a room, and people came in to periodically beat me. They asked me questions, I really can't remember." He squinted and looked away.

"Did you recognize anyone?"

"My memory is hazy."

That answered several of her questions. One, that taking Niall had been planned as an abduction. She was sure Uri used the explosion at the factory to hide the evidence. Additionally, it confirmed that Uri didn't want other Lasair members to know.

How many other people had been involved?

"Who else made it out? What happened to Kimber?" Niall asked, his voice going hoarse as he asked after his girlfriend. The same girlfriend who Arden suspected was working with Uri. Who'd turned a phaser on Arden and Dade and tried to kill them.

"I don't know." Talking about Kimber made her cranky. "The destruction burned so hot that a lot of the bodies were not recovered. They're unsure how many people died that day."

She tried to block out the feelings that immediately rose inside her. That the deaths were his fault. Arden had told him that very thing would happen. That there would be a collapse in the power structure between the Solizen, the govies, and the street gangs. And now without VitD, there was chaos. "She's probably gone."

Niall muttered, "She's alive."

"If you want to believe that." She didn't have the will to argue with him. What was the point? But maybe he was right. Kimber was slippery enough to get away and hide out somewhere, waiting for the next opportunity to strike.

He sat for a while, frowning. And then he retreated into that brooding silence where she wasn't sure whether he was paying attention.

She thought about informing him of Uri's betrayal and ask what her brother thought were Uri's ultimate plans for Lasair. But she also knew that if she did, Niall wouldn't tell her anything. He was still keeping things from her. Refusing to tell her the truth.

In the end, he was right. If she wanted an ounce of freedom, she had to start thinking ahead of the people who were trying to control her destiny, and start making the hard decisions. This was the first one: she wouldn't tell Niall about Uri until it suited her needs. She'd use her knowledge for leverage if she could. Arden had no doubt that she would figure out what was going on. Then she'd start playing her own game.

Chapter twenty-seven

Saben's father greeted Dade with a big hug. "It's nice to see you."

Dade knew the man meant it was nice that he was there and that he was wearing his real face. Not a synth-mask or a hood to shroud himself. Dade figured Hernim already knew he was alive, so there was no reason to hide anymore. He wasn't afraid of anyone recognizing him, except maybe the pap-drones. Dade didn't want to fully out himself yet. Not until he needed to make a public statement. The element of surprise would suit him well then.

If he meant to make a real change within the community, he needed to use his celebrity when it mattered and put his face to the projects that he supported. It would take a while to change his image, however.

Saben stood beside Dade. After greeting his family warmly, he looked around the area with a critical eye. "Things are coming along nicely."

The once-hollowed-out building had gone through a transformation. Dade had been coming with Saben to help. Every time they showed up, it looked better than the last time they were here. The people had made their temporary camps more permanent. Walls had been erected, both to keep out the bitter cold and to offer each family a bit of privacy. It looked as if a neighborhood had sprouted up out of the cavern of the skeleton building.

On the visicasts, there was talk of moving the displaced citizens to other cities. Yet nothing had been done. No one seemed to care about relocating them.

Dade wondered if anyone had seen the extent to which the new area had prospered. Because clearly, the people weren't leaving. They were digging in and creating a new life.

"You've made it just in time," Saben's father said. "The meeting is about to start."

"What meeting?" Dade asked.

There was a large group gathered in an unused open area. More people than he knew lived here. The crowd was made up of both men and women, but mostly they were young and physically fit. The backbone of the workforce.

A number of torches lit the area. At the far end, a makeshift stage had been erected. Several people were trying to get the crowd to stop talking and focus up front. Their voices echoed in the open structure, yet Dade couldn't make out exactly what was being said.

"We're discussing what we're going to do now that the city has no supply of VitD," Saben's father said.

Saben tensed. "It isn't a good idea to hold the meetings here. You'll draw attention to yourselves."

"It's the only place large enough," his father said. "Don't worry, the govies won't find out. We've been careful."

Dade agreed with Saben that this wasn't smart. The govies could ignore many things. But holding a public meeting would be like spitting in their face. The new settlement, the portion they'd so carefully begun to reconstruct, could be torn apart.

However, he had to be judicious about voicing his opinions. It wasn't his place to tell them how to live their lives.

"Come down and meet a few people," Saben's father offered.

"No," Saben said. "We need to be getting back."

"But you just got here."

Saben nodded. "To drop off supplies, but there're other things we need to do tonight."

"I understand, son. Be careful." He pulled Saben into a hug.

When Saben's father excused himself, Dade whistled low. "This isn't good."

"No. Though it does say a lot about how frustrated people are."

Dade nodded.

They stayed for a few more minutes, far enough away that they wouldn't be noticed. It was the first time that Dade had been able to observe the fallout up close. Honestly, he was surprised that it had taken this long to get people to question the rules so publicly.

Watching their body language, he noted that several were angry. They were the outspoken members who did most of the talking. But the others just looked scared. If this was an indication of what the city felt, the majority were still a long way off from doing anything about their circumstances.

As much as the people were frustrated, mostly they wanted their voices to be heard. They didn't want to fight. Or at least, the stirring anger could just as easily be put out with a few public programs.

Dade didn't want bloodshed. Too many would die, and that was a loss that could be avoided given the right circumstances.

The problem was determining who would end up on top of the power structure. There were the obvious choices: the govies could maintain power, the Solizen could snatch it, or any of the other gangs could rise, of course. Yet it was the murkiness of the other possible candidates that made Dade pause. He knew there were shadows in the Underworld who had enough power to make their bid. People like Crispin.

And then there was Clarissa. Perhaps this was what she was so concerned with. What she meant when she'd indicated that there were bigger stakes at play. If her ultimate goal could give these people a level of independence, then he would help her.

Dade needed to do something in order to shape the outcome of this fight. He felt deep inside that this was his calling. He didn't want to lead. He knew that for sure. But he could fight and help back the right person who would usher in new policies.

"You'd think people would learn by now," Saben said so that only Dade could hear. "We destroyed one planet with war, strangled the resources until they were gone. This planet was supposed to be a fresh start."

Dade snorted. "A fresh start to destroy more things."

"Humans always do."

Dade thought of the ships docked in the sky stations outside the planet. These people weren't wealthy enough to buy tickets to leave. They'd have to sell their lives away, and quite possibly the lives of their children. "They're going to suffer without VitD. It's a ticking bomb."

"We could jump to another city," Saben suggested. "I don't believe they're all without VitD even though that's what Mina thinks."

"You want to abandon these people?"

"We would come back." Saben stared hard at the crowd. "We could bring hope."

Dade was already shaking his head. "No, let's see how Mina's idea plays out. We'll steal what we can until then. And when we get our hands on the recipe, we'll figure out what to do."

"That's why I stayed with you. I knew that you'd become something special. That I could trust that you'd do something to help those I love."

Dade felt emotion stick in his throat. He swallowed past it and tried to joke. "You hooked your star to a lonely boy locked in a Tower."

Grunting, Saben gave him a rare smile. "It was the best decision I ever made."

Chapter twenty-eight

Arden stood in the dark hallway, waiting for Dade's return. She'd felt conspicuous. At times she heard shuffling from down the hall and expected Roan or Coco or even Mina to show up and ask her what she was doing. It was too early to turn in for the night. The others were still enjoying their downtime, and she was roaming the halls like a specter.

How did she turn into this person? Paranoia had become something she had to overcome daily. That had never been her. Now, she had to figure out a way to deal with that constant feeling pressing at her mind.

Dade and Saben weren't here. They'd left the compound once again. She'd been watching them come and go for a while now, wondering what they were up to. They were leaving more often lately. That more than anything else made her determined to finally deal with it. To understand what Dade was doing.

She'd refused to ask questions. Or at least had till now. At first because of stubbornness, she wanted Dade to volunteer the information, to include her. After that talk they'd had, she'd thought they'd moved forward and he would finally share his plans with her.

But clearly he hadn't. Or else she wouldn't feel like this.

Arden was nervous. And damn if that didn't beat all. Nerves were not something she generally felt unless it was in warning that something bad was going to happen. She'd never had a problem telling anyone else what she thought.

This situation was different. It was about her feelings for Dade. More than anything, she didn't want to screw up things with him. Though maybe she'd already done that. It was difficult to tell.

Waiting made those nerves jangle. They strung tight and nearly caused her to scream.

Dade and Saben were silent as they turned the corner into the sleeping areas. Yet she knew they were there, had been tuned into the shadows for so long that all she felt was a huge relief that they were back. Except for the knots inside her that seemed to tighten instead of releasing.

Dade fell still, his body tensing when he caught sight of her. "What are you doing here? Is something wrong?"

Arden tried to force a smile. It felt false and brittle. Possibly she was snarling more than smiling, and that wouldn't do any good. She didn't want this conversation to come across as an interrogation. Not when she knew she had to apologize too.

"Can I talk to you?" The words felt like dust in her mouth. Arden swallowed and shook out her hands. Then she forced them down. She was going to make herself vulnerable, but she needn't look as if she were panicking.

It was time. She'd done a lot of thinking about what Dade had said to her. About Niall and his accusations. She was acting selfishly, though not on purpose. But she could see how others would think that she made decisions that would be best for herself. The air needed to be cleared. She was sick to death of living like this. The stress was eating her alive.

If they were going into the CRC—if she was going to die—then she needed to know that there was nothing standing between them.

Saben and Dade looked at each other. And then Saben gave her a curt nod and continued on down the hallway.

"Sure," Dade said. The smile he gave her seemed genuine. Perhaps he had waited for her to come to him. It made her feel worse that he knew her well enough to know she'd needed time to come around. Perhaps she was every bit as selfish as Niall had accused her of being.

She was as much responsible for creating this rift between them as he was. Probably more so, if she was honest.

Why were they pulling apart? She didn't know. If she could answer that question, maybe other answers would come as well. The more she tried to hang on, the slipperier her connection to him felt. The relationship she wanted with him was just out of her grasp.

"I want to make plans. I want them to be solid between us. I want to know going into this job that we have a future after we leave here," she said.

"Of course we have a future."

She pressed a hand to her stomach as it twisted. "What if something happens when we do this crazy scheme of Mina's? What if one of us doesn't come out?" A coldness spread through her. "I don't want us to end like this. I can't go into the CRC feeling this way."

"What way?" He was calm when he asked, and she realized he was going to make her say it, that he wanted her to articulate her feelings aloud.

"I don't want to feel like you and I are separate people working different agendas. I want to work with you, Dade. I want to help you."

His eyes narrowed, speculatively.

Okay, so she was going to have to grovel some more, because she'd said that before and then had done nothing different. "I want to know everything you've been doing. It's obviously important to you since you're gone all the time."

"Why now? What has changed since the last time we spoke?"

Everything. Her life felt so different. She felt different. Focused again, as if she'd lost sight of what made her whole. The drive of revenge made for a sharp knife cutting through her bullshit.

She wanted vengeance. Lasair deserved this. Maybe not all of them did. But while they all weren't complicit, they'd all share in the same fate. Her anger had grown, become a thing inside her with teeth and a life of its own. She felt it eat at her from her inability to stop the back-stabbing she hadn't seen coming.

For now, her fury had to be focused. If she did something good, then maybe that would soothe the monster, promise it retribution. Uri would curse the day he crossed her.

It wasn't just her, though. Dade had changed too. When he'd come back to the compound after the confrontation with his father, his eyes had hardened. He was more serious, more determined to do . . . some-thing. Even though he insisted that speaking with his father hadn't hurt him, she knew he had to be devastated. She, if anyone, knew what it felt like to be betrayed by family.

"I spoke with Niall," she admitted. "He brought up a lot of my issues. It made me realize that I've been too focused on myself."

His silence spoke volumes.

"I'm sorry," she added. "I don't mean to cut you out. It's just, I get focused and don't see beyond it."

"I know," he said. "Though you need to realize that I was meant to be more than just your sidekick."

Arden blinked, shocked by that statement. "What do you mean? I don't treat you like a sidekick."

"You don't treat me like an equal either."

"Yes, I do."

He was already shaking his head. "You make decisions alone. You expect me to go along with them."

The roiling queasiness of her stomach twisted more. "I don't mean to."

He let out a long sigh. "Look, I get it. You've been working on your own for a while. You may have had Lasair, but it wasn't as if they micromanaged you. Working with me will be different. We're going to butt heads a lot. Probably have versions of this conversation over and over. But hopefully it will get better each time. And eventually trusting each other will come naturally."

"I want that." She licked her lips. Her whole mouth felt dry. She was messing this up. "I want to be a team: you, me, Saben."

"I've made some decisions in the past few days," he said. "This is more for me than bringing back the Ghost. That will only do so much. We have a chance to shape this city's future."

"You want to lead?"

"No, but I have a vested interest in who does, or at least helping take out those who will cause the most harm."

She nodded. That would benefit everyone. It wasn't something she'd concern herself with normally. But he was right, if they could manage to swing the power dynamic to someone more worthy of it, it would help her in the long run.

"I've also decided that my father needs to be dealt with," Dade said. "I'm moving on with my life. Starting over."

She understood that completely. It was exactly how she felt about Uri. Though it didn't sound like he was so focused on revenge. Rather, he sounded sad.

"I want to go with you to steal the VitD." The twisting in her gut had eased. She felt silly, though, asking for this. It was such a minor thing. "And I want to help you with everything else too, of course. Altering the power structure, taking out big targets, whatever you've got planned. But I want to do the small stuff with you too."

"That's what I wanted to hear." He pulled her into his room, grinning from ear to ear. "I have something for you."

They were alone in the room he shared with Saben and Roan. She immediately felt privacy settle over them. She liked these moments where it was the two of them, craved them. One thing they had to put on their to-do list was getting their own space.

He went over to a drawer and took something out. Bringing it to her, he bounced, excitement evident in each movement.

"What's this?" she asked. She held the mask in her hand. The material felt cold—almost wet. Though she knew when the red mask with horns was attached to her face, it wouldn't feel like that at all.

He smirked. "You know what it is."

A Ghost mask.

"For me?"

Nodding, he pulled her into his arms. "Of course."

"You trust me with it?" She couldn't believe it. He was sharing this with her. And that made her feel a growing warmth inside. It was reassuring, their connectedness. He'd put it all into motion before she'd asked. Anticipating that she'd want to go with him. "You planned this?"

"No, I'd hoped," he said, then winked.

She scrunched her nose, the word sounding foreign. "Hope."

Dade leaned forward to brush his lips lightly against hers. "Yeah, that thing that sometimes you have to rely on because there seems no other path forward?"

"That's logic."

Laughing harder, he kissed her again. She felt the warmth spread through her, banishing the last of her tension.

Arden clutched the mask in her hand as she wrapped herself around him. Melted into the sensations that now played riot in her body. They were the good kind of emotions this time, light and fun. The bubbling joy in her heart that made her feel giddy.

When they panted for breath, she teased, "So you're making me your sidekick?"

Dade's smile grew wide and dazzling. "I hadn't thought of it that way, but yes, I like the sound of that."

Arden laughed.

"I've made some decisions too," she said. It was time to acknowledge it.

"Okay, I'll help you with whatever you need."

"I want to go back. I'm going to take over Lasair."

He nodded as if he'd suspected as much.

"I don't just want to repay Uri. I want to take everything from him. And those people, my family, they don't deserve what has happened to them. They need to rebuild too."

"Done," he said. "It will help with my plans anyway if you're controlling the gang."

"Dade," she cautioned, "they're not—well, it's not going to be like you'd want. They're not going to suddenly live on the legal side of the line."

"I know." His gaze seemed calm, confident. "It's okay. We're not going to take control by following the rules. I know that."

They kissed again. This time slower and hotter. Before they got too carried away, she asked, "So we're going to get through this stupid CRC thing. We're both going to make it out alive. And then . . . ?"

"And then we're going to decide whose ass to kick first."

"That sounds like a most excellent plan," she agreed.

Then he kissed her until her toes curled.

CHAPTER TWENTY-NINE

Arden's back was pressed to the dumpster, her phaser at the ready. She leaned out, peering around the metal container to look over the street. The area was quiet. There was no movement that she could detect. Lasair had warehouses all over the city. She had chosen this one because it had the least foot traffic. Before she'd left, they kept it stocked to the brim with VitD that would be made into Shine at some point. She hoped that was still the case.

Dade was next to her, keeping track of the alley behind them. They were both squatting, keeping low behind the cover of the metal. And were dressed identically in black synth-suits and the Ghost's signature masks. Considering what they were about to do, Arden thought a statement was in order.

She'd never gotten such a rush on a job before. It was amusing, really. Of all the things she'd done, stealing VitD from Lasair and then giving that cargo away without any expectation of payment was turning out to be the most satisfying. Maybe Dade had a point. They could do good and get vengeance at the same time. Until she could oust Uri from Lasair, becoming a thorn in his side had to be enough. And she would do it with pleasure.

"You don't have to come with me," Dade said.

"Yes, I do." It was time to show him that she was on board with whatever he wanted, that her plans didn't trump his. That she was an equal partner.

"You don't have to prove anything to me," he said.

"That's not the only reason I'm doing it." She grinned and wiggled her eyebrows. "Maybe I just wanted to see you do your thing in a skintight suit."

He gave her a flat look. "You see me in a running suit all the time."

She gave a breathy sigh. "Yes, but we're always so busy. This time I'll have the opportunity to enjoy it."

He leaned forward and kissed her. It was fast but passionate, and it left Arden tingly. "Thank you for helping."

"Let's just hope they haven't changed where they keep this cache of VitD," she said.

She had considered how Uri would handle their stash and decided that it made no sense for him to arbitrarily move it. To make sure, they'd gone into Venz's system, and she'd had Saben check the cams in this part of the city. There was still a lot of foot traffic in this area. Arden had recognized most of the people, so she was fairly confident they were still using this warehouse.

Besides, there weren't that many places in Undercity to hide things. They couldn't just burn one they already had set up. It was unlikely that Uri would move all their product. Doing that on a large scale would be next to impossible.

So basically, they'd gambled this entire night on her hunch. It was a lot of work and effort, not to mention dangerous, to break into a warehouse that could yield nothing.

She checked the street one more time. "You ready?"

"After you."

They left their hiding place and approached the warehouse on swift, silent feet. Their phasers were out, and each watched one side of the street as they ran. She liked that they'd worked together so much at this point that they'd synced their movements, giving hand signals and acting like extensions of the other.

Two cams focused on the door. They were discreet, small, the red indicator light blacked over so that no one could tell it was on. Arden shot them out with her phaser. Lasair didn't have enough people to monitor them constantly. Eventually someone would notice, so they needed to move quickly.

Dade took out a datapad and began the unlocking code.

Arden kept her back to Dade while he worked. Stepped in close with her phaser directed into the dark street, ready for trouble.

He unlocked the door quickly, and then they were inside. They kept the lights off as they cleared the warehouse. Then went to work by glo-wand.

She raised her hand, tapping her mask to turn on her infrared eye shields. It was a new design by Venz, incorporating the halo-glasses within the mask much like he had his goggles. He'd made them in preparation for their break-in to the CRC. They'd be able to see maps, temperature readouts, detection screens—all while working their job. Plus it added night vision. She didn't feel bad about taking it out for a spin. She had to know if it worked as well as Venz claimed.

Arden looked at Dade and waited for his nod. Then they were off, moving through the warehouse. They slunk between stacks of boxes, clearing each row as they went.

The amount of stolen product inside was staggering. Normally Lasair didn't have this big a stockpile of VitD. Some they saved to use, but mostly they resold it as Shine. It was a brisk business. Making money meant keeping a productive turnaround time between stealing, making Shine, and reselling. This looked like they had hoarded VitD for some time. The boxes were packed all the way to the ceiling. She looked up, impressed at the sight. They could fill a hundred hoversleds, the flat hovercarriers that were used to haul heavy items throughout Undercity, and still not clear out this warehouse. What they'd take would barely make a dent in the cache.

Arden felt a twinge of frustration. She should have thought ahead and planned two hoversleds, one for the mission and one for profit. Her mind ran through the calculations of how much they could have made. After all, they needed to be able to support themselves after they got away from Mina. They couldn't leave with nothing *again*.

She'd nearly walked the length of the warehouse, checking behind stacks of boxes and moving from aisle to aisle, when she heard a click. The sound was faint. But in the silent, dark room, it sounded like the blast of a phase-shot.

It was followed by a hiss. Then another hiss and another as nozzles turned on throughout the room. Steamed air, thick and white, began to fill the warehouse. It cut off her vision. She was trapped inside the swirling mass. Blue lights clicked on along the ground, small glowing beacons that lined the aisles.

At the sound of the first hiss, Arden held her breath. She pulled out her air-breather, sticking it into her mouth and clicking it on. She let the pump expunge the air from the disk before she exhaled and then pulled in her first deep breath.

All around her was a noxious cloud of poison gas. She knew this trick. The fumes, once inhaled, would shut down a person's circulatory system in less than a minute. And then the person would die.

The poison was pervasive and corrosive. Her air-breather wouldn't be able to vent the poison for long. The poison ate at the nanotech, and it broke down systems that filtered it. Knowing that the breather would work for only a few minutes, and that it had to last while the poison cycled through the warehouse, she kept her breaths even. Too much air intake would cripple the breather prematurely.

Arden ran down the aisle to the outside wall, looking for a control panel. She pressed against the walls, hoping for something to open. Her fingers ran along the metal sheeting.

She had less than three minutes before her air-breather broke down. Her internal clock monitored the time. As each thirty-second chunk went by, she became a little more panicked. If she failed, they'd both die.

A blast of phase-fire lit the opposite side of the room. She jolted, startled. Her heart raced. At first she thought someone had shot Dade. But then another blast shot straight upward, hitting the ceiling of the warehouse, and melted a hole in the ceiling.

Arden realized that it was Dade's way of getting her attention and took off at a run. Her vision was compromised from the smoke, and the boxes made a maze of her path. She kept her hands in front of her so as not to crash into a wall of boxes, which further slowed her down.

She found Dade standing before an open panel. He was pushing numbers into the light board, his fingers flying. Yet it was clear that his actions were having no effect.

Shoving him out of the way, she set to work, trying to remember everything she was taught. Turning the gas off was far more complicated than it seemed. It required numerous codes to be input in the correct order within a set amount of time. Trouble was she was awful at remembering the order. Being under pressure didn't help.

On her first try, she must have entered the wrong sequence of numbers. When she pressed "Enter," a loud air horn blasted, and then the mist started blowing heavier.

Cursing herself, she tried not to let the frustration make her fingers clumsier than they already were. She had to start over. Her mind strung out endless combinations of numbers. And she knew her three minutes were almost up.

Her second try proved no more successful than the first.

Dade shifted uneasily beside her. She could feel his nervousness, but she could also feel his silent encouragement.

On her third try, she knew this was her last opportunity to get it right. Her air-breather vibrated its warning, nearing the end of its lifespan. Her hands were unsteady from adrenaline and fear. She shook them out, stretching her fingers before trying again.

Stress caused her breath to thin. She focused on her fingers and how they hit the light board, hoping with all her might that this was the right combination. If it wasn't, they'd be dead.

She could do this. Arden knew the right combination. She needed to think. To focus: on each number, each sequence. Concentrate only on that and let every other thought in her mind fall away. When the last number was entered, she pressed the button once more and waited. The moment was tense, and she felt herself balancing on the edge of panic.

The annoying air horn ended its horrific whine. And then the gas slowly stopped blowing. It was almost a full ten seconds before she realized she'd managed to turn it off.

They weren't out of trouble yet. The gas in the room still needed to be cleared. She set to work, turning on the decontamination filter. Just as she began the keystrokes to start that, their breathers gave a low, constant wail, indicating that they were on their last thirty seconds of air.

This would be close. She pounded away at the light board. She was nearly there.

Just a bit more.

Their breathers clicked off as she hit the final button.

The decontamination filter whirled to life.

There was a loud boom as the fan kicked on. It sucked the air up toward the ceiling vents. The suction was so intense that Arden felt the pull on her body. She grabbed the console and Dade's hand simultaneously, holding them in place. Dade reached forward and also grabbed the console. In the next minute they were both lifted off their feet.

One second, two seconds, ten seconds. Her lungs burned. She wanted to release her breath, draw in some new air, and fill her lungs. Her eyes watered. The strain from hanging on and not being able to breathe made her muscles shake. Her fingers began to slip. Arden gripped harder, fighting against the strain.

Around them, boxes flew through the air. Breaking open, their contents becoming flying missiles. Arden tucked her head between her outstretched arms, trying to protect herself from being knocked out.

Finally the decontamination filter kicked off. Everything crashed to the ground. Arden fell, her body crumpled. She pulled out her air-breather and panted in a series of deep breaths.

Dade took out his air-breather as well, and after he got his breath back, he grinned at her. He was sexy in the devil mask. It made his jaw look even more chiseled. "That was close."

Arden snorted. They hadn't loaded the VitD yet, and she was already exhausted.

She checked the time. They had less than a half hour till their appointed meet time with Saben. It would be cutting it close.

"Let's get to work." Dade stepped around the debris and made his way to the bay door.

They opened it and moved the hoversled inside.

Loading the boxes was tedious and backbreaking. Though physically exhausted, she pushed herself on, arms shaking with fatigue. They needed to get as much VitD as possible. Arden was determined to keep working, even though her lungs burned and her body protested.

Dade showed no signs of tiring, lifting without pause. She refused to look his way and get distracted.

Once the hoversled was loaded, they took a black tarp and covered the top. It would blend with the other hoversleds moving through the city. There would be cams that could track them, but at least it gave them a fighting chance of getting lost in the streets.

They were late. Hopefully Saben would still be at their designated spot. He'd take the hoversled to convene with the others who would pick up the merchandise and act as the middleman. The boxes of VitD would be broken down onto smaller hoversleds, which would then travel to other meeting places, only to be broken down again. From there, they'd be delivered to the hospitals and child centers Dade had advised. And, of course, the men and women who'd made a deal with Saben to deliver them would take a cut off the top as payment.

"Now there're two Ghosts?" The words were chilly, spoken in a deep, cruel voice. "How fortunate that you came together. Now I can kill the both of you and be done with this."

Arden's body seized. Then she turned. Her body felt like it was not hers, the sensation like that of an out-of-body experience.

There, standing in the aisle, was Uri. He had a phaser in his hand, aimed at her and Dade. His expression was thunderous. She saw the hatred in his eyes.

It felt as if she were looking into the face of a stranger. He appeared worn, ragged, more so than the last time she'd seen him. Being in charge hadn't done him any favors. She could have told him that would happen. That the weight of power usually crushed, especially when one was without friends or apparent loyalty.

Mariah stood behind him. She hung back, her eyes wide. She too had a phaser in her hand.

Arden hadn't heard them come in. They'd gotten the drop on her, and later she'd flail herself for it. For now, though, she didn't feel fear. There was no place inside her spooling pit of anger for that.

She didn't want this confrontation here, not now. There would be better times, after she slowly stripped away his life. Yet she couldn't waste this opportunity to at least taunt him a bit.

She took a step closer to Uri. Her hand reached up, and she ripped off her mask. Perhaps exposing herself was a dumb move. But she needed to. If she was going to destroy him, she wanted him to know why. Who was behind it. So that when he suffered, he could do nothing but think of her.

Uri's eyebrows rose. "Arden?"

"You betrayed us." Her body vibrated with pent-up rage that needed to escape. It stretched inside her, making her ache. "How could you do it?"

She didn't expect an answer, and he didn't give one, his only response the uptick of one corner of his mouth.

"From now until you die, I'll make every moment of your life miserable," she promised.

Dade moved then, his foot kicking the phaser out of Mariah's hand.

Arden didn't bother to reach for her own phaser. This was about her anger and aggression. Giving in to the need to feel the physical connection of pain. She got the first hit in, a solid punch to Uri's mouth followed by her arm knocking his phaser loose. It went flying with a clatter against the stone floor.

Uri returned the hit. Landing his blow against Arden's nose and mouth. She felt his knuckles connect. Felt the solidness of it and the bite as her skin separated. Blood filled her mouth. Her head snapped to the side, moving with the punch to lessen the impact.

Arden didn't have the strength he did, but she was smarter, faster. Skills she could use against him. She let the blow flow through her, already swinging her body around, her foot coming up. She kicked her boot into the side of his face and sent him flying.

Bloodthirst got the better of her. She pulled her phaser, aiming it at the center of Uri's chest.

"Arden, stop," Mariah screamed.

"Arden." Dade's voice was calmer, but it still had an edge to it. "Let's go."

Lowering her phaser a couple feet, Arden shot Uri in the leg. She wanted to end him even though it wasn't the best move. If she wanted to control Lasair, it had to be a public fight. Though not necessarily fair. Otherwise her former gang wouldn't accept her as its leader. She'd need support from the inside to pull this off.

Uri screamed as the blast shot through him, much to Arden's satisfaction.

"Arden," Dade said, repeating her name, softer this time. He held Mariah, choking off her air, his arm around her throat. His other hand pressed his phaser to her temple. "You don't want to kill him."

Mariah stopped fighting him. She stared at Uri, then turned her gaze to Arden. Tears streaked her cheeks, but she didn't beg for their lives.

Arden wished she would. Then at least she wouldn't feel the sour pit in her stomach as she made the decision she knew she had to.

She spoke directly to Uri. "I want you to suffer. I'll do everything in my power to see it happens."

Then she spat a wad of blood at his feet.

CHAPTER THIRTY

Dade sat at the glass table in the command center. Before him the vid-projector flickered, and he swallowed his frustration as he watched it. The meeting had already been scheduled, but dealing with the message that played had been a last-minute addition to the agenda. It was not something anyone in the room took lightly.

Well, besides Arden.

She sat beside him, doing nothing to temper the smug look on her face. Her arms were folded across her chest, and she leaned back in her chair indolently. Her feet were perched on the table beside her own personal hologram feed.

The room was silent as they watched the vid. The feed wavered, making the image crack and spit. It was clear how much damage Arden had done to Uri's face in the hologram. Half his face looked distorted, swollen, and broken. The contrast and the hollowness of the laser projection probably made it look even worse than it was.

Uri's expression was menacing. And though the vid was distorted, the vibration of his body came through with visual clarity. They'd pissed him off well and good. That hadn't been precisely Dade's plan, though it obviously had been Arden's.

"I want my stolen VitD." His lips were thin, curled over his teeth when he spoke. The entirety of the vid had been a venom-soaked rant.

"And I want Arden's head. If I don't get both within five days, I will declare war on you, Mina, and everyone who works for you."

The vid abruptly ended.

Inside the room, the atmosphere had risen to uncomfortable levels. Everyone was angry, though they all wore it differently.

Mina stood at the head of the table. Her arms were crossed over her chest. She'd paced during the feed, clearly upset and barely holding her agitation in check. The clearheaded frustration of a leader, even as she shot looks at Arden that promised a bloody beating.

Nastasia was imperious. Roan, seething. Coco was somewhere between frustrated and awestruck that Dade and Arden had pulled off a job of such a large scale right beneath their noses. While Annem looked sad but thoughtful.

Then there was Niall, who had been invited to the meeting because apparently he was going with them to break into the CRC. He too was pissed, but it looked like his anger wasn't focused on Arden. No, his rage was directed at the vid, at Uri. He could barely stay seated as he watched.

Dade didn't know what to make of Niall. He'd stayed in lockdown since they'd rescued him a few days ago. Dade didn't know if he was even recovered enough to do the job. Niall still had bruises, and his hands still shook at times.

They'd never spoken to each other. Even so, he didn't trust Niall. There was something off about the guy. While his detox may have been to blame—the mood swings, the dark brooding looks, the constant sweats, the rages—Dade thought it was more. There was an intensity about the guy that made Dade question his motives. And he always looked at Arden with speculation. Dade didn't want Arden to be a cornerstone in any of her brother's plans.

Arden, however, seemed to take Niall's presence in stride. Though she seemed more and more exhausted after every encounter with her brother.

Mina leaned forward, her knuckles pressed to the surface of the table. She looked at each of them and then said to Venz, "Replay it."

Venz was quick to do as she asked.

The feed started over. This time Dade focused less on the rantings of a madman and instead considered what Uri had requested.

Uri's threat was overreaching. Lasair's numbers were decimated. They were still regrouping. How did Uri think he stood a chance against Mina with her connections and artillery? Uri got his weapons from her. This guy was all bluster. If he meant business, he would have attacked and not bothered to send an empty threat first.

Uri hurled accusations, screaming, "That bitch broke into my warehouse and stole my shit."

"It wasn't his to begin with," Arden said under her breath.

No one but Dade heard her. He kicked her under the table. She turned to him and rolled her eyes. She could at least pretend that what Uri accused them of wasn't true. The vid contained no proof.

Regardless, Dade was thankful for Arden's help the night before. Together they could be an unstoppable force.

Uri continued. "I want her. I want my stuff. And I want the person she was with."

His focus strayed from the replay to watch Niall. He looked even more intense. His jaw clenched and his shoulder rolled. He didn't appear to even blink.

"Are we done listening to this yet?" Arden asked with a yawn. "He's a lunatic."

Mina waved at Venz to click off the feed. Her eyes narrowed, and she looked ready to kill. "What did you do?"

"The boy is crazy. Do you really think I would break into Lasair's warehouse?"

"Yes," Nastasia said.

Coco laughed. "I was going to offer congratulations. That douchebag got what was coming to him."

Mina sent Coco a withering glare. "Enough."

"Sorry, boss."

Then Mina was right back to grilling Arden. "What made you think it was a good idea to piss off Lasair? They want your head anyway. We have another mission that can't be compromised, and I can't have you running roughshod all over our plans and starting a war. You're on the eve of paying off Dade's debt and you pull this crap. Are you trying to destroy everything?"

Arden tilted her head. "You have us tracked, right? Did we leave the compound?"

Dade sighed, leaning back in his chair. He was exhausted. It would have been easy enough to deny the entire thing, and yet Arden was going out of her way to prove some kind of point.

He didn't think it was smart that Arden taunted Mina. Saben had bugged Venz's computer with a virus that Dade had gotten from Clarissa. It was a temporary fix made to look as if they'd stayed in the compound. Venz would find it eventually, and then Mina would explode and make this look like a tea party.

Arden didn't seem to care about future repercussions. "Do you have a vid-feed of us? Because I remember being asleep then. But I suppose sleepwalking is always a possibility."

"I do not appreciate your sarcasm," Mina said. "If you were asleep, why does your face look like it ran into a wall?"

"She has a good point," Dade agreed, amused.

"Not helping," Arden said.

Dade chuckled. "Sorry."

"Maybe that's what happened," Arden said after some thought. "I was sleepwalking, and I must have walked into a wall or a door." She shrugged. "Something."

"A wall shaped like a fist," Coco added helpfully.

Arden tapped a finger to her mouth. "That's a possibility."

"Why do we put up with her?" Roan asked. "We expect loyalty. Send her over to Lasair and be done with it."

"Loyalty," Dade scoffed. "We didn't choose to be here."

Mina finally took a seat. She leaned back in her chair, her elbows on the armrests, and steepled her fingers. "I could have left you to Crispin."

"At least with Crispin we knew what we were getting," Arden countered.

"We're offering friendship. A family," Nastasia said.

Arden shrugged. "I don't believe that."

Dade wasn't so sure. They'd been welcoming. And so far they hadn't done anything disloyal. Instead, Dade, Arden, and Saben had been the ones to break that bond.

Coco interrupted. "If they don't want to honor their commitment to us, then they need to be treated like the enemy."

"Agreed, we can't have them running around whenever they feel like it," Roan added.

Nastasia said quietly, "We're not locking anyone up."

Dade almost laughed since Niall had been locked up for the past week. He looked over at Niall, waiting for him to say something. But he wasn't paying attention. He kept his focus on the table with a scowl on his face.

"You invited us in." Arden smirked. "This is what I do."

Roan stood up, but Coco stood as well and held him back.

"Stop," she said to him. "Let Mina handle it."

Nastasia appeared the least ruffled, unlike Mina, nor was she like the overly aggressive Roan. She seemed more disappointed when she looked at them imploringly. "We are on the same side."

"What side is that?" Arden asked. "That's the problem, isn't it? Everyone thinks they're on a 'side,' and yet everyone is out for themselves."

Dade couldn't fault Arden's logic. She was right. Everyone was out for themselves. Yet he had hoped that they'd all pull together eventually.

And he hoped that these people would turn out to be as true as their word.

Mina sighed. It was a weighty sound. "This isn't going to resolve itself tonight. We need to focus on tomorrow and breaking into the CRC. Everyone needs to work together." She looked pointedly at Arden. "Because if we don't, we won't make it out alive."

CHAPTER THIRTY-ONE

Dade snuck up to the doors of the CRC, moving between the security cameras. Making sure he showed up as no more than a shadow was what he did best. His ability honed by years of stealing from his father. Still, his anxiety was high, keeping him alert.

At times he had to slither along the ground in a crawl. The outline of his body melted from one deep pool of black to the next. Dade's hood was up, his hybrid halo-glass mask on, and an air-breather in his mouth. He was covered from head to toe in a new specialty synth-suit Venz had created from the net-tech he'd invented to hide their vehicles. It worked on the same principles that the car had. Not exactly hiding Dade, but causing the gaze of anyone looking to slide past him.

Several feet from the door, he waited a beat, crouched against the side of the building. He used the time to catch his breath and steel his resolve. He would be seen when he moved toward the door. As soon as he got into place, he'd have seconds to set the charge sticks, and then they'd all be moving, the plan in motion.

Dade could see the countdown clock projected in the corner of the halo-glass. Each second gripped his muscles tighter. With the infrared, he could see Mina when she leaned out. She held a hand up, indicating five seconds, corresponding with his timer.

At the "go" signal, he shot toward the door, charge sticks already in his hands. There were more in the pouch of his belt.

He adhered them to the wall around the door frame. Stick after stick went onto the wall with quick precision. He spaced them apart as best he could. When he was done with the door, he continued down the length of the wall.

Dade used a lot of explosives. They weren't just making their way inside. This was a statement. The clock in the corner of his mask started flashing. He was out of time. He took the rest of the charge sticks and threw them near the door. They all had capacitors set to blow, their timers synced together through Venz's expertise.

And then he ran.

He ran so fast that his muscles burned. Sweat poured off him. His lungs heaved, trying to get enough air.

Dade threw himself behind the shelter of vehicles where Mina, Roan, and Saben were hiding. He leaned against the hovervan, gasping. His body curled down, waiting for the explosion.

"Dade is clear," Mina said to Nastasia.

Nastasia's answer was to count the last three seconds into their comm. He knew that Venz was doing the same for the other group. Nastasia and Venz were working in tandem to run tonight's dual operations. There was no room for error. Their job was to keep everyone alive.

Her voice hit "one" and then "zero" exactly at the same time the detonation lit up the black sky.

Dade's head was down. He covered the back of his neck, and his eyes were shut. Yet the searing white burst of the explosion blast still leaked through his closed lids. The hovervan lifted momentarily against his back, resettling with a thump. He felt the heat and the rush of displaced air. Smelled the burning stench of melted metal and moonglass.

A blaring siren cracked the silence.

They now had exactly ten minutes to get in and out before the govies showed up. Their movements were synchronized between both teams. Everything coordinated down to the second, relying on the govies' predictably timed reactions.

Nastasia reset the timer that appeared in the eye mechanism of their halo-glass masks and instructed, "Go."

They were up and running toward the exploded side of the building. Focused, and working as a team. The three of them fanned out. They were loaded with firepower. Dade had a large blast-phaser in his hands and another strapped to his back, and several knives strapped to his arms and legs. His hips and chest were weighed down with a number of Venz's concussion bombs.

Inside, the govies were waiting for them, grouped in the anticipated attack formation they were trained to organize into if the building was breached. Guards lined the halls, tucked into dugouts made for this purpose where they could conceal themselves while firing on the incoming enemy.

The three of them picked off the guards, alternating between their phasers and concussion bombs. Venz had outfitted their ears with a sonic dampener that broke up sound waves so they wouldn't affect their team. The bombs detonated, and the guards fell. Each squad they cleared moved them several feet forward.

Dade stopped at every hallway branch, securing it before moving on. They didn't want the govies to block them in. The guards ahead of them began to retreat.

"They've initiated their lockdown protocol," Mina said, confirming his thoughts.

"Nine minutes," Nastasia said over the comm, counting down the time.

Dade's gaze immediately flicked to the corner of his halo-glass to confirm. He let out a breath.

That reminder of the time forced them to move quicker. They worked just as steadily, yet there was a desperation that settled in.

He felt like he was part of their team. He didn't know if it was the time spent with them or the fact that he'd worked with them on other missions, but he anticipated their reactions now. They moved as if they were meant to fight together. It felt good, right in a way that had been slightly off-sync until now.

It made him think of Arden. Dade wanted to know how she fared. Wanted to ask after the other group, but knew that would interrupt the mission. At least he had Saben with him.

Being split up from her sucked. Still, maybe it was for the best. It would help him to keep a clear head while he worked. And he knew Arden didn't need him. Though that didn't stop him from wanting to keep her in his sight, just in case. He was sick of loss and didn't want to face it again.

They moved inward toward the center of the CRC. The building was a series of concentric circles. Each had a gate of highly concentrated metal that couldn't be cut through within the span of time they had.

The circles were designed so they could only be unlocked from the inside. Once the doors were shut, there was no path into the center. Anyone stuck between the circles would have to stay in that ring until whatever emergency was cleared and the locks were disengaged.

When they passed through the halls, every so often they would come across a metal door that was closed and sealed tight. It didn't matter that they had already been locked out from the core. That wasn't their destination. Instead they made their way around the outermost ring to the holding cells the govies used to detain and often torture high-value targets.

"Head for the unit tower," Mina directed Dade and Roan. She set herself up with Saben, facing the hall from either side.

Dade and Roan turned down a hallway, running. Each second counted. Roan moved as if he were stalking prey. He was a little reckless, but his aim was dead-on, hitting the govies in the center chest. Dade focused on keeping them moving in the direction of the unit tower while watching Roan's back.

He knew they had made it to the containment wing when the hallways were lined with white metal doors. Behind the doors, presumably, were citizens the govies had taken both for information and to experiment on.

Nastasia called through the comm just as they reached the guard tower, indicating how much time they had left on the countdown. "Seven minutes."

Time moved too swiftly. They were three minutes in, and they hadn't even reached the checkpoint for the second part of the plan. It set a fire under their asses. They both felt the push, cutting people down with a focused precision as they went forward.

At the unit tower, they cleared the halls around it. The tower sat in the center of four halls and was shaped like a hexagon. It had windows on all six sides of the enclosed room. From there, it controlled everything in the outermost ring.

There were two guards inside the tower behind the phaser-proof moonglass. They looked panicked, speaking frantically into their comm, and viewing feeds on large panels that monitored the rooms and hallways.

Roan walked around the kiosk, pointing his phaser through the moonglass at them. Of course, he didn't shoot; there'd be no point. He yelled, "Open up."

The guards—a young man and woman—yelled back. The man tapped things onto a light board while the woman pulled her weapon. They were both focused on Roan because he had begun to taunt them.

Dade went in the opposite direction, so he ended up at their backs. There was no time to finesse the door open. He slapped some charge sticks to the door's locking mechanism that he could arm by hand and had a less destructive area radius than the ones he'd used to blow a hole in the building.

He yelled, "Fire," at Roan, and stepped back for cover.

The blast blew the door out and threw the two guards inside onto the ground. It also took out several windows of moonglass. Shards were everywhere. Dade threw a concussion bomb into the hub just in case the two guards were still awake. They waited until it detonated before he and Roan ran inside.

He checked to make sure the guards were still breathing, while pulling electro-cuffs from his utility belt. They appeared to be mostly unhurt. Dade set about restraining them.

Roan was at the console. He had shut down the outgoing distress calls. Then he pulled up the panels to get a visual into the rooms to look for Crispin's girl. "There're no names on these files."

Dade stood up and started going through the vid-feeds alongside him. The women all looked the same: beaten and waiflike, as if they were close to death. There was nothing to distinguish them as individuals.

"I'll try to cross-reference them with the patient files," Dade suggested.

"No," Roan countered, "you plant the worm."

Dade fished out the tiny disk from his tool belt. He searched for the plug-in that Venz had described. Dade thought he was pretty tech savvy, but this was far above the kind of tech stuff he usually did.

Now looking at the console, he was skeptical of his ability to navigate it. There were glowing buttons and data screens everywhere. Venz had seriously underestimated their system.

He could guess at the usage of half the equipment. Some were screen vids of holding cells that Roan was hacking. Some ran the doors and locks in this grid of the compound. The other stuff he had no clue as to what it was for. That was the area he concentrated on. They had some serious gear, and he wondered if most of it had come from other cities. And if so, how far advanced in technology were they?

Each one of the systems in the CRC ran independently. That was part of the failsafe procedure. Once the innermost ring was locked down, no one would have access to any part of the system until it reset. He needed to get the worm into place before the shutdown reached the center.

Venz couldn't break in from the outside. That was why it was Dade's responsibility to plant the worm. It would allow those in the other group to get control of their section, to complete their task. Without it, they'd be vulnerable. The entire plan rested on this.

Arden needed him to be successful.

Dade's chest tightened to the point of pain. His breathing shortened, and he could feel dampness under his suit. He could not let them down. This plan would not spin into a death spiral on his watch.

Dade addressed Nastasia through the comm. "I don't know what I'm looking for. Nothing looks like an upload input." Everything was streamlined. There were no key inserts.

"There should be something." She repeated the directions Venz had given her. She didn't know any better than Dade. Neither of them was a technical wizard.

"There's not a single slot where I can key in."

"Let me get Venz. Hang tight," she said.

Beside Dade, Roan scanned the rooms. Roan's face had gone taut with narrowed eyes, and his mouth was pulled into a thin line. A string of curses punctuated the tense pause.

Venz came on the comm line. He spoke fast, his voice high with excitement as he asked Dade to explain everything he saw.

When Dade finally paused, Venz said, "You're going to have to do a slide-load. Since there's nowhere to uplink, we'll have to use a digi-stream."

"I thought you couldn't get into the system?" Dade asked.

"I can't, but you're local. You can send a signal out so that I can snag the server. I'll get you a code. Hang on while I set up a digi-stream transfer."

Dade's heart beat in his ears while he waited. His hands felt numb. And then as Venz read off the code, he forced his fingers to type it in as fast as it was relayed to him. After several lines of code, he took a single deep breath and sent the connector. There was a pause during which Dade felt like his insides were suspended.

Finally, the visiscreen registered an upload in progress.

The worm took longer to transfer than Dade thought it would. Lines of code crawled along the screen. The percentage slowed as time ticked by.

It didn't help that Nastasia constantly tracked their declining time. "Six minutes."

"Okay," Dade said under his breath, frustrated. At five minutes, they'd be locked out of the system.

Mina and Saben showed up then. Mina came jogging in while Saben had his blast-phaser pulled low, walking backward. He stood at the door to the unit tower as Mina stepped inside. From this point on, the four of them needed to stick together in case anything went sideways.

She looked around at the two bound guards unconscious on the floor, to the scrolling numbers in front of Dade. She nodded. "Good job."

"I got the room number," Roan said. His sounded relieved, and some of his swagger reappeared.

"Excellent. Get the patient file too," Mina said. "Make sure to get all the notes and a list of everything that was done to her."

Roan's eyebrows went high even as he began downloading the information. "I thought this was a grab."

"It is. But you never know when information will be useful. Better to have it if we need it." Mina stepped up between them and began to unlock all of the rooms.

In the hallway, Dade heard the swish-swish-swish of the opening metal doors. There was no movement at first. Dade wondered if the patients were too broken to escape. Then he began to see people, cautious at first, peering around the door frames as if they expected to get hit.

The worm still wasn't finished uploading. They had thirty seconds before they would be locked out of the system. He'd done all that he could and still didn't know if they'd make it.

Nastasia sounded down the final seconds. "Three, two—"

The system dinged the completion of the uploaded worm.

"One." Then Nastasia said, "Second phase is a go. Five minutes left until govie reinforcements arrive."

Chapter thirty-two

Arden waited until she heard the blast from outside the CRC before they moved. The explosion shook the area. The loud boom reverberated through the metal wall that they clung to. Their limbs stretched like stars. It shook her core as it moved through her, rattling her nerves as much as her body.

They were lodged in the air shaft. Arms and legs extended, pushing against the metal and clinging by grips from their gloves and boots, squeezing and pressing until the shaking stopped.

The second they stabilized, Arden released the suction on her gloves and toed loose her boots, then began to slide down the shaft, her hands and feet still pressed against the metal. She fell fast, gaining speed. Arden pushed outward with her hands and feet to slow her momentum. She felt every bit of the heat and burn, from both the friction and the strain on her muscles.

In the lead position, she was aware of the small window of time they had. They all had to hit the first doors before they began to close. Excitement thrummed from the near impossibility of it.

The halo-glasses in her mask overlaid a projection map to the air-ducting system. Its scrolling feed kept her in sync with the ducts she passed. On one side she had a digital read of their time clock, below that a projected countdown in feet to her target goal. It gave her a digital readout of how fast she was traveling and how many more seconds till she hit the offshoot.

They approached a corner where the ductwork turned into the building. It was a steep angle. At the rate they were dropping, difficult to maneuver. Arden pushed harder against the ductwork, feeling the drag. She couldn't miss the turn. There would be no time to climb their way back up. And if she continued sliding down this duct, they'd end up too far away from the door to the inner circle.

She was ready for the transition to throw her body off its trajectory. The burn registered with a greater intensity of pain. She could no longer ignore it. Her muscles felt like they were turning to jelly. She just needed to hang on another fifteen seconds.

Arden slowed even more, pushing with everything she had. At the duct, she stepped her foot out so that it would solidly hit the bottom and then allowed the momentum of her fall to carry her forward, sliding into the metal hole. Once inside, she twisted herself into a ball, then moved around to face the opposite way. It was tricky, she being tall and the space tight. Arden grunted with the effort.

Knowing this had to be done fast, she forced herself to twist out of the pretzel position she was in. Her breath was a hot cloud as it recycled back on her through the air-breather. The feeling of claustrophobia made her skin crawl. She wiggled and jerked and got herself situated.

Then she began to crawl as fast as she was able. Behind her, she heard the others moving, righting themselves as she had and crawling forward after her.

Traveling through the vent system and into the CRC set off all kinds of internal building alarms. Had the plan relied on infiltrating through the vents to gain access, they would have been stopped before they'd begun. But with the alarms already triggered, and the other group involved in a firefight in the outer ring of the building, it would be enough of a distraction to get them to the first inside ring door. They still had to be as quiet as possible. Even with the alarms blaring, if anyone heard them, they could easily shoot phase-fire into the ductwork.

Niall crawled directly behind her. His panting sounded loud in their metal coffin. He was too out of shape for this mission. Annem and Coco brought up the rear.

Her brother was slowing them down. She didn't know why he'd insisted on coming, but it hadn't been her call. And Mina had said that he needed to be there. Ever since the job had started and they'd gotten into position, he'd acted manic. There was a determination about him she hadn't seen in years. It struck her as odd. He hadn't been willing to share any information the entire time he'd been in the hideout and yet had volunteered to come to the CRC with them without so much as a blink of hesitation.

Arden didn't trust him. He was up to something.

While Arden tracked their way through the maze of steel twists, Coco and Annem were planting sleeping-gas bombs inside the ventilation system. This was the reason Venz had been assigned to their group. He had been unable to get the precise air-shaft coordinates to this part of the ventilation system prior to their infiltration. He switched back and forth between Annem and Coco, giving them instructions while directing Arden through the maze of metal. Using the feed they sent him, Venz told Annem and Coco where to place the sleeping bombs so they would have the most coverage once the air filter kicked on. It was a lot of guesswork. Arden just hoped Venz chose correctly, because they didn't have another shot at this.

Venz was still speaking with Annem and Coco when Arden came to a section where she didn't know which way to turn.

Niall crawled up behind her. "Make a right." His direction was decisive and confident, and sounded exactly like it had when he'd been the Lasair leader.

She didn't question the order, her body already turning into the adjoining duct. It was like old times, easy to follow his orders. Trusting that Niall knew the plan, that he had it figured out ten steps ahead.

Where had they gone wrong, the two of them? She still loved him, but their relationship felt different. Cautious. Deep down, she knew that he'd fail her again because his priorities were always different than hers.

At the next vent, she stopped to get a location reading. She scanned between the grate to get a visual of the hall they were perched over. Relieved when it appeared they were moving in the right direction.

How did Niall know? There was no way he had been inside the CRC. Yet he spoke with the confident authority of someone who had inside knowledge. That should have been impossible.

There had to be a reason everyone wanted Niall, a reason why they'd kept him alive and tortured him. She was damned well going to find out what that was.

At the next turn, Niall said, "This one. It's the closest we're going to get."

She used her halo-glasses to first check the mapping location. And then when she calculated that Niall was right, she used them again to check the heat sensor to make sure the hall was clear before she pushed the grate out of the ceiling. They didn't have time to mess with anyone here. There was less than sixty seconds to get to the first door.

"How are you doing?" Venz asked.

"Exiting the vents," Arden said. She knocked loose the air-shaft cover and dropped down into the hallway. She pulled her phaser, keeping watch on the hall while the others dropped after her.

Coco was the last through.

There weren't any guards in the hall. It seemed that they'd stuck to their tactical training: a squad going forward to Dade's group, while the rest had fallen back into the next circle.

"Thirty seconds," Niall said, indicating the time they had left before the first gate closed.

They ran down the empty hall.

At the gate, they encountered a group of guards. Arden and Niall engaged in a phase-fight with them, while Coco and Annem slid past and into the gate to take care of the guards on the other side.

"It's closing," Annem screamed.

Arden nudged Niall to run, then followed. For a second, she shot back at their pursuers, and then leapt and slid past the door just as the gate shut. The gears ground together as the lock clicked into place.

"Gate one is locked," Arden said into the comm to Venz as she pushed herself up and ran with Niall for the next gate.

Coco and Annem were already ahead, trying to clear their path through more guards. It might give them enough time to get to the next gate before that closed too. They ran past Coco and Annem, who were engaged in a phase-fight, through the second gate, and continued at a dead run to the third gate. There they took on the next set of guards.

Annem alerted them through the comm to Venz that they'd made it to the third gate, and soon they were flying past Arden and Niall to the fourth. They played that back and forth all the way to the sixth gate.

The sixth gate was halfway shut as Arden and Niall ran up to it. Coco and Annem were still outside the gate, shooting wildly. There wasn't enough time to deal with all the guards here. There were too many. They had to focus on slipping through before it closed.

There was no thought to Arden's actions. This was their only chance. If they didn't get in, they'd be stuck between gates five and six, waiting for someone to come and arrest them. They wouldn't even have to leave the CRC before they were tortured.

Arden pounded through the guards, shooting as she ran. She got as near as she could to Coco and Annem before she ducked for cover. Then she took as many crazy shots as she could, knowing her life depended on it. They were outnumbered, the fight brutal.

The door was three-fourths closed. The siren blared as a warning that the door was about to lock.

Venz counted down the seconds. "Nine . . . eight . . ."

"Get inside," Arden shouted to the others. And then she couldn't worry about anyone else. She focused on shooting every guard she saw. Her breath came out in staccato pants as she reached for the last of her endurance.

She ran. Hot phase-fire seared past her. Close enough to feel the blowback of the displaced air. But Arden kept running, her legs pumping.

"Three . . . two . . ."

She slammed through the door that was just wide enough for her to get through sideways. The metal scraped her hip. She gasped with pain and knew that it would leave a deep bruise.

"One," Venz said.

The door lock clicked into place.

Arden looked up, at first disoriented. She gasped and swallowed, trying to wet her mouth. The lockdown had been completed. They were inside the center zone. Their movements would no longer be tracked. This room was cut off from the city—from the grid. It was the only place that the cams and vid-feeds truly couldn't reach. The doors wouldn't be opened till the threat was cleared and the coding was reset.

It also meant they were on their own. Venz was no longer able to communicate through the comm.

All four of them had made it inside. Niall was standing at the far end of the hall, checking for more guards. To her right, Annem lay on the ground with Coco beside her.

Arden pushed to her feet and walked over.

Annem lay still. A large knife stuck out of the back of her shoulder. Her breathing had shallowed, and she seemed on the verge of passing out. Blood collected in a small pool beneath her.

"We have to pull the knife out," Arden said.

Coco was shaking her head. "She could lose more blood that way."

"Think," Arden snapped. "How are we going to get her out of here with a knife in her back? It has to be done."

She nodded at Arden's words, and then reached to extract the knife. The wound gushed blood. Coco immediately tried to stanch it with her hands.

Arden pulled a med kit from her pack, and between the two of them, they field-patched her as best they could. Coco worked silently, her hands steady. A rock. But Arden could tell that her focus was shot. It was on Annem, not the mission.

Niall was standing to the side, observing. "It's deep."

"She's gonna be okay," Arden said to assure Coco. They were just words, probably lies at that. Yet she felt better saying them.

Above them, the air-filtering system kicked on with a loud groan. And then in succession their sleep bombs detonated. Smoke filled the hallways with a soft swish and a billowing white cloud. Their air-breathers filtered it out, leaving their group as the only people currently on their feet within the center unit.

Niall picked up Annem, slinging her over his shoulder.

Bodies lay on the floors of the hallway, asleep from the gas. They'd fallen where they stood, their limbs askew. Most of them were scientists, dressed in green and blue scrubs or lab coats. But some guards were interspersed with the scientists.

The hub was located in the center of the facility. It was a large room full of metal tables with lab equipment. On one side of the room, there was a whirring bank of machines collecting and collating data. On the other were the consoles that ran the central station. This was the brain of the CRC. They couldn't log into the system yet. Once the shutdown protocol had been enabled, it blocked off access to the computers within the lab. Plus, there wasn't remote access—yet.

Both problems would be solved once the worm that the other group uploaded spread its virus through the system. Then they'd have access to all of the CRC and would be able to open the door to any room.

CHAPTER THIRTY-THREE

Dade watched in horror as chaos erupted in the women's wing. Or rather, girls' wing, since everyone kept here was young, horrifyingly so.

The doors along the hall were open. After the first few patients who'd escaped their rooms started making a ruckus, other patients streamed into the hallway. Some screamed, pulling at their hair or running broken nails down their faces. Others wandered, running into one another and falling over. They yelled, swinging wildly to avoid things only they could see.

It was loud. One girl's scream led to two, to four, to eight girls joining her until the sound rippled throughout the space. Some grabbed their heads, shaking them back and forth, emitting keening, wailing cries.

The girls wore white hospital gowns that wrapped around them and tied at the side. They were one-size-fits-all, with so much material that they were voluminous on the girls' emaciated bodies.

The girls were disheveled and looked brittle. Nests of hair matted thickly on their heads. Self-made scratches hatched their skin. Purple and green bruising segmented around their wrists and ankles from where they'd likely been strapped down. Their feet were bare and dirty with overgrown toenails that had yellowed.

But when he looked into their eyes, Dade's stomach squeezed. Their gazes were vacant. Whatever horror they faced was inside their minds.

Dade wasn't sure they were aware they were in the hall. They looked haunted. A vital piece had broken inside them.

Dade was careful not to jostle them as he made his way through the mass of bodies. A couple girls stumbled into him and, unbalanced, started to fall. He caught them. His hands bruising their thin skin even though he tried to be careful.

They'd never get out. Never be free again. This place was supposed to be impregnable, and Dade was sure that after this it would be. He wanted to take all of them with him. Let them escape. They deserved lives free of torture.

Even as he thought this, he knew that he couldn't help them. They wouldn't make it two feet outside before they were stopped. And what would he do with them even if he could get them out? They had broken minds. It was far too late to help them.

He could end up here if his father had his way. All it would take was one misstep. Then he'd be locked away forever, broken and tortured. Worse, they could take Arden or Saben. His chest burned at the thought.

Mina led the way to the target's room.

At the door, Roan slipped by her and went inside first. Then Mina and Saben. Dade was the last one into the room. He was surprised to find the girl they were looking for still inside. He'd thought that if she'd escaped into the hall as the others had done, they might lose her.

The girl lay on her thin mattress with her back toward the door. She was curled forward, her body hunched. The cotton gown she wore dipped low on her back, showing each knot of her spine.

Unlike the matted nests of the others, her golden hair had been braided to keep it away from the sides of her skull. The hair three inches above her ears had been shaved, and a line was cut into her head. He could see the cut had been restitched with black med thread. It wasn't a neat job, the knots clumpy and uneven.

Mina leaned over the girl, touching the pulse at her neck.

"Is she alive?" Dade asked.

Roan snorted. "Wouldn't that be ironic if she wasn't?"

Dade growled at him, about to tell him he was an asshole, when Mina said, "Barely."

Mina turned the girl gently onto her back.

She moved her hands to the girl's head, turned her face, and used her thumbs to open the girl's eyes and check her pupils. "They've drugged her with something."

"It's probably for whatever they did to her head," Roan said. "It looks pretty brutal."

Dade stepped forward to get a better look. There was dried blood on the mattress beneath her head, indicating there was a similar wound on the other side. He swallowed back the sourness creeping up his throat.

The girl appeared broken. Her sallow skin did nothing to hide the bruising. There were yellow stains around her nose, the corners of her lips, and her neck. He wondered if the bruises were caused by some kind of medical device.

She didn't move when Mina shook her. Or when Mina slid back the gown to check the rest of her body. Her arms were covered in open, oozing bedsores. Clearly she'd been here for a while. Then there was the deeper bruising around her torso. One or two places looked like a boot print.

Dade swallowed, trying not to be sick. He turned away.

"What have they done to you, Kallow?" Mina whispered. Her voice was sad, full of a deep emotion that Dade had never heard from Mina.

He wondered who the girl was, especially since Crispin wanted her and Mina knew her. She'd clearly been treated worse than the others. What had earned her that cruelty? And why had they kept her alive?

"I need the suit," Mina said.

Saben stepped forward and pulled it from his pack.

"Thank you." She cleared her throat. "Saben and Roan, you watch the halls. Dade, I need your help."

She put undergarments on the girl before Dade walked over.

Mina's gaze had never slipped from Kallow since they'd entered the room. The way she was caring for her spoke of a previous friendship.

She ran her hand over Kallow's cheek, then said to Dade, "Hold up her legs for me."

He did as he was told, holding her weight as Mina worked the suit onto the girl. It wasn't skintight as it should be. The girl was too frail for that. And yet, it was an effort to get her dressed.

Something bothered Dade, set him on edge in a way he couldn't explain. It was like an echo, something he should remember and yet did not. The feeling got stronger the longer he stared at Kallow.

He felt as if he should know this girl. She seemed familiar. Or maybe she just had that sort of face, because try as he might, he could not place her.

It frustrated him enough to ask, "Who is she?"

"It doesn't matter."

But it did. He knew it did. "Tell me."

Mina sighed. "She should look familiar."

The words didn't register as they should have. It was like Mina spoke into the tunnel of his memory. Yet the connection still wasn't there.

Running her fingers over the girl's cheek, Mina turned Kallow's head. This side looked even worse than the other. What made his breath stutter, though, was the sun-star tattooed on the skin behind her ear. Clearly visible on Kallow's shaved head. The cut and the sutures had bisected the middle of the sun.

It would scar that way, a broken sun-star. The shape mangled. If it didn't follow the trajectory of the cut on the other side, he would have presumed that whoever did it had desecrated the tattoo on purpose.

If he'd known her, it had been years ago, perhaps when he was a child. How could any of the Solizen be missing? Did the Solizen know that one of their own was kept here? Had they sanctioned this? Dade felt a kinship with her even if he didn't know her. It made him want to protect Kallow even more.

"Who?" he pressed, knowing that Mina knew. That she was purposely not telling him.

"Your sister."

The words didn't even register. He was already shaking his head. The denial came hot and fast. He felt his hands begin to shake. "Impossible. She died when I was ten."

"Obviously not."

Dade swallowed. He couldn't deal with this revelation. It didn't make sense. One day she'd disappeared out of his life, and he'd been told . . . Well, he'd been told endless lies. "What does Crispin want with her?"

"I don't know," Mina said. She carefully tucked the girl's hair back into the hood before she pulled it over the back of her head. Then gently smoothed the strands in.

The words rang hollow to Dade. Yet he couldn't help but think she knew exactly what would happen once they handed Kallow over.

"You didn't ask?"

"It's not my business."

Dade swallowed back his rising anger, knowing that now that he had found his sister, he couldn't let her go. "Is Crispin going to hurt her?"

Mina looked up at that. "No, I promise."

"If he does, I'll rescue her a second time."

Her gaze seemed sincere as she spoke. "I promise, Dade. She won't suffer in Crispin's hands. He'll take care of her."

Over the comm, Venz broke in. "The govies just pulled up. They're surrounding the building."

"We need to go," Mina said.

CHAPTER THIRTY-FOUR

Alarms screamed. Their piercing sounds breached the air, making Arden's head throb. Lights in the corridors and rooms flashed blue, strobing the walls with continuous blinks of color. The vid-projectors along the console went blank, their foggy images dissipating into the air.

And then nothing.

It was quiet. The alarms shut off, but the whirling lights remained on: blue-white-blue-white.

The machines lining the console didn't restart as Venz had said they would. He'd assured them that once the other team loaded the worm, it would force the system to reload and they'd have access to the station. Yet everything remained off.

They waited and . . . nothing.

She fought her rising panic. None of them had the skills to figure out how to crack into the system. Everything was centralized. If the worm didn't work, if the other team hadn't loaded it in time, then— well, she wouldn't go down without a fight.

It would be horrible to come all this way and not get what they sought, a waste of their lives. But she had no compunction against killing them instead of surrendering. She'd already done that to get in. If they caught her, she'd be dead anyway or locked up here and tortured. Might as well take out a few before she died.

Arden was just deciding how best to make her last stand when the console kicked on. Then the visiprojectors hummed to life. The vapor appeared, forming into images. A long display flashed across the projection, a series of numbers that continued to scroll and grow and change over the seconds. All stuff she didn't understand. And then the screen flicked twice, and the system opened and looked normal. In the center of the screen, the CRC logo twirled.

"Oh, thank the moons," Arden hissed out.

The worm had worked. The release of tension made her feel a little sick, like being chucked out of a building without light wings.

Arden stepped up to the console, and her fingers flew on the light board. She opened all the doors within the center capsule. They didn't know which room the formula would be kept in, and there was no time to be precise about it. Once that was done, she turned back to the others.

They each had their assigned duties. Annem was supposed to do all the system stuff. There were a lot of files to be located and data to be collected. They might be here for the VitD recipe, but that didn't mean Mina wasn't going to make the most of their time and access there. Venz had gone over all the details with Annem. They'd worked through as many scenarios as Venz could think of.

The other three—Arden, Niall, and Coco—were supposed to find the recipe.

But now it appeared that wasn't going to happen. Annem was pale, her body curled on the floor. She hadn't woken up.

Coco sat beside her. She'd removed the top corner of Annem's suit so she could get better access to her shoulder. Her hands worked over Annem's wound, using a second tube of quick-seal to stabilize her shoulder as much as possible, then wrapping gauze around the wound.

Time was their enemy. Niall was already at the door to the hub, gazing at Arden balefully. If they didn't have Annem to break into the system, then that part of the plan would get scrapped. It wasn't the focus of this mission anyway. Mina would have to deal with it.

"Coco," Arden said, "we need to go."

Coco finished redressing Annem but didn't look up. The bandage under the suit made Annem's shoulder bulky. "I was there when Venz taught Annem the system. What if I break into it, instead? I can get the files. It's the only choice we have."

It wasn't, not really. They could decide not to retrieve information from the mainframe. It was only a data-mining expedition anyway, to see if there was anything they could use in the future. Mina would complain about the lost opportunity, but then Arden had also overheard Mina tell Coco not to let Niall out of her sight. She had sounded very explicit with her warning.

"You need to go with them, I'll be fine." Annem's voice was no more than a whisper. Her eyes closed. It surprised Arden that she'd woken. Arden had thought for sure the pain would knock Annem out for a good long while.

"I'm not leaving you," Coco said, her words mostly a sob. She shook her head repeatedly in disbelief and frustration. "They can figure it out. When the doors open again, you and I have to make it out of the CRC. So I'm going to stay here and work this system and make sure you stay alive."

She was trusting the most important part of the mission to Niall and Arden. Coco gave Arden a look of warning, her eyes narrowing as she then looked at Niall. "Don't screw up."

Niall and Arden unloaded their equipment, leaving behind their blast-phasers and packs, only taking their sidearms and knives with them. They needed to move swiftly and the extra weight would slow them down.

The halls were lined with rooms, and all the doors were open. Bodies were slumped in most of them. They walked with their phasers at the ready, checking each room in case the sleeping gas didn't vent correctly.

Arden had a general idea of what they were looking for, a cabinet of sorts perhaps. Somewhere the govies would label and store physical specimens. She moved into each room, clearing it fast. If it didn't look like it contained what she wanted, they moved on.

The VitD formula could be kept anywhere. It could be any size for that matter. Mina hadn't been specific, despite Arden's pushing her for answers. Though she did tell Arden not to worry, that she'd know it when she saw it. Whatever that meant.

Irritation clawed at Arden. She worked her way down the hall with no clear direction. They could look for days without success. She'd know it when she saw it—*whatever*. Only knowing scattered pieces of a plan irritated her to the core. Arden didn't understand why everything had to be so damned secretive.

She liked to collect secrets too. Yet she'd never sent people on a mission blind. Hadn't thought Mina would either. Arden couldn't stop the curl of betrayal from forming inside her soul.

The center ring of the CRC was a lot larger and more intricate than she'd been led to believe. They'd made it through one hall and started on another. Arden poked her head into a couple of rooms. They looked like offices or lab facilities, nowhere to hide something important.

She'd suspected that the job would be hard, but she was losing faith that they'd find the recipe. Then bad scenarios started playing through her mind, and she noted everything that could go wrong. Annem was already hurt. Maybe the recipe wasn't here either. Perhaps this whole plan was a ruse for something else. She wouldn't put that past Mina. And if that turned out to be the case, she was going to make Mina pay.

Arden paused to sweep another room. When she stepped back into the hall, she saw Niall turning a corner far ahead.

At first he had pretended to check the rooms on the other side of the hall from her. That had morphed into only lazy glances as he'd passed them by. She'd thought it meant that he was as frustrated as she was with the search. Now he walked as if he'd honed in on something and knew exactly where to go.

She ran after him.

Niall ignored every open door. His head was dipped forward, and his stride had picked up. At the next turn, he stopped. Closed his eyes as if he were thinking about something. His head bobbed up and down in tune with whatever information was in his head. And then he made a left turn, followed shortly by another right.

Arden kept pace with him. She wanted to ask him all sorts of questions, the first of which was, "How do you know what you're looking for?" Instead, she kept her mouth shut and watched. Arden didn't want to remind him she was there. She couldn't risk him ditching her and taking the recipe for himself.

Niall was another person with deep, untold secrets.

Damn him.

The question of why she wanted to repair their relationship taunted her. Just because he was family didn't mean he deserved her loyalty and trust. He'd done nothing to earn it. Had disrespected it at every turn. And yet here he was again, clearly manipulating all of them.

There was a pleased sort of grin on his face, a smirk that she hadn't seen in years. He wanted to be here.

She walked directly behind him when he finally entered a room. And then she stopped in her tracks.

This room was some kind of vault. The walls were shiny with metal. Drawers in all shapes and sizes were cut into the walls. Some were large rectangles, some were thin, and others were small squares. All packed together so that they touched seam to seam, stacking from floor to ceiling. The light in the room reflected off the surfaces, making the room shine with blinding silver.

Arden squinted.

Just like Mina had predicted, she'd know it when she saw it. If any room held the secrets, it was here, embedded in the city's core. Now to figure out which box they needed. That would be a mess. There wasn't a label or numbering system on the drawers.

They didn't have time to check and open every box. She wondered what was in all the other drawers. What vast secrets were the govies hiding?

Two hunched figures were on the floor. Both unconscious from the gas. They were older and dressed in the scrubs all the scientists wore. The male closer to her had hit his head. There was a bit of blood smeared on the rack beside him at about hip height as if he'd smacked it as he fell. Arden saw only the legs and shoes of the other.

Niall was quiet beside her. His arms crossed over his chest as he stared at the wall. His gaze tracked the boxes. It looked as if he counted, starting at the top left and then down a specific row. He reached out his hand. It hovered over a drawer, then lowered to the one below it. He caressed the metal.

His grin was in full force now. Then he looked back at the two scientists.

Arden watched him with narrowed eyes. "Something you're not telling me?"

But of course he didn't answer.

Niall walked over to the closest scientist, the one with the head wound, then dragged him over to the wall. He stepped closer to the drawer. It was thin, and long, about a foot and a half in width. The metal was shiny under his fingers, yet it didn't take on his prints. He traced the edge with one hand before reaching down to lift the scientist's palm. The box was low enough that Niall only had to prop up the scientist's back so that his palm could reach the metal.

When the scientist's palm connected, the drawer slid silently open on hidden tracks.

Arden stepped to Niall's side to peer into the drawer along with him. The interior was lined with soft black material. Spheres rested atop it in several rows, each in its own divot. Every sphere had been etched with a different symbol. The spheres were small, pocketable. They were no bigger than the palm of her hand.

Niall ran his finger over the etched symbols, obviously looking for one in particular.

Bastard. He'd known exactly what they were looking for this whole time. All her assumptions that he'd planned this were now coming painfully true. Would she ever learn to shield herself against him?

He pulled out one of the spheres, holding it between his fingers. Twisting it in front of him as he examined it. His eyes squinted, but she saw in them his excitement, his burning triumph.

Arden reached out and snatched the sphere from his hand. She wanted a closer look at it, but more than that, she didn't trust him with it.

Niall looked up at her in surprise. Almost as if he'd forgotten she was there. Then his expression morphed into anger. He reached out to take the sphere back, but Arden stepped away.

She kept her hand curled in toward her chest until she was out of grabbing distance. The sphere was lighter than she'd imagined, almost weightless. She hadn't had a clear idea what they'd be looking for, but this mirrored bit of nothing wouldn't have been what she'd envisioned.

Arden twisted it as Niall had, wondering how to open it. The two symbols on its surface were concave. There was also a bit of a dip along the surface, bisecting the two symbols as if the sphere could separate in half. She pushed her glove-covered fingernail against one of the inset symbols, but nothing happened. Arden reached down to her calf for her knife, intending to dig the blade into the etching.

Niall reached forward but stopped just short of touching it. "Don't. If you try to break into it, the liquid inside will dissolve the tech-chip."

Arden paused. Placed the tip of her knife against the metal, standing immobile. "And the tech-chip does what?"

"Holds the recipe, of course."

But if that were true, wouldn't someone—anyone—on this godforsaken planet remember how it was made? No. If there was a tech-chip, the recipe was so much more than just how to make VitD.

Niall held his hand out for the sphere.

She ignored it. Arden reached down to slide her knife back, keeping her gaze on Niall. Then she stood up and slid the sphere into her utility belt. "We've got what we came for. Time to go."

Niall stood there and looked at her, the hatred he felt for her naked on his face. Tension vibrated between them, though he didn't make a move toward her.

Arden forced herself not to react. To stay just as calm as he appeared to be. She kept her breathing even, her hand open and loose at her side.

He gave her a tight smile, then turned back to the drawer and extracted another two spheres. His choice wasn't random. Niall stopped and started several times searching for specific shapes.

"What are those?" she asked as he slipped two of the spheres into his own utility belt.

"It's not your concern."

She wanted to press him on the spheres. Mina was after the VitD recipe. He was clearly after something else.

Niall turned to the door. "Right, let's go."

Arden hesitated, but Niall had already exited the room.

She followed, realizing he hadn't turned back toward the center of the maze where Coco and Annem waited for them. Instead, he'd turned the opposite way, going deeper into the halls. This time he didn't pretend not to know where he was going. Niall navigated with the surety of having been here before.

She ran after him. He didn't slow or wait for her to catch up. A couple of times she lost him around a corner before sighting him again.

She became afraid of where he was headed. That this was a trap. And yet, she still followed and clung tight to her caution.

Arden skidded to a halt when he finally entered a room. She peered inside, realizing it was a refrigeration room. A clear heavy plastic covered the doorway. In spite of it, cold air seeped out.

She pushed past the plastic and stepped inside, cautious in case he was waiting to jump her. Arden's hand slid to her phaser.

The room was filled with open shelving with rows of vials and containers of liquid. Some looked to be blood samples, perhaps, and others various kinds of serums. She saw a wall of locked cabinets with moonglass doors. Inside were even more specimens. These looked like drug samples of some kind. Everything in the room was clearly labeled and kept with a neat efficiency.

She didn't see Niall right away. She stepped farther into the room and began to travel the length of it, looking down each aisle. She found him near the back, staring into a shelf. His hands moved over the vials there.

"What is this place?" What she really wanted to know was what dangerous liquid he was trying to find.

"Why do you think Mina wanted the recipe?" Niall asked her, instead. He didn't even bother to look up from what he was doing. "She saved Dade and put this all in motion. They could have easily infiltrated the CRC without him."

Arden was silent.

"She wanted you," Niall said.

Arden shook her head. "She wanted *you*. And she needed me to bring you here. Because you knew which sphere to take." She probably even hoped that Arden would convince Niall to join them so she could pick his brain of all his secrets.

Niall grinned at her toothily. "She didn't know that I'd come happily because it serves my purpose. But you did, you suspected."

Arden's lips flattened. She had. She should have said something, told Dade or Mina her suspicions. At least then they could have planned for this. Because there was no doubt she was about to be betrayed. Her blood roared in her ears, but she forced herself to ask, "Letting me know what you've done here serves your purpose too, doesn't it? So tell me, then, what is it that you want?"

"I want you to consider your life," he bit out. "Just like I've been saying all these years. What is Mina going to do with the recipe? Are you going to let her take it from you? Sit back and watch as she becomes the most powerful woman on this planet?"

She had considered that. But she wasn't about to share her thoughts with him. "Are you saying you want me to join you in . . ." She paused and looked around. Then she raised an eyebrow. "In whatever it is you're doing?"

Niall ignored her, turning away. He looked through another rack of vials.

Arden saw a blinding shade of red. She was sick of being ignored and treated as if she didn't deserve any explanation. That ended now. She took out her phaser and shot the shelving next to him, sending glass and liquid exploding.

Niall jumped back. Then let out an audible breath and glared at her. "Was that necessary?"

She shrugged. "I wanted your attention."

He turned away from her to another shelf, scanning its contents quickly. There were vials of liquid in shades of red, blue, yellow, green. Some of the formulas were thick, some bubbly, some shining as if they had stars inside.

"What are we doing here, Niall?"

"Getting our freedom back."

Arden scrunched her nose. "Freedom? From whom?"

"From everyone." He was tucked within the shelf. She couldn't see his head as he moved the contents around. Then he grunted in success. Pulling back, he held a vial in his hand.

The liquid inside was metallic silver. It looked thick, sticking to the sides like syrup, leaving traces of residue, as it swirled around. Lights, like glowing embers of starlight, seemed to shoot through. They were mesmerizing.

There wasn't a name on it that she could see. Out of everything here, the vial Niall wanted wasn't labeled. That made her nervous and set her heart to pounding.

"What are you going to do with it?" she asked.

He gave her an enigmatic look. Then he flicked the end so that the needle protruded, extending a thumb depressor on the other side. He held it upside down and flicked the moonglass while subtly pushing at the thumb gauge to remove air bubbles.

She stood frozen, not fully believing what he was about to do. But when he moved the injector to his arm, she cried, "Don't."

Niall didn't stop.

Arden felt as if the air had been sucked from her body. She couldn't believe it. She knew he was going to do something, but not this.

His face crumpled—eyes squinting, then flying wide in pain. He cried out, a wet, hoarse sound. Then he shifted on his feet, stumbling, before dropping to the floor.

She was on him in an instant, trying to ease him over to check whether he was still breathing. His body began to shake in her hands, and then he screeched in agony. She pushed back his head, making sure his airway was clear.

Then he stopped moving. His eyes had rolled back into his head. His mouth went slack.

"Niall." She shook him, needing him to wake up. There was no way she could get him back to the others. They already had to worry about Annem. She couldn't carry him by herself.

Arden checked his pulse.

Panic crawled up her chest. It clogged her throat, lodging there. What was she supposed to do? She didn't like Niall much, but she didn't want him to die either.

Niall sucked in a deep breath. His eyes shifted and rolled, and then squeezed shut. He hacked a deep cough that ended in a wheeze.

Arden sat back on her butt, too surprised to feel relief. She reached forward. "Niall?"

It took him a while to answer, to eventually look at her. His eyes were clear, though shadowed with pain. He let out a deep groan. "I didn't expect it to hurt that bad."

"Are you crazy?" she yelled. She wanted to hit him, though she knew that wouldn't do any good. Instead of taking her anger out physically, she helped him sit up. It was far less satisfying. "What did you inject?"

He stared at her for what felt like forever, but was probably only a second. Then he pushed her away and stood up on shaky feet. "It dissolves the tracker Mina implanted and eats the govies' data sensor, too. It eats anything that's been implanted in the body. I'm completely off the grid now. The govies can't find me. Mina can't find me. I'm free." He took off his blackout band and let it fall to the ground. "I won't need that anymore."

Normally, uncovering the data chip that lay beneath that skin would immediately put Niall back onto the grid for the govies to track if they weren't inside the CRC. But if he was right, he was no longer on it. He'd become completely unregistered and untrackable. And, if he was caught, it meant certain death.

Arden blinked. The information slowly clicked itself into place. Freedom. He'd meant freedom from everything, everyone. Quick on the heels of that understanding, another realization struck. That meant he couldn't go back to Mina's hideout. She had been clear that no one could get in without a tracker.

Narrowing her eyes, Arden got to her feet.

"I'm giving you a chance to come with me," Niall said.

Her thoughts spun with all the possibilities. It wasn't like she wanted to stay. She didn't like the fact she'd been manipulated by Mina. But there was Dade to consider. She wouldn't leave him. "Why would you want me to go with you? You don't trust me. You've made that clear."

He considered her, an unreadable expression on his face. "Because if you don't, then I will be forced to kill you."

Arden swallowed hard at his words. Not that she was afraid. It was at the finality of the statement. That he could make it in the first place. "I can't go with you."

Niall snarled. He held his hand out. "Fine, your death is on you. Now, give me the sphere."

Like hell.

Arden rolled her eyes. "You really think I'm going to do that?"

Niall snatched his phaser from the side of his hip and pointed it at the center of her chest. His eyes were manic, bright and feverish. "Do it, or I'll shoot you and take it. I'm not leaving here without it."

Arden sucked in a harsh breath. She looked from him to the phaser and back again. Fury heated her from the inside out. She felt the warmth in her belly and in the stain on her cheeks. How dare he threaten to kill her.

Her hands lifted halfway. She kept her palms open. Arden had been right not to trust him. She snatched her own phaser from her hip and aimed it at him. "I won't stop you from leaving with the other two spheres."

She didn't promise not to collect them later.

"I don't think so, little sister." He grinned. "Unlike me, you won't shoot."

"Wouldn't I?"

"You've gone soft," he continued to taunt. "I've watched you. You let emotion rule you now. You should know better."

Arden frowned. What could she say to that? It was true. Perhaps she was weak.

"Now, hand over the sphere," he said.

"No."

And then . . . he pulled the trigger.

Arden blinked. Damn, he really did it. He really shot at her. She couldn't believe it.

Niall's brow scrunched, and he pulled the trigger again.

Arden went from disbelief to frustration in a flash. She may have been weakened by emotions, but she wasn't irrational. "I took out the phaser core of your sidearm. You really should do a pre-op check, you know."

She had suspected something but hadn't really believed it. Unfortunately, her fears had come true. It broke her heart. He'd tried to kill her.

"You sent me in here without a weapon? What if I'd been shot?" Niall threw his phaser away.

"Calm down. Your blast-phaser worked. Good thing you left it in the hub with Coco and Annem," Arden said with a laugh, referring to the long battle-phaser, and not the small sidearm phaser he'd discarded. "It looks like I was right. You tried to shoot me. I don't regret that choice at all."

"You know, Arden," he said in that condescending voice that grated on her nerves, "you need to get your shit together."

"Excuse me? I'm the one with the phaser on you, remember?" She shook it at him as a reminder.

"Figure out who you are and stop blindly following people." Then he turned and walked out of the room, saying as he left, "You're on your own. Good luck."

She didn't stop him. He'd been right about that too. She couldn't shoot him. She had changed somehow. Perhaps she'd become a kinder person. Right now that was aggravating.

Arden sighed. There he went, always walking out of her life.

Chapter thirty-five

Arden made it back to the center hub. She was slightly out of breath, and her body shook. Pausing at the door before entering the room where Coco and Annem waited, she took a moment to focus her thoughts. She pushed aside everything she felt, the anger and resentment, the pain of having been betrayed yet again. *Damn Niall.* She was going to murder him. And screw him for forcing her to make that decision. Blood on her hands was one thing, yet killing her brother would go past what her conscience could easily forgive. But eventually she'd have to do it because he'd make it necessary.

He'd been right. She would always hesitate to kill him. Even though Arden knew she would have to when the time came, the thought of killing her brother made the aching, yawning pit in her stomach roil with acid.

Not that she could think about it now. That jerk had better make it out of here, because she wanted to have that showdown.

Annem hadn't moved from the floor. Her breathing was still punctuated with short staccato inhales. She'd lost too much blood. Coco had done her best to stanch it, yet it had soaked into the fabric of the suit and left smears on the floor.

Arden wondered whether their plan would work if Annem's suit was damaged that much. They'd have to try regardless.

Coco stood at the console with her back to the door. Her fingers were moving swiftly across the light board, gathering as much intel as possible. And yet she kept glancing over to Annem to make sure she was okay.

The alarms had started again, and the pulsing blue lights switched to red.

"They're opening the ring doors," Arden said. "They'll get to the center soon enough. We need to go."

Coco startled and turned around. She looked at Arden, then looked behind her, nose crinkling. "Where's Niall?"

Arden shook her head. Sometimes words were difficult. How could she explain his betrayal toward her? He'd betrayed their group too. There was always the sense of familial guilt whenever he let her down, even if the blame didn't belong to her.

Coco scowled. "That prick."

"Agreed."

"You know I'm going to kill him, right?"

Arden sighed. "So am I."

"Okay, just wanted to make sure we were on the same page." Coco turned back around to the console and quickly finished her task, then made sure the CRC logo appeared as if the mainframe had just been booted.

Arden went to Annem and knelt beside her. She put Annem's air-breather back on and pulled up the extra fabric in her neck cowl so that there was no exposed skin anywhere on her body. Then she did the same for herself.

This was a terrible place to try out Venz's new suits. They'd tested them in the hideout, sure. If they were caught, the worst that could happen here was not death. It was capture. That made Arden's anxiety skyrocket.

He'd fashioned them using the net-tech he'd created to hide their hovervan. As long as every bit of skin was covered, they should be near-invisible, blending in with their surroundings. Except of course, if the illusion was broken, they'd just have to fight their way out. The halo-glass and air-breather were covered in a thin fabric coating as well. He'd also woven in a shield to cut off their heat signature, then calibrated the halo-glass so that they could see one another.

By all accounts, it should work. The govies' gaze should slide off them, and they'd simply walk out as long as they didn't draw attention to themselves.

Though that also meant that they had to leave behind their blast-phasers. Any weapon that had to be hand carried was ditched in order not to break the illusion. It didn't leave them completely without weapons, however. Arden still had two phasers at her hip, and two knives at her calves. All four were in sheaths of net-tech. They would have to stay hidden, unless it all went to shit.

Once they were suited up, Arden activated her net-tech. Coco did the same. Arden looked over at her to make sure the halo-glass could get a read. There was a fuzzy shimmer around Coco. Her features were distorted. But Arden could see her shape, and that was enough.

"I've got a lock on you," Arden said.

Coco looked to Arden. "Same."

Then they turned on Annem's suit. At first she went shimmery too. But then it started to flicker.

Coco swore.

The damage that Annem's suit had taken must have broken the weave, making it unable to connect the circuit. "Did you close the hole in the back?"

"No," Coco said.

"We need to bind it together."

"With what?"

Arden looked around. Her gaze landed on the open med kit. "Do you have any more quick-seal?"

Coco dumped the contents of the box on the ground, rifling around until she found a tube. "It's meant to hold skin."

"Well, it needs to hold fabric till we can get the hell out of here. Then it can fall apart for all I care."

Arden pulled Annem so that her front faced Arden, her back to Coco. Reaching around Annem, Arden gathered the fabric and pulled it together. The fabric curled back, wanting to separate.

Annem moaned.

Coco went to work sealing up the fabric, whispering encouragement to Annem as she did so. She leaned forward to blow on the quick-seal in an attempt to dry it faster.

Annem's blinking suit went shiny with a hazy glow.

"We don't have much time." Arden was already moving Annem to stand, while still keeping her in her arms.

She shifted to one side while Coco came up on the other. Together they lifted Annem between them. Annem cried out as her arm was lifted over Coco's shoulder.

"I know," Coco crooned. "But I can't carry you by myself."

It took them some trial and error to start moving out of the room. They stood by the door leading into the next set of rings, waiting for it to open. Annem was slung between them. Her head dipped forward, and Arden could hear her panting.

Arden felt her hot breath venting back to her inside the air-breather. Her body was tense, but she held it still, allowing no movement to ruin the illusion of the net-tech.

Waiting was the worst. If she could move, if she could be doing something, then she wouldn't feel so useless.

She used the time to map out their route in her head, to prepare herself for any eventuality. They had to get through the entire facility in order to escape into the city. Her heartbeat pounded as she mentally calculated the distance. They'd take each ring efficiently, watching for traps. All the doors would be open. There would be hundreds of govies roaming the halls.

It wasn't about speed. It was about calculation and avoidance. Though it was a bit difficult to sneak through the halls with an injured person.

Arden had no doubt the others were safe. They only had to make it out of the first ring to cross to the outside. That could be done easily enough simply by slipping past the first wave of govies.

She, Coco, and Annem could do this too. They were strong. Yet if anything happened, she knew the others had the same philosophy she did. It was get out of here or die. There were no other options.

Finally the door to the next ring opened. Govies poured in. They were suited up with blast-phasers. They wore their govie-greens with helmets and phase shields pulled down to cover their faces.

Arden felt her tension wind up, and yet a calm also settled over her. A peacefulness that let her know that they were about to do something amazing. The high of adrenaline was starting to spike in her system, and she grinned.

They waited until the door was clear enough to move through it three people wide. It became a jigsaw getting through the maze of hallways. They'd have to back up sometimes or turn sideways. Often having to press against the wall for minutes at a time until it was clear enough for them to move through.

Two rings from the exit, Coco said in a whisper through the comm, "We're leaving a blood trail."

Arden looked over her shoulder. The blood from Annem's wound had soaked through the suit. She glanced at the floor. It wasn't bad, a few drops every so many feet. Then she checked the wall they'd been pressed against and saw the smear.

Fantastic.

It wouldn't be long until that would be seen. The trail led straight to them. "We need to move faster."

Coco nodded, and they increased their speed to a near run. They started taking more risks. Slinking through even tighter spaces. They no longer waited for areas to be empty, instead simply striding past govies who were still clearing rooms. There was no time for caution.

Movement stirred in the halls. She could feel the alertness before she heard the alarm, the squeak of instructions given to the govies. Arden heard someone say, "Blood."

Her heart raced and her body pumped. Straining her muscles, she pushed them harder. The three of them didn't bother moving silently anymore. The words *Get out, get out, get out* played a drumbeat in Arden's head.

They had made it to the last ring when Annem groaned and then fell. She slipped down between Coco and Arden, her knees hitting the floor.

Arden clawed at Annem with nearly numb fingers, her grip loosened from holding on too long. Her breath caught in her throat.

On Annem's other side, Coco did the same, reaching for Annem. They moved together, pulling Annem up, although now she felt as if she weighed even more. Her body was completely limp. She couldn't walk at all any longer. They'd have to carry her the rest of the way.

"They're in the corridor." A shout followed by a phase-blast nearly took Arden's head off. She ducked, her hand reaching for her phaser. She returned the blast.

It was chaos.

Coco pulled her phaser too. They were shooting, and running, and hauling Annem's prone body between them. Arden doubted any of their blasts made contact.

The govies shouted. Telling one another to shoot where their eyes couldn't focus. The illusion of invisibility was broken.

"We're not going to make it," Coco panted.

"Yes, we are." And they were because she was not going to die here. Arden had too much to live for. They were in the last ring, and they just had to make it through the blast hole. But there were too many govies congregated there. "I think it's time for plan B."

Coco nodded. "On three."

Arden nodded, and counted down. The original net-tech the suit was made from would have taken out the car if anyone had tampered with it. Venz had done some restructuring. The modified version wouldn't blow them up, instead emitting a shock wave that would knock out everything surrounding them.

Together Arden and Coco engaged their suits. There was a flash of light followed by a high-frequency sound that wiped out the govies closest to them. They fell, washing out like a ripple in a puddle before the girls. The nearest went down first. Followed by those behind them, and so on, until the entire group surrounding the exit lay on the ground. Arden could see blood trailing out the closest govies' ears. She turned away.

"Run," she said through bloodless lips. And they took flight, because their lives depended on it.

CHAPTER THIRTY-SIX

The door slid open, letting out the balmy air from inside. The church was kept warm, welcoming. Though Arden always felt that she should be a better person to enter this place. Or at least she should *want* to be a better person. Accepting that life was full of crap and then scraping to survive was the antithesis of believing that everything would work out in the end.

But she didn't look down on others for needing the peace that came with this place. It comforted Dade. She was glad for that. Sometimes she wished she could also believe in some sort of steady presence in her life.

Arden stepped into the vestibule. Annem still hung between her and Coco. Annem's head lolled on Coco's shoulder. She'd come to after they'd made it out to the streets, but in the last quarter mile, she'd passed out again and they'd had to carry her.

The streets had been silent. Arden had heard only the splash of their feet on the cold, wet stone as they'd hurried up the front steps. The lights were dim in deference to the lateness of the hour. Though it was always dark in the Levels. Inside, the church was just as quiet. It was around two in the morning, but the front doors remained unlocked. She wasn't sure if there even was a lock.

Still, despite the empty streets and the time, it was dicey to meet here and not somewhere more private. But there was a purpose to it. As expected, the govies had shut down the streets around the CRC. Arden and the group had known that for at least a few hours, there would be no way to get out of the district without tipping off their location. And they knew they had to stay in the Levels. They couldn't take their prey, the one whom Nastasia and Venz would bring soon, down into Undercity.

They'd needed a place with deniability. The church wasn't bugged, and the city's cameras couldn't monitor them inside. As long as they stayed in the public areas, the church was open to all and therefore couldn't be held responsible for their nefarious activities if they were discovered there.

Arden, Coco, and Annem entered the main sanctuary and started down the aisle. Flickering candles left most of the expanse shadowed, and she didn't see any priests. It smelled of age, candle wax, and lingering spices from the ceremonial smoke. She often thought this was what God must smell like if he was real.

Annem moaned softly. It would be hours until they could get her to a medical facility where she could get looked at properly. Father Benedict would have medical supplies. Hopefully they would stabilize her in the meantime.

They headed toward where Mina, Roan, and Saben were using a pew near the front. The girl they'd rescued lay on a bench, Mina leaning over her. Arden was too far away to see the girl properly over the high seat back. But she saw that they'd covered her with a blanket, and she looked worse than Annem.

Arden looked around the sanctuary for Dade and couldn't find him. Anxiety tightened her chest. Her heart stuttered to a hard pulsing beat. She refused to believe that something had happened.

They were halfway down the center aisle when Roan looked up. He took them in for a full heartbeat before he made a low sound of distress at the state of Annem. That snagged Mina's attention, whose sharp gaze snapped up. Saben, who'd been loitering near the raised dais at the front, straightened and stepped their way.

Then it was a blur of action.

Roan was the first to get to them. His arm slipped around Annem, pulling her into him. Annem's head lolled against his chest, and then Roan scooped her up under her knees.

Coco quickly stepped after them, not letting Roan get too far ahead as he went toward the bench where they'd placed the other girl.

"What happened?" Mina asked Coco, turning to follow as well.

Arden sagged. She was exhausted. The night felt like it had stretched on for hours, and sleep was still a long way off. She pulled at reserves that she didn't quite have.

Saben stepped up beside her. "Are you okay?"

"I will be." She tried not to let her fear bleed into her question. "Where's Dade?"

"He's in the back. Father Benedict isn't doing well."

There was relief that Dade hadn't been hurt. On the heels of that, she felt bad for Father Benedict. And for Dade, who would be devastated when the priest died. Father Benedict was more of a father to Dade than his own had been. A confidant, someone who provided a place where Dade could feel peace.

Father Benedict suffered from Violet Death. He'd been sick the last time Arden had seen him. His skin molded with the purple veining, open sores swallowing up his body. She hadn't thought that he had much time to live then. Without any medical shipments, he must have gone downhill even further. She knew Dade would take it hard and blame himself. Especially since he hadn't been delivering regular VitD supplies here.

Arden didn't want to face the others quite yet. She wandered down the pews and sat at the back of the church. Her exhaustion didn't help with everything else that weighed on her. Too wrapped up in taking care of Annem, they hadn't noticed Niall wasn't there. But the confrontation was coming. And Arden didn't have enough mental stamina to deal with it.

She watched as they got Annem situated and fussed over her. Another blanket appeared to drape over the girl. She heard Mina murmur reassurance to Coco. "She'll be okay for now. Don't worry, she'll make it."

Coco squeezed her eyes shut and nodded. She was kneeling beside Annem's head. And then she bent low so that Arden couldn't see her anymore behind the bench.

Regret was an oppressive thing. It squeezed her. Taunted her. Told her that no matter how hard she tried and what choices she made, the outcome would always be this: brokenness. It was not fair. But then, her entire life hadn't been fair. She'd have to deal with it as she always did, by moving forward.

Mina slid out of the bench where the two girls lay and made her way up the aisle. Her gaze was intense, pinning Arden like a bug to a board. As Mina's gaze slid off her to check the rest of the sanctuary, Arden knew what was coming next.

Arden didn't want this to be a confrontation, and the best way to avoid it was to act like it didn't matter. She leaned back, sprawled her legs, and forced herself to relax against the wood. The pew bit into her back, reminding her not to get too comfortable.

"Where is he?" Mina asked, assuming Niall had bailed.

It wasn't the wrong assumption, clearly. But it still pissed Arden off. She honestly couldn't say why. Perhaps it was because she'd tried to give Niall a chance even when he'd proven himself untrustworthy. And she usually was suspicious of everyone. It felt like a reflection on her judgment.

Arden shrugged. "I don't know."

There was nothing to say. No excuses to be given. She hadn't been privy to Niall's plan. He'd ditched her once again and left her to pick up the pieces of his betrayal.

Roan had followed Mina up the aisle. His teeth were gritted, and he made to step around Mina. "Why did you let him go?"

Mina stuck out her arm and held him back.

Arden snorted. If they thought she had control over Niall, then they were more ridiculous than she was. She refused to take the blame. Arden gave them a quick rundown of what happened. Leaving out the fact that Niall had nicked the two other spheres and that he'd used the serum to burn out all his trackers. And perhaps she embellished the end a little bit. Maybe "forgot" to tell them that she'd neutralized Niall's phaser and let him walk out the door.

She didn't think it was wrong not to tell them. Call it self-preservation. Since Mina kept secrets from her, it was only fair. Until Arden figured out what was really going on, she'd keep her mouth locked up tight.

"What did you want me to do?" Arden asked. She wasn't about to sit here and be lectured by Roan.

"Shoot the bastard?" he said sarcastically.

Yes, there would have been immediate satisfaction for frying his lying, deceiving ass. She honestly wished she'd at least wounded him a little. But she would let him walk out that door again, given the same circumstances. He had things and information she wanted, and he served her purpose better alive.

Alive and not with Mina.

Which perhaps circled right around to where her frustration came in. Arden had realized that after today, she needed to start playing the long game. Dade's read of the situation made sense to her. He was right. If she wanted to win, she needed to be the one in charge of making the decisions in her life.

While Roan bitched, Mina frowned. She wasn't happy. That was evident. But she wasn't really surprised either. Not if she'd told Coco to watch him. Arden wondered if anything shook her, if she wasn't already three steps ahead. If Mina ended up being Arden's opponent, she wasn't sure who would win. Mina wouldn't be an easy enemy to defeat.

Mina watched Arden with those too-calculating eyes. Seeing what?

Arden wasn't sure she wanted to know. She locked gazes with Mina.

Then Roan said, "Tell me you at least got the sphere."

The question allowed her to look away from Mina. That she could answer honestly. "I did."

"He didn't take it?" Mina's eyes narrowed.

"He tried to."

"Probably let her get away with it because he needed us to open it," Roan muttered. "The bastard will come back for it."

Arden pulled the sphere from her utility belt. She held it out in the palm of her hand. "Here."

Mina looked from the sphere to Arden. Then her shoulders relaxed slightly. "Let's hope this is the one we want."

Roan snickered. "Right? Because I'm not going back."

Mina reached forward and plucked the sphere from Arden's palm. She inspected it. Pinching it, holding it close to her face. She stuck her fingernail into the grooves.

Roan looked over her shoulder. His eyes gleamed, and Arden could tell that he wanted to pluck it out of Mina's hand but he didn't dare. "Now all we have to do is open it."

CHAPTER THIRTY-SEVEN

Dade heard shouting when he stepped into the sanctuary from the back rooms of the church. He'd left Father Benedict, not knowing if it was the last time he'd ever see him. His heart sat heavy, and he didn't know how to process the loss.

He breathed out in frustration. He'd deal with this one last thing on this never-ending night, and then he could crawl into bed.

The yelling focused him. He watched as Venz and Nastasia stepped in from the vestibule, wrangling a trussed-up man between them. The man's hands were electro-cuffed behind his back, and there was a hood over his face. He had a good deal of weight on the slim-built pair. As he fought, the two struggled to keep him still. He cursed, promising world-ending retribution. They weren't empty threats. His voice sounded loud in the cavernous sanctuary, echoing back at them.

Nastasia said, "Shut it or I'll gag you," and gave him a push.

Dade didn't need to get any closer to know who it was they had. The man had been in his Sky Tower practically every day of his childhood.

They led Nakomzer halfway down the church to the opposite side from where Kallow and Annem reclined. Roan and Mina stepped forward to help.

Roan shoved the man down onto the pew. "You could have tranked him."

"Then we'd have to carry him," Nastasia said sourly.

Nakomzer made a noise as he fell into the seat. He immediately tried to get up, but Roan just pushed him down again. Mina, Roan, Venz, and Nastasia formed a blockade around him, boxing him in with their bodies.

Dade was weary. This confrontation with Nakomzer was necessary, yes, but he didn't want to watch it. Tonight had been a tumult of emotions. Seeing the pain of the people held inside the CRC. The overwhelming knowledge of finding out his sister was alive. Wondering what the govies had done to Kallow. Worried that he couldn't figure out a way to keep Crispin from taking her. Knowing that he couldn't save Father Benedict's life. He felt useless and he hated it.

His gaze sought out the only person he wanted to be with right now.

Arden sat at the back of the church apart from the rest. She looked up, and their gazes met. Her eyes glittered as she stood and walked the aisle toward him.

His feet moved. He wanted to be with her and couldn't wait. He needed her closeness. Wanted to hold her, to give some solidness to his life, to tie him to this place. His emotions were too out of order, and he needed an anchor.

Arden looked exhausted, perhaps a little broken. Her gaze was alert, but the pockets of her eyes were bruised. Sadness felt like a deep part of her. It had been growing for a while. He knew she struggled with it. But perhaps after whatever had happened tonight, she no longer could hold it back.

He realized he hadn't seen Niall yet. A quick glance around confirmed he wasn't there. Dade frowned and gave her a questioning look. She rolled her eyes in response.

They met in the aisle. He opened his arms, and she fell into them. Holding her was a balm to his soul. He was oblivious to everyone and everything, savoring the moment. He breathed her in as he tucked her closer. When he felt like they'd both regained some modicum of peace, he leaned down and kissed her.

It was a kiss of reassurance, of connection. More deepness of feeling than passion. His hands gently wound through her hair as she tipped her head back to meet him. Kissing her was like finding his other half, the mingling of breath and souls.

He pulled back.

She pressed her forehead against his chest and breathed out. "I want something different."

Dade wasn't sure what she meant, though he understood the sentiment. He wanted something different too.

He squeezed her tight and kissed the top of her head. Then he turned to lay his cheek against her crown. His head was turned now, toward the bench where he knew they'd laid out Kallow, and he realized that there was more than just one girl lying on the pew.

Kallow was still passed out, her eyes closed, her face tormented. He could see the bite of pain between her brows as if she were trapped in the nightmare of her mind. He wondered if she'd ever wake up.

It surprised him to see Annem on the pew just beyond her. Her body was twisted, so he couldn't get a good sense of how she'd been hurt. Coco leaned over her, her face pressed close to Annem's, whispering soft words, while her hand stroked Annem's hair.

Emotions clogged his throat. That could just as easily have been Arden lying there. He asked, "What happened?"

"What always happens." There was a deep bitterness in her words.

Dade was glad Arden had been spared, even if that made him self-ish. He remembered how broken she'd been after the joint refinery, and he didn't want to live that over again. Not now, and not ever.

The struggle at the other end of the church stole his attention. Nakomzer was shouting now.

Dade sighed. "I suppose we should go."

Arden nodded and pulled away.

Hand in hand, they walked to where the others held Nakomzer on the bench. Arden and Dade stood in the main aisle near the group. Neither of them wanted to get involved in the interrogation.

The others hadn't removed Nakomzer's blindfold. Most likely wouldn't. And they waited him out until he calmed down or at least realized he wasn't about to be rescued.

"Thank you for coming," Mina finally said when there was silence.

Nakomzer tilted his head to the side. "I know you." The words were muffled behind the hood.

She snorted. "Probably."

Dade was impressed that she didn't care whether he could place her. Her ability to navigate the city was unparalleled, and she clearly had no concern that Nakomzer could ruin that. She was one of the better-known dealers. Often shifting from being "legitimate" to deal in the more nefarious side of trade. She had access to public places like the skyport. Nakomzer would hunt her once he got away. She wouldn't be so careless unless she had another plan.

He swallowed. No, he'd never allow that to happen. Not that he had a particular fondness for Nakomzer, but he didn't believe in cold-blooded murder either. He'd probably feel the need to rescue Nakomzer. And he didn't owe that man anything.

"What am I doing here?" Nakomzer demanded. His tone was the same as always, dripping with authority, even if he was trussed up.

"You have something I need," Mina said.

Nakomzer shook his head. "I won't help you. You will get nothing from me. *Nothing*. And when I find out who you are, you're dead."

Mina gave a rare, genuine laugh, bright and throaty. "Such lofty threats. But it's all right, we don't need your cooperation." She pulled her knife out from the sheath at her side. "We just need your blood."

"Couldn't we have done this without him?" Venz looked a little sick.

Mina smiled at him. "It has to be fresh from the source. There's a temperature requirement, and it counts the nano-bite particles in the cells. I'm sure he takes nanites to counteract a correct reading if we stored a blood sample."

Nakomzer started to thrash again. He moved so far down the pew that Roan had to step in to shove him back into place.

"There's no way you'll keep it." Obviously he knew that they needed his blood to open the sphere, and that they had the sphere in the first place. "They'll find it. They'll find *you*. And when they do, you're all dead."

"I'm shaking," Mina said dryly. Then she instructed Roan and Nastasia, "Hold him."

Nakomzer really started struggling then. He shifted and swore. Yet he couldn't get away from the hands grasping him. They pushed him down onto the bench so that his chest rested against it while the palms of his hands were upturned in the electro-cuffs.

Venz had stepped back from the action, his eyes wide and his mouth open.

Mina took the knife, slicing the fleshy part of Nakomzer's palm. The blood welled up, liquid scarlet dripping off the side of his flesh. Dade could tell that she cut deeper than necessary. To let Nakomzer know that she could do whatever she wanted and he couldn't stop her.

Nakomzer yelped.

This wasn't the real danger he faced, though. The cut could easily be med-sealed. It was the after, whatever Mina's plan turned out to be, that he should save his strength for.

Mina wiped the blade on her pant leg and then returned it to its sheath. Then she brought out the small silver sphere. Dade wanted to get a closer look at it, but he stayed back.

Gripping Nakomzer's hand, she rolled the sphere in the blood, coating it.

Then Dade stepped forward. His breath quickened.

The others had crowded around as well. Nakomzer, all but forgotten, gave up and slumped onto the pew.

Mina held her palm out flat, the sphere resting in the center. Its surface appeared solid. The blood pooled in its deep grooves, red turning to black before it soaked into the sphere and disappeared. There were two clinking sounds and then a mighty crack along the seam between the symbols, splitting the sphere into two.

Dade had expected something hidden inside that would change his world. Not this small black square. It looked like a piece of broken plastic. Like something he'd throw away if he didn't know better. Nothing he'd ever seen before, a tech-chip of some sort.

Venz's eyes gleamed. It was the first time Dade could remember him looking somewhat close to predatory.

Arden held out her hand. "May I see it?"

To her credit, Mina didn't hesitate to hand over the bit of plastic.

Arden squinted at the small black square. She held it up in front of her and twisted it this way and that.

A gust of wind from the vestibule pulled away Dade's attention. The front door had opened. From where he stood, he couldn't yet see who'd entered the church.

Arden turned as well, lowering her hand. She was the closest to the door and stepped forward to intercept the visitor. She stopped near the archway, and her body went rigid. Then she moved her hand to the side for her phaser.

Dade groaned as Crispin strolled in.

CHAPTER THIRTY-EIGHT

Dade couldn't fully wrap his head around what he saw. He'd known that they'd have to deal with Crispin soon, but he hadn't expected to do so tonight. Perhaps he should have. This was the perfect place to ambush them, especially if Crispin knew they had just pulled off the job.

Crispin swaggered into the church and down the aisle as if he owned the place. He looked happy—jolly even. He held his hands wide in greeting. "Hello, my friends."

An icy chill slid down Dade's back, and he found himself frozen. The others, aside from Arden, didn't go for their weapons. He understood why they couldn't fight here. The reasons for him were personal. He could never use a phaser in this sacred church. He owed Father Benedict everything. To destroy this church would hurt him, and Dade would never do that.

The others were more pragmatic: it wasn't good business to fight on neutral ground.

Which left them defenseless.

That didn't mean that Crispin was without weapons. He was dressed in a flashy burgundy tunic with a single phaser on his hip. It looked as if he'd just come from a party. He wore no fighting attire, not even a synth-vest. But then, he didn't need to. His other weapons followed behind him.

The Twins flanked his side. Their eyes glowed with bloodlust, and they wore daggerlike smiles. Not far behind them, another three mercenaries entered the church.

There was rustling in the back of the building, and Dade turned to see yet more armed mercenaries enter from the back of the nave.

They were boxed in.

Pressure built inside Dade. He nearly screamed with it. Whatever Crispin wanted couldn't be good, not with the backup he'd come with. He'd stacked the deck in his favor.

Dade swallowed back his frustration and tried to breathe. Breathe, focus, and wait. It was all he could do.

Arden looked pissed. Her mouth was a slash across her face, and her brow a thundercloud. Her body had gone preternaturally still, her expression promising Crispin she'd gut him where he stood.

A discordant note struck in Dade when he realized Mina wasn't surprised to see Crispin. Or at least she didn't appear to be. That could mean many things, for she was adept at hiding her thoughts. Still, if she had any idea this would happen, she should have warned him.

Mina said smoothly to Crispin, "I said I'd bring her to you."

No, no, no. Dade wasn't prepared to do this now. He needed time to plan, to figure out how to keep Kallow away from him.

Crispin's tone was still cheerful, and the smile never wavered. "I was in the neighborhood and thought I'd save you the trip."

It was difficult to tell who the most dangerous person was in the room. The tension ratcheted up with each lethal smile and well-placed word. Yet all Dade felt was sickness wash over him. His mind swam with it.

Crispin's gaze slid to the front of the church where Kallow lay. He made no move to retrieve her, and no emotion broke his genial expression. The question of who Kallow was to him, someone he cherished or someone he hated, was not answered. Dade wanted to know—needed to know. Knew that would make the difference in everything. That he might be willing to chance this if she was dear to Crispin.

"What do you want with her?" Dade forced himself to ask.

Crispin smiled, though it wasn't his usual jovial facade. This one was softer. "We have unfinished business, she and I."

That didn't sound good, but it didn't sound terrible either. Dade was torn. He had no way to stop this.

Crispin flicked his hand for a mercenary to retrieve Kallow. The big hulking man moved gracefully in spite of his size.

When he reached the pew, Coco moved aside silently but kept her body in front of Annem, blocking her from view. Her gaze remained level, and her body coiled. Her lips pulled slightly back from her teeth.

The man picked up Kallow. It was a gentle movement, as if she weighed nothing. She was still swaddled in the blanket that the priests had given her. Her body looked infinitely tiny. The man tucked her close and then walked past them all as he carried her out of the church.

Dade watched his every step, wanting that last glimpse of his sister. If only he'd known who she was. If only he had a plan to save her. But he was trapped by circumstance.

"What does that mean, that you have unfinished business?" Dade pressed. He barely dared to breathe. He felt his body grow colder as the minutes ticked steadily on.

"It means she will be a guest. I will take care of her and bring her back to good health. Provided she wakes." There was a frown on Crispin's face that Dade had never seen him wear.

The others watched, transfixed. All of them waiting for this farce to get to the point. Each of them unsure of Crispin's next move.

"I don't believe you."

"Dade," Mina said softly, "I told you, he won't hurt her. They were together."

The words should have calmed him. Instead, they struck like a bolt of electricity through him. Dade heard the "were" in that explanation and the caution in Mina's voice. He'd come to learn her subtle cues meant much more than the words she said. Crispin and Kallow may have once been lovers, but it seemed that a falling-out had happened. It did little to ease Dade's suspicion of Crispin. "I won't let you take her."

Crispin ignored Dade until the girl was outside the church. Once the front door slid shut, he addressed him. "Then it's just as well you're coming with us. After all, two Solizen in my power are better than one."

"What?" Arden growled beside Dade.

"I'm here for my collateral," Crispin said. "There's still a debt owed, after all."

"What are you talking about?" Dade asked. He should be more concerned, but honestly, he wasn't. This was his way to watch her. Kallow needed him. Whatever else, he could make sure she wasn't hurt and figure out a way to break them both out.

"I agreed to let you help Mina for a price. I never said she could keep you. You made a bargain with me, and that still stands."

The words hit Dade's ears, and yet they didn't make sense. He thought over that day in Crispin's office. *A service for a service*, every word echoing in his head. There had never been an agreement to zero out Saben's debt. He cursed himself ten times a fool. How could he have not realized? No matter. He'd figure out a way to pay off that debt too. Either way, this worked out better for him. He was willing to go as Crispin's sacrifice.

"You only get one of them," Mina said. "Dade was paying off Saben's debt, so you can't have him."

"No." Crispin's grin spread wider. "Dade negotiated time. I have a signed contract. He's mine too."

Dade held his tongue. He wanted to tell everyone it was okay. That he wanted to go. But that wasn't the right way to play this. Not if he wanted to have the element of surprise, to work his way through Crispin's defenses from the inside. He had to be smart, pragmatic. Start thinking like a crafty thug—like Crispin.

Arden's voice was hard when she said, "Too bad both of them aren't here."

Dade blinked, the words surprising him. He turned his head and realized that Saben was gone. He felt relief. If he couldn't be there for Arden, then Saben would. Yes, he felt the lightness enter him. This was truly how it should be.

For the first time since he'd entered the sanctuary, Crispin looked irritated. His eyes narrowed at Dade. "He'll be found soon enough. For now, it's time to go."

"He's not leaving." And in a flash, Arden had removed her phaser and pointed it at the center of Crispin's head.

Seven other phasers pointed back at her in the next heartbeat.

She didn't look intimidated. "I have no problem dying, because you'll be dead first. Seems like a good deal to me."

Mina's crew members didn't raise their weapons. They didn't surrender either, but it was clear they took direction from Mina, who stood relaxed.

Arden wouldn't back down. She would fight for him. But Dade couldn't have bloodshed here. And her death was not a consequence he could live with. He wished he could tell her it was okay.

A fight wasn't what Dade wanted. Not death, not a phase-fight. Crispin had brought too many people with him. They were outgunned. And Mina wasn't going to stand with them. Her people weren't going to take the fall for him. And he wasn't letting Kallow out of his sight.

Dade felt the world closing in around him. He knew his options were limited. This was the only choice, the one with tactical advantage. He understood what he had to do.

"Arden, lower your weapon," Mina said. It was a command, but that didn't make any difference. Arden didn't follow orders on a good day. And now? Dade didn't have to read Arden's mind to tell that she'd put Mina in the enemy category too.

He selfishly wanted to hold her before he left. Wanted to kiss her goodbye. To feel her skin again one last time so that he could remember in the days, weeks, maybe months ahead what it felt like to have her in his arms. To explain to her that this was his decision. It was one he had to make.

Instead of giving in to that weakness, he raised his head and looked directly at Crispin. "I'm ready to go."

"Dade, no," Arden said with a gasp.

He looked at her and felt his face go soft. He wanted her to know he loved her. Hoped she could read his love and that she knew that he counted on her to come get him and Kallow.

"It's going to be okay," he said.

She shook her head, but pressed her mouth in a thin line, refusing to speak.

"Good," Crispin said. "Let's go. We're done here."

The Twins came up on either side of Dade. They didn't touch him. He knew they wouldn't unless he resisted.

Arden's face was a mask of fury. "Stay safe," she whispered as he stepped forward.

Dade kept his head high as he walked out. And didn't look back even once. He knew it would break his heart.

CHAPTER THIRTY-NINE

Arden didn't move when they left. She was caught up in a web of indecision and numb anger, and the tension ransacked her body. But as soon as the frigid blast of air from the open door hit her skin, it wiped that web clean, breaking it to dust. Fury burned through her, setting her loose. And with it, all her common sense melted away as well.

She wanted to go after Dade. When she found him at Crispin's, she had no idea what she'd do. Maybe she'd slash Crispin's face off, or maybe she'd gut him. Both sounded equally good. As long as she could let out the rage that boiled free.

They had to physically restrain her. Roan, Mina, and Nastasia moving as one, blocking and crowding her. Their hands were as soothing as they were insistent on keeping her there.

Arden tried to shake them off. Her body fighting harder, the outrage of his leaving clouding her thoughts. She understood that he went to avoid needless death. Part of her even agreed with it.

But, no. Arden would not let this happen. Dade was not going to be taken from her.

Mina kept repeating her name, louder each time.

Arden felt like she was going to explode. That churning, hot, overwhelming feeling invaded every part of her. It affected her ability to breathe—to think.

He was gone.

The numbness she retreated into after Colin's death, the numbness she'd grasped for when Dade left, could no longer be found. There was no more indecision. No time to let things take their natural course.

Blood—that was what she wanted. She'd paint the world with it if she had to. Vengeance would be hers.

"Let me go," Arden snarled.

"You need to calm down," Mina said. Her voice was steady. She tried to step in front of Arden. "You can't force this right now. Stop and think."

"Don't tell me what I can't do," Arden said. "You knew he'd be taken."

Mina nodded once. "I knew it was a possibility."

Her admission shredded Arden's soul. She turned her head away, not able to look at Mina. Afraid what she'd do if she focused her anger there.

Arden took a breath. She closed her eyes and centered. When she let her body relax, they released her, though they were still too close for her liking. Gripping tight on the tether that kept her anger from exploding, she said, "We have to get him back."

"I understand that you want Dade, but . . ." Mina hesitated. "We can't help you. I'm sorry."

Angry. Fury. Heat.

Arden swallowed it all. She had to be smart about this. This was about saving Dade. Nothing else mattered. Not Mina. Not her group or their fear of a turf war. She didn't need them. Arden could do this alone.

Nakomzer, who Arden had forgotten was there, sneered, "It won't matter. You'll all pay with your lives for what you've done."

Mina glanced to the pew where he now sat after righting himself. Then she silently gave Nastasia an order with a nod of her head.

Nastasia stepped over to him and hit Nakomzer in the back of the head with the butt of her phaser. When he slumped over like a sack of discarded trash, she blew out a breath. "He's annoying."

Arden swallowed back a wild laugh. She had to get out of there before she cracked in half.

Straightening, she looked Mina in the eye. Held her gaze and poured her promises for retribution into it. Then she shouldered past her and walked down the aisle. Since Crispin was well gone by then, no one stopped her when she strode out of the church.

Arden was not surprised when Saben met her on the street. He fell into step beside her as they rounded the corner and crossed into the next district, putting as much distance between themselves and the church as she could manage.

When she'd felt the air change inside the church, when that door had opened, a twist in her gut warned her. Arden had turned and caught Saben's eye. Like the flick of a light, she'd known who it was going to be and whom he was there for. Saben had been at the front of the church, the only one of them who had a chance of getting out. He'd taken a step toward them, but she'd given him a sharp shake of her head. Then she'd looked to the nave, where there was a secret exit, and prayed he'd do as she'd asked.

Thankfully, Saben had obeyed. Even though it must have killed him to leave them vulnerable. But she couldn't very well rescue both Dade and Saben on her own. And with his acquiescence, Saben had earned her trust.

"You're going to get him," he said.

"Yes." It wasn't a question, and she didn't treat it as one. They already had their phasers and new net-tech running suits. That was good, because they weren't going back to get the rest of their things.

Dade and she had plans. This was only a temporary setback. A *very* temporary one. They were going to get out of this mess, and then they were going to wreak havoc on the city, just as they'd agreed to. The ass-kicking line, though, had just moved Crispin to the top of the list. Arden didn't have any doubt about her abilities.

As she walked, her body protested the strain of the day. They needed a little downtime if they were going to do this, a chance to recover and reassess. They needed to organize.

Saben seemed to echo her thoughts. "We can't follow them."

"Not tonight," she agreed. "But we're going to get Dade back no matter what it takes."

Saben gave her a feral smile.

"We're gonna need some friends," she said. "Mina won't help."

"I have some ideas for that."

Arden was sure she wouldn't like those ideas because they weren't hers to begin with, but she agreed anyway. Beggars couldn't be choosers. If Saben trusted them, she could too. It was time that she learned to work with a group, especially if she planned to lead Lasair.

She turned off the skywalk and into a dark passageway. Arden opened her palm. Inside lay a small black tech-chip.

"Is that—?" Saben's voice was full of awe and steel.

"Why would we leave this? After all, we went to so much trouble to steal it."

Saben shook his head, clearly impressed. "She'll kill you for this."

Arden gave a nonplussed shrug. "I'm sure she'll try."

Saben stared at the black square. His gaze was fixed, intense. "Do you know anyone who can read it?"

"No. Do you?"

His mouth twisted. "No."

Arden shut her palm and tucked away the bit of plastic. Her connections were burned, both with Lasair and with Mina. They'd figure out how to read the tech-chip later.

"For now, we focus on payback," she said. "Everything else can wait until we retrieve Dade and show them—my family, Mina—that we're not to be messed with. That we can stand on our own without them."

Saben smirked. "And that is your plan? To go against them all?"

She nodded. "To make them suffer. They deserve it."

Arden dug into her pack and pulled out two vials of liquid silver. She'd stolen them from the cold storage after Niall left. It had been a swift decision. But the need for it had come sooner than she had expected.

Holding them up to Saben for his inspection, she told him, "This will burn all nanotech in our bodies." Then, thinking back to Niall's reaction when he'd injected it, she added, "It will burn us too."

His eyes went dark, contemplative. "If we leave their group, we'll have no protection for a while. We can still choose to go back. Give the tech-chip to Mina. It's not too late."

But it was too late. She wouldn't place her life in the hands of another again. It was time to forge their own path.

"I'm sure," she said.

She handed over one of the vials and took another for herself. They both prepared the serum. And then stared at each other, needles to their skin.

"On three?" she asked.

Saben nodded.

The countdown was quick, and then the liquid burned. Worse than she'd imagined that it would. It felt like her whole body had gone supernova. Cutting out all her thoughts and whiting out her emotions. Arden embraced it. Letting the lack of control, of being burned and forged anew, embrace her.

And then there was satisfaction. An awakening feeling of power.

Distantly she realized that she'd fallen to the ground. She lay there, panting. Her watery eyes blinked open, taking in the static cloud moving around her, swallowing her body in its mists.

She'd had enough of death and destruction on other people's terms. It was time for her to make the world explode. They would all pay.

ACKNOWLEDGMENTS

I'm lucky to have many amazing people in my life.

A big thank-you to my mom, Beckie, who listens to me complain about every step of the writing process. Who is my sounding board for every new idea that flits through my head, and reads my first drafts (and second, and third . . .). Thank you for suffering with me!

Thank you to my dad, Mike, who thinks every idea comes from him. I'm glad I got your genes.

My life wouldn't be complete without my family. Steven, Seth, and Rebekah, thank you for giving me the time and space and encouragement to follow my dreams. You make my life fun.

As always, a big thank-you to my agent, Carlisle Webber. You've been incredibly supportive and all-around awesome. Here's to many more projects together.

To my editor, Adrienne Procaccini, thank you for believing in me. You've been a delight to work with. I don't know how I got so lucky.

Amara Holstein, you are amazing. Thank you for pushing me farther than I thought I could go with this book.

Thank you to my publishing team: Brittany Jackson, Courtney Miller, Kim Cowser, Kristin King, and those members whom I don't connect with but who I know have had a hand in making this book come to life. I'm so very blessed to be working with such a dedicated group of people.

I'd love to give a huge thank-you to the women in my life who encourage me in each step of the writing process: Anissa Maxwell, Laura Goodson, Danielle McIlroy, Heather Nordell, Mary Lynn, Deanna Kaech, Katie Smith, and Cam Williams.

And finally to my readers, I wouldn't have a career without you. Thank you so much for buying this book and supporting me.